The Tidal Wave and Other Stories

by

Ethel M. Dell

The Tidal Wave and Other Stories
by Ethel M. Dell

Copyright © 2024

ISBN: 978-93-62768-61-2

Published by

DOUBLE 9 BOOKS

2/13-B, Ansari Road
Daryaganj, New Delhi – 110002
info@double9books.com
www.double9books.com
Tel. 011-40042856

This book is under public domain

ABOUT THE AUTHOR

From 1911 to 1939, Ethel May Dell Savage, better known by her pen name Ethel M. Dell, was a British writer of more than 30 bestselling romance novels and several short tales. Dell was born on August 2, 1881, to a middle-class family in Streatham, a London neighborhood. Her father was a clerk in the City of London, and she has an older sister and brother. Dell began writing stories at a young age, and many of them have been published in popular journals. Her stories were primarily romantic in nature, set in the British Raj and other former British colonial territories. Some thought her stories were too sexual. Dell worked on her first novel, The Way of an Eagle, for several years before releasing it with T. Fisher Unwin after being rejected by eight other publishers. The book was part of Unwin's First Novel Library, a series that celebrated a writer's first novel. The Way of an Eagle was first published in 1911 and went through thirty printings by 1915. In 1922, Ethel married Lieutenant-Colonel Gerald Tahourdin Savage, who resigned his service at the time of their marriage, leaving Dell as the family's sole support. Despite negative reviews from reviewers, she built a loyal fan base and earned between £20,000 and £30,000 per year. Her husband was loyal to her and zealously protected her privacy.

CONTENTS

CHAPTER I
STILL WATERS

Rufus the Red sat on the edge of his boat with his hands clasped between his knees, staring at nothing. His nets were spread to dry in the sun; the morning's work was done. Most of the other men had lounged into their cottages for the midday meal, but the massive red giant sitting on the shore in the merciless heat of noon did not seem to be thinking of physical needs.

His eyes under their shaggy red brows were fixed with apparent concentration upon his red, hairy legs. Now and then his bare toes gripped the moist sand almost savagely, digging deep furrows; but for the most part he sat in solid contemplation.

There was only one other man within sight along that sunny stretch of sand—a small, dark man with a shaggy, speckled beard and quick, twinkling eyes. He was at work upon a tangled length of tarred rope, pulling and twisting with much energy and deftness to straighten out the coil, so that it leaped and writhed in his hands like a living thing.

He whistled over the job cheerily and tunelessly, glancing now and again with a keen, birdlike intelligence towards the motionless figure twenty yards away that sat with bent head broiling in the sun. His task seemed a hopeless one, but he tackled it as if he enjoyed it. His brown hands worked with a will. He was plainly one to make the best of things, and not to be lightly discouraged—a man of resolution, as the coxswain of the Spear Point lifeboat needed to be.

After ten minutes of unremitting toil he very suddenly ceased to whistle and sent a brisk hail across the stretch of sand that intervened between himself and the solitary fisherman on the edge of the boat.

"Hi—Rufus—Rufus—ahoy!"

The fiery red head turned in his direction without either alacrity or interest. The fixed eyes came out of their trance-like study and took in the blue-jerseyed, energetic figure that worked so actively at the knotted hemp. There was something rather wonderful about those eyes. They were of the deep, intense blue of a spirit-fed flame—the blue of the ocean when a storm broods below the horizon.

He made no verbal answer to the hail; only after a moment or two he got slowly to his feet and began leisurely to cross the sand.

The older man did not watch his progress. His brown, lined face was bent again over his task.

Rufus the Red drew near and paused. "Want anything?"

He spoke from his chest, in a voice like a deep-toned bell. His arms hung slack at his sides, but the muscles stood out on them like ropes.

The coxswain of the lifeboat gave his head a brief, upward jerk without looking at him. "That curly-topped chap staying at The Ship," he said, "he came messing round after me this morning, wanted to know would I take him out with the nets one day. I told him maybe you would."

"What did you do that for?" said Rufus.

The coxswain shot him a brief and humorous glance. "I always give you the plums if I can, my boy," he said. "I said to him, 'Me and my son, we're partners. Going out with him is just the same as going out with me, and p'raps a bit better, for he's got the better boat.' So he sheered off, and said maybe he'd look you up in the evening."

"Maybe I shan't be there," commented Rufus.

The coxswain chuckled, and lashed out an end of rope, narrowly missing his son's brawny legs. "He's not such a soft one as he looks, that chap," he observed. "Not by no manner of means. Do you know what Columbine thinks of him?"

"How should I know?" said Rufus.

He stooped with an abrupt movement that had in it a hint of savagery, and picked up the end of rope that lay jerking at his feet.

"Tell you what, Adam," he said. "If that chap values his health he'll keep clear of me and my boat."

Everyone called the coxswain Adam, even his son and partner, Rufus the Red. No two men could have formed a more striking contrast than they, but their partnership was something more than a business relation. They were friends—friends on a footing of equality, and had been such ever since Rufus—the giant baby who had cost his mother her life—had first closed his resolute fist upon his father's thumb.

That was five-and-twenty years ago now, and for eighteen of those years the two had dwelt alone together in their cottage on the cliff in complete content. Then—seven years back—Adam the coxswain had unexpectedly tired of his widowed state and taken to himself a second wife.

This was Mrs. Peck, of The Ship, a widow herself of some years' standing, plump, amiable, prosperous, who in marrying Adam would have gladly opened her doors to Adam's son also had the son been willing to avail himself of her hospitality.

But Rufus had preferred independence in the cottage of his birth, and in this cottage he had lived alone since his father's defection.

It was a dainty little cottage, perched in an angle of the cliff, well apart from all the rest and looking straight down upon the great Spear Point. He tended the strip of garden with scrupulous care, and it made a bright spot of colour against the brown cliff-side. A rough path, steep and winding, led up from the beach below, and about half-way up a small gate, jealously padlocked in the owner's absence, guarded Rufus's privacy. He never invited any one within that gate. Occasionally his father would saunter up with his evening pipe and sit in the little porch of his old home looking through the purple clematis flowers out to sea while he exchanged a few commonplace remarks with his son, who never broke his own silence unless he had something to say. But no other visitor ever intruded there.

Rufus had acquired the reputation of a hermit, and it kept all the rest at bay. He had lived his own life for so long that solitude had grown upon him as moss clings to a stone. He did not seem to feel the need of human companionship. He lived apart.

Sometimes, indeed, he would go down to The Ship in the evening and lounge in the bar with the rest, but even there his solitude still wrapped him round. He never expanded, however genial the atmosphere.

The other men treated him with instinctive respect. He was powerful enough to thrash any two of them, and no one cared to provoke him to wrath. For Rufus in anger was a veritable mad bull.

"Leave him alone! He's not safe!" was the general advice and warning of his fellows, and none but Adam ever interfered with him.

Just recently, however, Adam had begun to take a somewhat quizzical interest in the welfare of his son. It had been an established custom ever since his second marriage that Rufus should eat his Sunday dinner at the family table down at The Ship. Mrs. Peck—Adam's wife was never known by any other title, just as the man's own surname had dropped into such disuse that few so much as knew what it was—had made an especial point of this, and Rufus had never managed to invent any suitable excuse for refusing. He never remained long after the meal was eaten. When all the other fisher-lads were walking the cliffs with their own particular lasses, Rufus was wont to trudge back to his hermitage and draw his mantle of solitude about him once more. He had never walked with any lass. Whether from shyness or surliness, he had held consistently aloof from such frivolous pastimes. If a girl ever cast a saucy look his way the brooding blue eyes never seemed aware of it. In speech with womenkind he was always slow and half-reluctant. That his great bull-like physique could by any means be an object of admiration was a possibility that he never seemed to contemplate. In fact, he seemed expectant of ridicule rather than appreciation.

In his boyhood he had fought several tough fights with certain lads who had dared to scoff at his red hair. Sam Jefferson, who lived down on the quay, still bore the marks of one such battle in the absence of two front teeth. But he did not take affront from womenkind. He looked over their heads, and went his way in massive unconcern.

But lately a change had come into his life—such a change as made Adam's shrewd dark eyes twinkle whenever they glanced in his son's direction, comprehending that the days of Rufus's tranquillity were ended.

A witch had come to live at The Ship, such a witch as had never before danced along the Spear Point sands. Her name was Maria Peck, and she was the daughter of Mrs. Peck's late lamented husband's vagabond brother—"a seafaring man and a wastrel if ever there was one," as Mrs. Peck was often heard to declare. He had picked up with and eventually married a Spanish pantomime girl up London way, so Mrs. Peck's information went, and Maria had been the child of their union.

No one called her Maria. Her mother had named her Columbine, and Columbine she had become to all who knew her. Her mother dying when she was only three, Columbine had been left to the sole care of her wastrel father. And he, then a skipper of a small cargo steamer plying across the North Sea, had placed her in the charge of a spinster aunt who kept an infants' school in a little Kentish village near the coast. Here, up to the age of seventeen, Columbine had lived and been educated; but the old schoolmistress had worn out at last, and on her death-bed had sent for Mrs. Peck, as being the girl's only remaining relative, her father having drifted out of her ken long since.

Mrs. Peck had nobly risen to the occasion. She had no daughter of her own; she could do with a daughter. But when she saw Columbine she sucked up her breath.

"My, but she'll be a care!" was her verdict.

"She don't know—how lovely she is," the dying woman had whispered. "Don't tell her!"

And Mrs. Peck had staunchly promised to keep the secret, so far as lay in her power.

That had happened six months before, and Columbine was out of mourning now. She had come into the Spear Point community like a shy bird, a little slip of a thing, upright as a dart, with a fashion of holding her head that kept all familiarity at bay. But the shyness had all gone now. The girlish immaturity was fast vanishing in soft curves and tender lines. And the beauty of her!—the beauty of her was as the gold of a summer morning breaking over a pearly sea.

She was a creature of light and laughter, but there were in her odd little streaks of unconsidered impulse that testified to a passionate soul. She would flash into a temper over a mere trifle, and then in a moment flash back into mirth and amiability.

"You can't call her bad-tempered," said Mrs. Peck. "But she's sharp—she's certainly sharp."

"Ay, and she's got a will of her own," commented Adam. "But she's your charge, missus, not mine. It's my belief you'll find her a bit of a handful before you've done. But don't you ask me to interfere! It's none o' my job."

"Lor' bless you," chuckled Mrs. Peck, "I'd as soon think of asking Rufus!"

Adam grunted at this light reference to his son. "Rufus ain't such a fool as he looks," he rejoined.

"Lor' sakes! Whoever said he was?" protested the equable Mrs. Peck. "I've a great respect for Rufus. It wasn't that I meant—not by any manner o' means."

What she had meant did not transpire, and Adam did not pursue the subject to inquire. He also had a respect for Rufus.

It was not long after that brief conversation that he began to notice a change in his son. He made no overtures of friendship to the dainty witch at The Ship, but he took the trouble to make himself extremely respectable when he made his weekly appearance there. He kept his shag of red hair severely cropped. He attired himself in navy serge, and wore a collar.

Adam's keen eyes took in the change and twinkled. Columbine's eyes twinkled too. She had begun by being almost absurdly shy in the presence of the young fisherman who sat so silently at his father's table, but that phase had wholly passed away. She treated him now with a kindly condescension, such as she might have bestowed upon a meek-souled dog. All the other men—with the exception of Adam, whom she frankly liked—she overlooked with the utmost indifference. They were plainly lesser animals than dogs.

"She'll look high," said Mrs. Peck. "The chaps here ain't none of her sort."

And again Adam grunted.

He was fond of Columbine, took her out in his boat, spun yarns for her, gave her such treasures from the sea as came his way—played, in fact, a father's part, save that from the very outset he was very careful to assume no authority over her. That responsibility was reserved for Mrs. Peck, whose kindly personality made the bare idea seem absurd.

And so to a very great extent Columbine had run wild. But the warm responsiveness of her made her easy to manage as a general rule, and Mrs. Peck's government was by no means exacting.

"Thank goodness, she's not one to run after the men!" was her verdict after the first six months of Columbine's sojourn.

That the men would have run after her had they received the smallest encouragement to do so was a fact that not one of them would have disputed. But with dainty pride she kept them at a distance, and none had so far attempted to cross the invisible boundary that she had so decidedly laid down.

And then with the summer weather had come the stranger—had come Montagu Knight. Young, handsome, and self-assured, he strolled into The Ship one day for tea, having tramped twelve miles along the coast from Spearmouth, on the other side of the Point. And the next day he came again to stay.

He had been there for nearly three weeks now, and he seemed to have every intention of remaining. He was an artist, and the sketches he made were numerous and—like himself—full of decision. He came and went among the fishermen's little thatched cottages, selecting here, refusing there, exactly according to fancy.

They had been inclined to resent his presence at first—it was certainly no charitable impulse that moved Adam to call him "the curly-topped chap"—but now they were getting used to him. For there was no gainsaying the fact that he had a way with him, at least so far as the women-folk of the community were concerned.

He could keep Mrs. Peck chuckling for an hour at a time in the evening, when the day's work was over. And Columbine—Columbine had a trill of laughter in her voice whenever she spoke to him. He liked to hear her play the guitar and sing soft songs in the twilight. Adam liked it too. He was wont to say that it reminded him of a young blackbird learning to sing. For Columbine was as yet very shy of her own talent. She kept in the shallows, as it were, in dread of what the deep might hold.

Knight was very kind to her, but he was never extravagant in his praise. He was quite unlike any other man of her acquaintance. His touch was always so sure. He never sought her out, though he was invariably quite pleased to see her. The dainty barrier of pride that fenced her round did not exist for him. She did not need to keep him at a distance. He could be intimate without being familiar.

And intimate he had become. There was no disputing it. From the first, with his easy *savoir-faire*, he had waived ceremony, till at length there was no ceremony left between them. He treated her like a lady. What more could the most exacting demand?

And yet Adam continued to call him "the curly-topped chap," and turned him over to his son Rufus when he requested permission to go out in his boat.

And Rufus—Rufus turned with a gesture of disgust after the utterance of his half-veiled threat, and spat with savage emphasis upon the sand.

Adam uttered a chuckle that was not wholly unsympathetic, and began deftly to coil the now disentangled rope.

"Do you know what I'd do—if I was in your place?" he said.

Rufus made a sound that was strictly noncommittal.

Adam's quick eyes flung him a birdlike glance. "Why don't you come along to The Ship and smoke a pipe with your old father of an evening?" he said. "Once a week's not enough, not, that is, if you—" He broke off suddenly, caught by a whistle that could not be resisted.

Rufus was regarding the horizon with those brooding eyes of vivid blue.

Abruptly Adam ceased to whistle. "When I was a young chap," he said, "I didn't keep my courting for Sundays only. I didn't dress up, mind you. That weren't my way. But I'd go along in my jersey and invite her out for a bit of a cruise in the old boat. They likes a cruise, Rufus. You try it, my boy! You try it!"

The rope lay in an orderly coil at his feet, and he straightened himself, rubbing his hands on his trousers. His son remained quite motionless, his eyes still fixed as though he heard not.

Adam stood up beside him, shrewdly alert. He had never before ventured to utter words of counsel on this delicate subject. But having started, he was minded to make a neat job of it. Adam had never been the man to leave a thing half done.

"Go to it, Rufus!" he said, dropping his voice confidentially. "Don't be afraid to show your mettle! Don't be crowded out by that curly-topped chap! You're worth a dozen of him. Just you let her know it, that's all!"

He dug his hands into his trousers pockets with the words, and turned to go.

Rufus moved then, moved abruptly as one coming out of a dream. His eyes swooped down upon the lithe, active figure at his side. They held a smile—a fiery smile that gleamed meteor-like and passed.

"All right, Adam," he said in his deep-chested voice.

And with a sidelong nod Adam wheeled and departed. He had done his morning's work.

CHAPTER II
THE PASSION-FLOWER

"Where's that Columbine?" said Mrs. Peck.

A gay trill like the call of a blackbird in the dawning answered her. Columbine, with a pink sun-bonnet over her black hair, was watering the flowers in the little conservatory that led out of the drawing-room. She had just come in from the garden, and a gorgeous red rose was pinned upon her breast. Mrs. Peck stood in the doorway and watched her.

The face above the red rose was so lovely that even her matter-of-fact soul had to pause to admire. It was a perpetual wonder to her and a perpetual fascination. The dark, unawakened eyes, the long, perfect brows, the deep, rich colouring, all combined to make such a picture as good Mrs. Peck realised to be superb.

Again the pure contralto trill came from the red lips, and then, with a sudden movement that had in it something of the grace of an alighting bird, Columbine turned, swinging her empty can.

"I've promised to take Mr. Knight to the Spear Point Caves by moonlight," she said. "He's doing a moonlight study, and he doesn't know the lie of the quicksand."

"Sakes alive!" said Mrs. Peck. "What made him ask you? There's Adam knows every inch of the shore better nor what you do."

"He didn't ask," said Columbine. "I offered. And I know the shore just as well as Adam does, Aunt Liza. Adam himself showed me the lie of the quicksand long ago. I know it like my own hand."

Mrs. Peck pursed her lips. "I doubt but what you'd better take Adam along too," she said. "I wouldn't feel easy about you. And there won't be any moonlight worth speaking of till after ten. It wouldn't do for you to be traipsing about alone even with Mr. Knight—nice young gentleman as he be—at that hour."

"Aunt Liza, I don't traipse!" Momentary indignation shone in the beautiful eyes and passed like a gleam of light. "Dear Aunt Liza," laughed Columbine, "aren't you funny?"

"Not a bit," maintained Mrs. Peck. "I'm just common-sensical, my dear. And it ain't right—it never were right in my young day—to go walking out alone with a man after bedtime."

"A man, Aunt Liza! Oh, but a man! An artist isn't a man—at least, not an ordinary man." There was a hint of earnestness in Columbine's tone, notwithstanding its lightness.

But Mrs. Peck remained firm. "It wouldn't make it right, not if he was an angel from heaven," she declared.

Columbine's gay laugh had in it that quality of youth that surmounts all obstacles. "He's much safer than an angel," she protested, "because he can't fly. Besides, the Spear Point Caves are all on this side of the Point. You could watch us all the time if you'd a mind to."

But Mrs. Peck did not laugh. "I'd rather you didn't go, my dear," she said. "So let that be the end of it, there's a good girl!"

"Oh, but I—" began Columbine, and broke off short. "Goodness, how you made me jump!" she said instead.

Rufus, his burly form completely blocking the doorway, was standing half in and half out of the garden, looking at her.

"Lawks!" said Mrs. Peck. "So you did me! Good evening, Rufus! Are you wanting Adam?"

"Not specially," said Rufus. He entered, with massive, lounging movements. "I suppose I can come in," he remarked.

"What a question!" ejaculated Mrs. Peck.

Columbine said nothing. She picked up her empty watering-can and swung it carelessly on one finger, hunting for invisible weeds in the geranium-pots the while.

Mrs. Peck was momentarily at a loss. She was not accustomed to entertaining Rufus in his father's absence.

"Have a glass of mulberry wine!" she suggested.

"Columbine, run and fetch it, dear! It's in the right-hand corner, third shelf, of the cupboard under the stairs. I'm sure you're very welcome," she added to Rufus, "but you must excuse me, for I've got to see to Mr. Knight's dinner."

"That's all right, Mother," said Rufus.

He always called her mother; it was a term of deference with him rather than affection. But Mrs. Peck liked him for it.

"Sit you down!" she said hospitably. "And mind you make yourself quite at home! Columbine will look after you. You'll be staying to supper, I hope?"

"Thanks!" said Rufus. "I don't know. Where's Adam?"

"He's chopping a bit of wood in the yard. He don't want any help. You'll see him presently. You stop and have a chat with Columbine!" said Mrs. Peck; and with a smile and nod she bustled stoutly away.

When Columbine returned with the mulberry wine and a glass on a tray the conservatory was empty. She set down her tray and paused.

There was a faintly mutinous curve about her soft lips, a gleam of dancing mischief in her eyes.

In a moment a step sounded on the path outside, and Rufus reappeared. He had been out to fill her watering-can, and he deposited it full at her feet.

"Don't put it there!" she said, with a touch of sharpness. "I don't want to tumble over it, do I? Thank you for filling it, but you needn't have troubled. I've done."

"Then it'll come in for tomorrow," said Rufus, setting the can deliberately in a corner.

Columbine turned to pour out a glass of Mrs. Peck's mulberry wine.

"Only one glass?" said Rufus.

She threw him a quizzing smile over her shoulder. "Well, you don't want two, do you?"

"No," said Rufus slowly. "But I don't drink—alone."

She gave a low, gurgling laugh. "You'll be saying you don't smoke alone next. If you want someone to keep you company, I'd better fetch Adam."

She turned round to him with the words, offering the glass on the tray. Her eyes were lowered, but the upward curl of the black lashes somehow conveyed the impression that she was peeping through them. The tilt of the red lips, with the pearly teeth just showing in a smile, was of so alluring an enchantment that the most level-headed of men could scarcely have failed to pause and admire.

Rufus paused so long that at last she lifted those glorious eyes of hers in semi-scornful interrogation.

"What's the matter?" she inquired. "Don't you want it?"

He made an odd gesture as of one at a loss to explain himself. "Won't you drink first?" he said, his voice very low.

"No, thank you," said Columbine briskly. "I don't like it."

"Then—I don't like it either," he said.

"Don't be silly!" she said. "Of course you do! I know you do! Take it, and don't be ridiculous!"

But Rufus turned away with solid resolution. "No, thanks," he said.

Columbine set down the tray again with a hint of exasperation. "You're just like a child," she said severely. "A great, overgrown boy, that's what you are!"

"All right," said Rufus, propping himself against the door-post.

"It's not all right. It's time you grew up." Columbine picked up the full glass, and, carrying it daintily, advanced upon him. "I suppose I shall have to make you take it like medicine," she remarked.

She stood against the door-post, facing him, upright, slender, exquisite as an opening flower.

"Drink, puppy, drink!" she said flippantly, and elevated the glass towards her guest's somewhat grim lips.

The sombre blue eyes came down to her with something of a flash. And in the same moment Rufus's great right hand disengaged itself from his pocket and grasped the slim wrist of the hand that held the wine.

"You drink—first!" said Rufus, and guided the glass with unmistakable resolution to the provocative red lips.

She jerked back her head to avoid it, but the doorpost against which she stood checked the backward movement. Before she could prevent it the wine was in her mouth.

She flung up her free hand and would have knocked the glass away, but Rufus could be prompt of action when he chose. He caught it from her and drained it almost in the same movement. Not a drop was spilt between them. He set down the glass on a shelf of the conservatory, and propped himself up once more with his hands in his pockets.

Columbine's face was burning red; her eyes literally blazed. Her whole body vibrated as if strung on wires. "How—dare you?" she said, and showed her white teeth with the words like an angry tigress.

He looked down at her, a faint smile in his blue eyes. "But I don't drink—alone," he said in such a tone of gentle explanation as he might have used to a child.

She stamped her foot. "I hate you!" she said. "I'll never forgive you!"

"A joke's a joke," said Rufus, still in the tone of a mild instructor.

"A joke!" Her wrath enwrapped her like a flame. "It was not a joke! It was a coarse—and hateful—trick!"

"All right," said Rufus, as one giving up a hopeless task.

"It's not all right!" flashed Columbine. "You're a bounder, an oaf, a brute! I—I'll never speak to you again, unless—you—you—apologise!"

He was still looking down with that vague hint of amusement in his eyes—the look of a man who watches the miniature fury of some tiny creature.

"I'll do anything you like," he said with slow indulgence. "I didn't know you'd turn nasty, or I wouldn't have done it."

"Nasty!" echoed Columbine. And then her wrath went suddenly into a superb gust of scorn. "Oh, you—you are beyond words!" she said. "You had better get along to the bar and drink there. You'll find your own kind there to drink with."

"I'd rather drink with you," said Rufus.

She uttered a laugh that was tremulous with anger. "You've done it for the first and last time, my man," she said.

With the words she turned like a darting, indignant bird, and left him.

Someone was entering the drawing-room from the hall with a careless, melodious whistle—a whistle that ended on a note of surprise as Columbine sped through the room. The whistler—a tall, bronzed young man in white flannels—stopped short to regard her.

His eyes were grey and wary under absolutely level brows. His hair was dark, with an inclination—sternly repressed—to waviness above the forehead. He made a decidedly pleasant picture, as even Adam could not have denied.

Columbine also checked herself at sight of him, but the red blood was throbbing at her temples. There was no hiding her agitation.

"You seem in a hurry," remarked Knight. "I hope there is nothing wrong."

His chin was modelled on firm lines, but there was a very distinct cleft in it that imparted to him the look of one who could smile at most things. His words were kindly, but they did not hold any very deep concern.

Columbine came to a stand, gripping the back of a chair to steady herself. "Oh, I—I have been—insulted!" she panted.

The straight brows went up a little; the man himself stiffened slightly. Without further words he moved across to the door into the conservatory and looked through it. He was in time to see Rufus's great, lounging figure sauntering away in the direction of the wood-yard.

Knight stood a moment or two and watched him, then quietly turned and rejoined the girl.

She was still leaning upon the chair, but she was gradually recovering her self-control. As he drew near she made a slight movement as if to resume her interrupted flight. But some other impulse intervened, and she remained where she was.

Knight came up and stood beside her. "What has he been doing to annoy you?" he asked.

She made a small, vehement gesture of disgust. "Oh, we won't talk of him. He is an oaf. I dare say he doesn't know any better, but he'll never have a chance of doing it again. I don't mix with the riff-raff."

"He's Adam's son, isn't he?" questioned Knight.

She nodded. "Yes, the great, hulking lubber! Adam's all right. I like Adam. But Rufus—well, Rufus is a bounder, and I'll never have anything more to say to him."

"I think you are quite right to hold your head up above these fisher fellows," remarked Knight, his grey eyes watching her with an appraising expression. "They are as much out of place near you as a bed of bindweed would be in the neighbourhood of a passion-flower." His glance took in her still panting bosom. "I think you are something of a passion-flower," he said, faintly smiling. "I wonder at any man daring to risk offending you."

Columbine stood up with the free movement of a disdainful princess. "Oh, he's just a lout," she said. "He doesn't know any better. It isn't as if you had done it."

"That would have been different, would it?" said Knight.

She smiled, but a sombre light still shone in her eyes. "Quite different," she said with simplicity. "You see, you're a gentleman. And—gentlemen—don't do unpleasant things like that."

He laughed a little. "You make me feel quite nervous. What a shocking thing it would be if I ever did anything to forfeit your good opinion."

"You couldn't," said Columbine.

"Couldn't!" He repeated the word with an odd inflection.

"It wouldn't be you," she explained with the utmost gravity, as one stating an irrefutable fact.

"Thank you," said Knight.

"Oh, it's not a compliment," she returned. "It's just the truth. There are some people—a few people—that one knows one can trust through and through. And you are one of them, that's all."

"Is that so?" said Knight. "You know, that's rather—a colossal thing—to say of any one."

"Then you are colossal," said Columbine, smiling more freely.

Knight turned aside, and picked up the sketch-book he had laid upon the table on entering. "Are you sure you are not rash?" he said, rather in the tone of one making a remark than asking a question.

"Fairly sure," said Columbine.

She followed him. Perhaps he had foreseen that she would. She stood by his side.

"May I see the latest?" she asked.

He opened the book and showed her a blank page. "That is the latest," he said.

She looked at him interrogatively.

"I am waiting for my—inspiration," he said.

"I hope you will find it soon," she said.

He answered her with steady conviction. "I shall find it tonight by moonlight at the Spear Point Rock."

Her face clouded a little. "I believe Adam is going to take you," she said.

"What?" said Knight. "You are never going to let me down?"

She smiled with a touch of irony. "It was the Spear Point you wanted," she reminded him.

"And you," said Knight, "to show the way."

Something in his tone arrested her. Her beautiful eyes sank suddenly to the blank page he held. "Adam can do that—as well as I can," she said.

"But you said you would," said Knight. His voice was low; he was looking full at her. He saw the rich colour rising in her cheeks. "What is it?" he said. "Won't they let you?"

She raised her head abruptly, proudly. "I please myself," she said. "No one has the ordering of me."

His grey eyes shone a little. "Then it pleases you—to let me down?" he questioned.

Her look flashed suddenly up to his. She saw his expression and laughed. "I didn't think you'd care," she said. "Adam knows the lie of the quicksand. That's all you really want."

"Oh, pardon me!" said Knight. "You are quite wrong, if you imagine that I am indifferent as to who goes with me. Inspiration won't burn in a cold place."

She dropped her lids, still looking at him. "Isn't Adam inspiring?" she asked.

"He couldn't furnish the particular sort of inspiration I am needing for my moonlight picture," said Knight.

He spoke deliberately, but his brows were slightly drawn, belying the coolness of his speech.

"What is the sort of inspiration you are wanting?" asked Columbine.

He smiled with a hint of provocation. "I'll tell you that when we get there."

Her answering smile was infinitely more provocative than his. "That will be very interesting," she said.

Knight closed his sketch-book. "I am glad to know," he said thoughtfully, "that you please yourself, Miss Columbine. In doing so, you have the happy knack of pleasing—others."

He made her a slight, courtly bow, and turned away.

He left her still standing at the table, looking after him with perplexity and gathering resolution in her eyes.

CHAPTER III
THE MINOTAUR

"Not stopping to supper even? Well, you must be a darned looney!"

Adam sat down astride his wood-block with the words, and looked up at his son with the aggressive expression of a Scotch terrier daring a Newfoundland.

Rufus, with his hands in his pockets, leaned against the woodshed. He made no reply of any sort to his father's brisk observation. Obviously it made not the faintest impression upon him.

After a moment or two he spoke, his pipe in the corner of his mouth. "If that chap bathes off the Spear Point rocks when the tide's at the spring he'll get into difficulties."

"Who says he does?" demanded Adam.

Rufus jerked his head. "I saw him—from my place—this afternoon. Tide was going down, or the current would have caught him. Better warn him."

"I did," responded Adam sharply. "Warned him long ago. Warned him of the quicksand, too."

Rufus grunted. "Then he's only himself to thank. Or maybe he doesn't know a spring tide from a neap."

"Oh, he's not such a fool as that," said Adam.

Rufus grunted once again, and relapsed into silence.

It was at this point that Mrs. Peck showed her portly person at the back door of The Ship.

"Why, Rufus," she said, "I thought you was in the front with Columbine."

Rufus stood up with the deference that he never omitted to pay to Adam's wife. "So I was," he said. "I came along here after to talk to Adam."

Mrs. Peck's round eyes gave him a searching look. "Did you have your mulberry wine?" she asked.

"Yes, Mother."

"You were mighty quick about it," commented Mrs. Peck.

"Yes, he's in a hurry," said Adam, with one of his birdlike glances. "Can't stop for anything, missus. Wants to get back to his supper."

"I never!" said Mrs. Peck. "You aren't in that hurry, Rufus, surely! Just as I was going to ask you to do something to oblige me, too!"

"What's that?" said Rufus.

Mrs. Peck descended into the yard with a hint of mystery. "Well, just this," she said confidentially. "That there Mr. Knight, he's a very nice young gentleman; but he's an artist, and you know, artists don't look at things like ordinary folk. He wants to get a moonlight picture of the Spear Point, and he's got our Columbine to say she'll take him there tonight. Well, now, I don't think it's right, and I told her so. But, of course, she come out as pat as anything with him being an artist and different-like from the rest. Still, I said as I'd rather she didn't, and Adam had better take him, because of the quicksand, you know. It wouldn't be hardly safe to let him go alone. He's a bit foolhardy too. But Adam's not so young as you, Rufus, and he was out before sunrise. So I thought as how maybe you'd step into the breach and take Mr. Knight along. Come, you won't refuse?"

She spoke the last words coaxingly, aware of a certain hardening of the young fisherman's rugged face.

Adam had got off his chopping-block, and was listening with pursed lips and something of the expression of a terrier at a rat-hole.

"Yes, you go, Rufus!" he said, as Mrs. Peck paused. "You show him round! I'd like him to know you."

"What for?" said Rufus.

Adam contorted one side of his face into something that was between a wink and a grin. "Do you good to go into society," he said. "That's all right, missus, he'll go. Better go and ask Mr. Knight what time he wants to start."

"Wait a bit!" commanded Rufus.

Mrs. Peck waited. She knew that her stepson was as slow of speech as his father was prompt, but she thought none the less of him for that. Rufus was solid, and she respected solid men.

"It comes to this," said Rufus, speaking ponderously. "I'll go if I'm wanted. But I'm not one for shoving myself in otherwise. Maybe the chap won't be so keen himself when he knows he can't have Columbine to go with him. Find that out first!"

Mrs. Peck looked at him with an approving smile. "Lor', Rufus! You've got some sense," she said. "But I wonder how Columbine will take it if I says anything to Mr. Knight behind her back."

Adam chuckled. "Columbine in a tantrum is one of the best sights I know," he remarked.

"Ah! She don't visit her tantrums on you," rejoined his wife. "You can afford to smile."

"And I does," said Adam.

Rufus turned away. There was no smile on his countenance. He said nothing, but there was that in his demeanour that clearly indicated that he personally was neither amused nor disconcerted by the tantrums of Columbine.

He followed Mrs. Peck indoors, and sat down in the kitchen to await developments. And Adam, whistling cheerfully, strolled to the bar.

Mrs. Peck had to dish up the visitor's dinner before she could tackle him upon the subject in hand. She trotted to and fro upon her task, too intent for further speech with Rufus, who sat in unbroken silence, gazing steadily before him with a Sphinx-like immobility that made of him an impressive figure.

The beefsteak was already in the dish, and Mrs. Peck was in the act of pouring the gravy over it when there sounded a light step on the stone of the passage and Columbine entered.

She had removed her sun-bonnet and donned a dainty little apron. The soft dark hair clustered tenderly about her temples.

"Oh, Aunt Liza," she said, "if I didn't go and forget that Sally was out tonight! I'm sorry I'm too late to help with the dinner. But I'll take it in."

She caught her breath at sight of the massive, silent figure seated against the wall, but instantly recovered her composure and passed it by with an upward tilt of the chin.

"You needn't trouble yourself to do that, my dear," rejoined Mrs. Peck, with a touch of tartness. "I'll wait on Mr. Knight myself. You can lay the supper in the parlour if you've a mind to be useful. There'll be four to lay for."

Columbine turned with something of a pounce. "No, there won't! There'll be three," she said. "If that—oaf—stays to supper, I go without!"

"Good gracious!" ejaculated Mrs. Peck.

Rufus came out of his silence. "That's all right. I'm not staying to supper," he said.

"But—lor' sakes!—what's the matter?" questioned Mrs. Peck. "Have you two been quarrelling?"

"No, we haven't!" flashed Columbine. "I wouldn't stoop. But I'm not going to sit down to supper with a man who hasn't learnt manners. I'd sooner go without—much."

Rufus remained absolutely unmoved. He made no attempt at self-justification, though Mrs. Peck was staring from one to the other in mystified interrogation.

Columbine turned swiftly and caught up a cover for the savoury dish that steamed on the table. "You'd better let me take this in before it gets cold," she said.

"No; put it on the rack!" commanded Mrs. Peck. "There's a drop of soup to go in first. And, Columbine, my dear, I don't think it's right of you to go losing your temper that way. Rufus is Adam's son, remember, and you can't refuse to sit at table with him."

"Leave her alone, Mother!" For the second time Rufus intervened. "I've offended her. My mistake. I'll know better next time."

His deep voice was wholly devoid of humour. It was, in fact, devoid of any species of emotion whatever. Yet, oddly enough, the anger died out of Columbine's face as she heard it. She turned to the tablecloth-press and began to unwind it in silence.

Mrs. Peck sniffed, and took up the soup-tureen.

As she waddled out of the kitchen Columbine withdrew the parlour tablecloth and turned round.

"If you're really sorry," she said, "I'll forgive you."

Rufus regarded her for several seconds in silence, a slow smile dawning in his eyes. "Thank you," he said finally.

"You are sorry then?" insisted Columbine.

He shook his great bull-head, the smile still in his eyes. "I wouldn't have missed it for anything," he said.

There was no perceptible familiarity in the remark, and Columbine, after brief consideration, decided to dismiss it without discussion. "Well, let it be a lesson to you, and don't you ever do such a thing again!" she said severely. "For I won't have you or any man lay hands on me—not even in fun."

"All right," said Rufus.

He thrust his hands deep into his pockets as if to remove all cause of offence, and was rewarded by a swift smile from Columbine. The storm had blown away.

"I'll lay for four after all," she said, as she whisked out of the room.

Rufus was still seated in solitary state in the kitchen when Mrs. Peck returned from the little coffee-room where she had been serving her guest.

She peered round with caution ere she came close to him and spoke.

"It's as you thought. He don't want to go with either you or Adam."

Rufus's face remained unchanged; it was slightly bovine of expression as he received the news. "We'll both get to bed in good time then," was his comment.

Mrs. Peck's smooth brow drew in momentary exasperation. She had expected something more dramatic than this.

"I'm glad you're so easily satisfied," she said. "But let me tell you—I'm not!"

She paused to see if this piece of information would take more effect than the first, but again Rufus proved a disappointment. Neither by word nor look did he express any sympathy.

Mrs. Peck continued, it being contrary to her nature to leave anything to the imagination of her hearers. "If he'd been content to go with one of you, I wouldn't have given it another thought. Goodness knows, I'm not of a suspicious turn. But the moment I mention the matter, he turns round with his sweetest smile and he says, 'Oh, don't you trouble, Mrs. Peck!' he says. 'I quite understand. Miss Columbine explained it all, and I quite see your point. It ought to have occurred to me sooner,' he says, smiling with them nice teeth of his, 'but, if you'll believe me, it didn't.' And then, when I suggested maybe he'd like you or Adam to go with him instead, it was, 'No, no, Mrs. Peck. I wouldn't ask it of 'em. I couldn't drag any man at the chariot-wheels of Art. If I did, she would see to it that the chariot was empty.' He most always talks like that," ended Mrs. Peck in an aggrieved tone. "He's that airy in his ways."

A sudden trill of laughter from the doorway caused her to straighten herself sharply and trot to the fireplace with a guilty air.

Columbine entered, light of foot, her eyes brimful of mirth. "You're caught, Aunt Liza! Yes, you're caught!" she commented ungenerously. "I know exactly what you were saying. Shall I tell you? No, p'raps I'd better not. I'll tell you what you looked like instead, shall I? You looked exactly like that funny old speckled hen in the yard who always clucks such a lot. And Rufus"—she threw him a merry glance from which all resentment had wholly departed—"Rufus looks—and is—just like a great red ox."

"Don't you be pert!" said Mrs. Peck, stooping stoutly over the fire. "Get a duster and dust them plates!"

Columbine laughed again with her chin in the air. She found a duster and occupied herself as desired.

Her eyes were upon her work. Plainly she was not looking at Rufus, not apparently thinking of him. But—very suddenly—without changing her attitude, she flashed him a swift glance. He was looking straight at her, and in his blue eyes was an intense, deep glow as of flaming spirit.

Columbine's look shot away from him with the rapidity of a swallow on the wing. The colour deepened in her cheeks.

"P'raps he's almost more like a prize bull," she said meditatively. "Perhaps he's a Minotaur, Aunt Liza. Do you think he is?"

"My dear, I don't know what you're talking about," said Mrs. Peck, with a touch of acidity.

Columbine laughed a little. "Do you know, Rufus?" she said.

She did not look at him with the question; there was a quivering dimple in her red cheek that came and went.

"I'd like to know," said Rufus with simplicity.

"Would you, really?" Columbine polished the last plate vigorously and set it down. "The Minotaur," she said, in the tone of a schoolmistress delivering a lecture, "was a monster, half-bull, half-man, who lived in a place like the Spear Point Caves, and devoured young men and maidens. You live nearer to the Caves than any one else, don't you, Rufus?"

Again she ventured a darting glance at him. His look was still upon her, but its fiery quality was less apparent. He met the challenge with his slow, indulgent smile.

"Yes, I live there. I don't devour anybody. I'm not—that sort of monster."

Columbine shook her head. "I'm not so sure of that," she said. "But I dare say you'd tame."

"P'raps you'd like to do it," suggested Rufus.

It was his first direct overture, and Columbine, who had angled for it, experienced a thrill of triumph. But she was swift to mask her satisfaction.

She tossed her head, and turned: "Oh, I've no time to waste that way," she said. "You must do your own taming, Mr. Minotaur. When you're quite civilised, p'raps I'll talk to you."

She was gone with the words, carrying her plates with her.

"She's a deal too pert," observed Mrs. Peck to the saucepan she was stirring. "It's my belief now that that Mr. Knight's been putting ideas into her head. She's getting wild; that's what she is."

Knowing Rufus, she expected no response, and for several seconds none came.

Then to her surprise she heard his voice, deep and sonorous as the bell-buoy that was moored by the Spear Point Reef.

"Maybe she'd tame," he said.

And "Goodness gracious unto me!" said Mrs. Peck, as she lifted her saucepan off the fire.

CHAPTER IV
THE RISING TIDE

A long dazzling pathway of moonlight stretched over the sea, starting from the horizon, ending at the great jutting promontory of the Spear Point. The moon was yet three nights from the full. The tide was rising, but it would not be high for another two hours.

The breakers ran in, one behind the other, foaming over the hidden rocks, splashing wildly against the grim wall of granite that stood sharp-edged to withstand them. It was curved like a scimitar, that rock, and within its curve there slept, when the tide was low, a pool. When the tide rose the waters raged and thundered all around the rock, but when it sank again the still, deep pool remained, unruffled as a mountain tarn and as full of mystery.

Over a tumble of lesser rocks that bounded the pool to shoreward the wary might find a path to the Spear Point Caves; but the path was difficult, and there were few who had ever attempted it. For the quicksand lay like a golden barrier between the outer beach and the rocks that led thither.

It was an awesome spot. Many a splinter of wreckage had been tossed in over the Spear Point as though flung in sport from a giant hand. And when the water was high there came a hollow groaning from the inner caves as though imprisoned spirits languished there.

But on that night of magic moonlight the only sound was the murmurous splash of the rising waves as they met the first grim rocks of the Point. Presently they would dash in thunder round the granite blade, and the sleeping pool would be turned to a smother of foam.

On the edge of the pool a woman's figure clad in white stood balanced with outstretched arms. So still was the water, so splendid the moonlight, that the whole of her light form was mirrored there—a perfect image of nymph-like grace. She sang a soft, low, trilling song like the song of a blackbird awaking to the dawn.

"By Jupiter!" Knight murmured to himself. "If I could get her only once—only once—as—she—is!"

The gleam of the hunter was in his look. He stood on the rocks some yards away from her, gazing with eyes half-shut.

Suddenly she turned herself, and across the intervening space her voice came to him, half-mocking, half-alluring, "Have you found your inspiration yet?"

"Not yet," he said.

She raised her shoulders with a humorous gesture, "Hasn't the magic begun to work?"

He came towards her, moving slowly and with caution. "Don't move!" he said.

She waited for him on the edge of the pool. There was laughter in her eyes, laughter and the sublime daring of innocence.

He reached her. They stood together on the same flat rock. He bent to her, in his eyes the burning worship of beauty.

"Columbine!" he said. "Witch! Enchantress! Queen!"

The red blood raced into her face. Her eyes shone into his with a sudden glory—the glory of the awaking soul. But the woman-instinct in her checked the first quick impulse of surrender.

She made a little motion away from him. She laughed and veiled her eyes from the fiery adoration that flamed upon her. "The magic is working—evidently," she said. "What a good thing I brought you here!"

"Yes; it is a good thing," he said, and in his voice she heard the deep note of a mastery that would not be denied. "Do you know what you have done to me, you goddess? You have opened the eyes of my heart. I am dazzled. I am blinded. I believe I am possessed. When I paint my picture—it will be such as the world has never seen."

"Hadn't you better begin it?" whispered Columbine.

He held out his hand to her—a hand that was not wholly steady. "Not yet," he said. "The vision is too near, too wonderful. How shall I paint the rapture that I have hardly yet dared to contemplate? Columbine!"

His voice suddenly pleaded, and as though in answer she laid her hand in his. But she did not raise her eyes. She palpitated from head to foot like a captured bird.

"You are not—afraid?" he whispered.

"I don't know," she whispered back. "Not of you—not of you!"

"Ah!" he said. "We are caught in the same net. There is nothing terrible in that. The same magic is working in us both. Let it work, dear! We understand each other. Why should there be anything to fear?"

But still she did not raise her eyes, and still she trembled in his hold. "I never thought," she faltered, "never dreamed. Oh, is it true?"

"True that you are the most beautiful creature that this earth contains?" he said, and his voice throbbed upon the words. "True that the very sight of you turns my blood to fire? Aphrodite, goddess and sorceress, do you doubt that? Wait till you see my picture, and then ask! I have found my inspiration tonight—yes, I have found it—but it is so immense—so overwhelming—that I cannot grasp it yet. Tonight, dear, just for tonight—let me worship at your feet! This madness must have its way. In the morning I shall be sane again. Tonight—tonight I tread Olympus with the Immortals."

He was drawing her towards him, and Columbine—Columbine, who suffered no man's hand upon her—was yielding slowly, but inevitably, to the persuasion of his touch. Just at the last, indeed, she made a small, wholly futile attempt to free herself; but the moment she did so his hold became the hold of the conqueror, and with a faint laugh she flung aside the instinct that had prompted it. The next instant, freely and splendidly, she raised her downcast face and abandoned herself utterly to him.

To give without stint was the impulse of her passionate, Southern nature, and she gave freely, royally, that night. The magic that ran in the veins of both was too compelling to be resisted. The girl, with her half-awakened soul, the man, with his fiery thirst for beauty, were caught in the great current that sweeps like a tidal wave around the world, and it bore them swiftly, swiftly, whither neither he in his restlessness nor she in her in experience realised or cared. If the sound of the breakers came to them from afar they heeded it not. They were too far away to matter as yet, and Knight had steered a safe course for himself in troubled seas before. As for Columbine, she knew only the rapture of love triumphant, and tasted perfect safety in the holding of her lover's arms. He had won her with scarcely a struggle, and she gloried with an ecstasy that was in its way sublime in the completeness of her surrender. On such a night as that it seemed to her that the whole world lay at her feet, and she knew no fear.

The still pool slept in the moonlight, a lake of silver, unspeakably calm. Beyond the outstretched blade of rock the great waters rose and rose. The murmur of them had swelled to a roar. The splash of them mounted higher and ever higher. Suddenly a crest of foam gleamed like a tongue of lightning at the point of the curve. The pool stirred as if awakening. The moonlight on its surface was shivered in a thousand ripples. They broke in a succession of tiny wavelets against the encircling rocks.

Another silver crest appeared, burst in thunder, and in a moment the pool was flooded with tossing water.

"Do you see that?" whispered Columbine. "It is like my life."

They stood together under the frowning cliff and watched the wonder of the pool's awakening. Knight's arm held her close pressed to his side. He could feel the beating of her heart. She stood with her face upturned to his and all the glory of love's surrender shining in her eyes.

He caught his breath as he looked at her. He stooped and kissed the red, red lips that gave so generously. "Is my love as the rising tide to you, sweet?" he murmured.

"It is more!" she answered passionately. "It is more! It is the tidal wave that comes so seldom—maybe only once in a lifetime—and carries all before it."

He pressed her closer. "My passion-flower!" he said. "My queen!"

He kissed the throbbing whiteness of her throat, the loose clusters of her hair. He laid his hot face against her neck, and held it so, not breathing. Her arms stretched upwards, clasping him. She was panting—panting as one in deep waters.

"I love you! I love you!" she whispered tensely. "Oh, how I love you!"

Again there came the thunder of the surf. The waters of the pool leapt as if a giant hand had churned them. The foam from beyond the reef overspread them like snow. The whole world became full of the sound of surging waters.

Knight opened his eyes. "The tide is coming up fast," he said. "We must be getting back."

She clung closer to him. "I could die with you on a night like this," she said.

He crushed her to his heart. "Ah, goddess!" he said. "You couldn't die! But I am only mortal, and the tide won't wait."

Again the swirling breakers swept around the Point. Reluctantly she came to earth. The pool had become a seething whirl of water.

"Yes," she said, "we must go, and quickly—quickly! It rises so fast here."

Sure-footed as a doe over the slippery rocks, she led the way. They left the magic place and the dazzling tumble of moonlit water, the dark caves, the enchanted strand. Progress was not easy, but Knight had been that way before, though only by day. He followed his guide closely, and when presently they emerged upon level sand, he overtook and walked beside her.

She slipped her hand into his. "It's the lie of the quicksand that's puzzling," she said, "if you don't know it well."

"I am in thy hands, O Queen," he made light reply. "Lead me whither thou wilt!"

She laughed — a low, sweet laugh of sheer happiness. "And if I lead you astray?"

"I would follow you down to the nethermost millstone," he vowed.

Her hand tightened upon his. She paused a moment, looking out over the stretch of sand that intervened between them and the little fishing-quay. He had safely negotiated that stretch of sand by daylight, though even then it had needed an alert eye to detect that slight ooziness of surface that denoted the presence of the sea-swamp. But by night, even in that brilliant moonlight, it was barely perceptible. Columbine herself did not trust to appearances. She had learnt the way from Adam as a child learns a lesson by heart. He had taught her to know the danger-spot by the shape of the cliffs above it.

After a very brief pause to take her bearings, she moved forward with absolute assurance. Knight accompanied her with unquestioning confidence. His faith in his own luck was as profound as his faith in the girl at his side. And the tumult in his veins that night was such as to make him insensible of danger. The roar of the rising tide exhilarated him. He walked with the stride of a conqueror, free and unafraid, his face to the sea.

Unerringly she led him, but she did not speak again until they had made the passage and the treacherous morass of sand was left behind.

Then, with a deep breath, she stopped. "Now we are safe!"

"Weren't we safe before?" he asked carelessly.

Her eyes sought his; she gave a little shiver. "Oh, are we ever safe?" she said. "Especially when we are happy? That quicksand makes one think."

"Never spoil the present by thinking of the future!" said Knight sententiously.

She took him seriously. "I don't. I want to keep the present just as it is — just as it is. I would like to stay with you here for ever and ever, but in another half-hour—in less—the tide will be racing over this very spot, and we shall be gone." Her voice vibrated; she cast a glance behind. "One false step," she said, "too sharp a turn, too wide a curve, and we'd have been in the quicksand! It's like that all over. It's life, and it's full of danger, whichever way we turn."

He looked at her curiously. "Why, what has come to you?" he said.

She caught her breath in a sound that was like a sob. "I don't know," she said. "It's being so madly happy that has frightened me. It can't last. It never does last."

He smiled upon her philosophically. "Then let us make the most of it while it does!" he said. "Tonight will pass, but—don't forget—there is tomorrow."

She answered him feverishly. "The moon may not shine tomorrow."

He laughed, drawing her to him. "I can do without the moon, queen of my heart."

She went into his arms, but she was trembling. "I feel—somehow—as if someone were watching us," she whispered.

"Exactly my own idea," he said. "The moon is a bit too intrusive tonight. I shan't weep if there are a few clouds tomorrow."

She laughed a little dubiously. "We couldn't cross the quicksand if the light were bad."

"We could get down to the Point by the cliff-path," he pointed out. "I went that way only this afternoon."

"Ah! But it is very steep, and it passes Rufus's cottage," she murmured.

"What of it?" he said indifferently. "I'm sure he sleeps like a log."

She turned from the subject. "Besides, you must have moonlight for your picture. And the moon won't last."

"My picture!" He pressed her suddenly closer. "Do you know what my picture is going to be?"

"Tell me!" she whispered.

"Shall I?" He turned gently her face up to his own. "Shall I? Dare I?"

She opened her eyes wide—those glorious, trusting eyes. "But why should you be afraid to tell me?"

He laughed again softly, and kissed her lips. "I will make a rough sketch in the morning and show it you. It won't be a study—only an idea. You are going to pose for the study."

"I?" she said, half-startled.

"You—yes, you!" His eyes looked deeply into hers. "Haven't you realised yet that you are my inspiration?" he said. "It is going to be the picture of my life—'Aphrodite the Beautiful!'"

She quivered afresh at his words. "Am I really—so beautiful?" she faltered. "Would you think so if—if you didn't love me?"

"Would I have loved you if you weren't?" laughed Knight. "My darling, you are exquisite as a passion-flower grown in Paradise. To worship you is as natural to me as breathing. You are heaven on earth to me."

"You love me—because of that?"

"I love you," he answered, "soul and body, because you are you. There is no other reason, heart of my heart. When my picture of pictures is painted, then—perhaps—you will see yourself as I see you—and understand."

She uttered a quick sigh, clinging to him with a hold that was almost convulsive. "Ah, yes! To see myself with your eyes! I want that. I shall know then—how much you love me."

"Will you? But will you?" he said, softly derisive. "You will have to show me yourself and your love—all there is of it—before you can do that."

She lifted her head from his shoulder. The fire that he had kindled in her soul was burning in her eyes. "I am all yours—all yours," she told him passionately. "All that I have to offer is your own."

His face changed a little. The tender mockery passed, and an expression that was oddly out of place there succeeded it. "Ah, you shouldn't tell me that, sweetheart," he said, and his voice was low and held a touch of pain. "I might be tempted to take too much—more than I have any right to take."

"You have a right to all," she said.

But he shook his head. "No—no! You are too young."

"Too young to love?" she said, with quick scorn.

His arm was close about her. "No," he answered soberly. "Only so young that you may—possibly—make the mistake of loving too well."

"What do you mean?" Her voice had a startled note; she pressed nearer to him.

He lifted a hand and pointed to the silver pathway on the sea. "I mean that love is just moonshine—just moonshine; the dream of a night that passes."

"Not in a night!" she cried, and there was anguish in the words.

He bent again swiftly and kissed her lips. "No, not in a night, sweetheart. Not even in two. But at last—at last—*tout passe!*"

"Then it isn't love!" she said with conviction.

He snapped his fingers at the moonlight with a gesture half-humorous, yet half-defiant. "It is life," he said, "and the irony of life. Don't be too generous, my queen of the sea! Give me what I ask—of your graciousness! But—don't offer me more! Perhaps I might take it, and then—"

He turned with the words, as if the sentence were ended, and Columbine went with him, bewildered but too deeply fascinated to feel any serious misgiving. She did not ask for any further explanation, something about him restrained her. But she knew no doubt, and when he halted in the shadow of the deserted quay and took her face once more between his hands with the one word, "Tomorrow!" she lifted eyes of perfect trust to his and answered simply, "Yes, tomorrow!"

And the rapture of his kisses was all-sufficing. She carried away with her no other memory but that.

CHAPTER V
MIDSUMMER MORNING

It was two mornings later, very early on Midsummer Day, that Rufus the Red, looking like a Viking in the crystal atmosphere of sky and sea, rowed the stranger with great, swinging strokes through the fishing fleet right out into the burning splendour of the sun. Knight had entered the boat in the belief that he was going to see something of the raising of the nets. But it became apparent very soon that Rufus had other plans for his entertainment, for he passed his father by with no more than a jerk of the head, which Adam evidently interpreted as a sign of farewell rather than of greeting, and rowed on without a pause.

Knight, with his sketch-book beside him, sat in the stern. He had never taken much interest in Rufus before; but now, seated facing him, with the giant muscles and grim, unresponsive countenance of the man perpetually before his eyes, the selecting genius in him awoke and began to appraise.

Rufus wore a grey flannel shirt, open at the neck, displaying a broad red chest, immensely powerful, with a bull-like strength that every swing of the oars brought into prominence. He had not the appearance of exerting himself unduly, albeit he was pulling in choppy water against the tide.

His blue eyes gazed ever straight at the shore he was leaving. He seemed so withdrawn into himself as to be oblivious of the fact that he was not alone. Knight watched him, wondering if any thoughts were stirring in the slow brain behind that massive forehead. Columbine had declared that the man was an oaf, and he felt inclined to agree with her. And yet there was something in the intensity of the fellow's eyes that held his attention, the possibility of the actual existence of an unknown element that did not fit into that conception of him. They were not the eyes of a mere animal. There was no vagueness in their utter stillness. Rather had they the look of a man who waits.

Curiosity began to stir within him. He wondered if by judicious probing he could penetrate the wall of aloofness with which his companion seemed to be surrounded. It would be interesting to know if the fellow really possessed any individuality.

Airily he broke the silence. "Are you going to take me straight into the temple of the sun? I thought I was out to see the fishing."

The remote blue eyes came back as it were out of the far distance and found him. There came to Knight an odd, wholly unwonted, sensation of smallness. He felt curiously like a pigmy disturbing the meditations of a giant.

Rufus looked at him for several seconds of uninterrupted rowing before, in his deep, resounding voice, he spoke. "They won't be taking up the nets for a goodish while yet. We shall be back in time."

"The idea is to give me a run for my money first, eh?" inquired Knight pleasantly.

He had not anticipated the sudden fall of the red brows that greeted his words. He felt as if he had inadvertently trodden upon a match.

"No," said Rufus slowly, speaking with a strangely careful accent, as if his mind were concentrated upon being absolutely intelligible to his listener. "That was not my idea."

The spirit of adventure awoke in Knight. There was something behind this granite calmness of demeanour then. He determined to draw it forth, even though he struck further sparks in the process.

"No?" he said carelessly. "Then why this pleasure trip? Did you bring me out here just to show me—the 'Pit of the Burning'?"

His eyes were upon the dazzling glory of the newly risen sun as he threw the question. Rufus's massive head and shoulders were strongly outlined against it. He had ceased to row, but the boat still shot forward, impelled by the last powerful sweep of the oars, the water streaming past in a rush of foam.

Slowly, like the hammer-strokes of a deep-toned bell, came Rufus's voice in answer. "It wasn't to show you anything I brought you here. It was just to tell you something."

"Really?" Knight's interest was thoroughly aroused. He became alert to the finger-tips. There was something in the deliberate utterance that conveyed a sense of danger. A wary gleam shone in his eyes under their level brows. It was one of his principles when dealing with an uncertain situation never to betray surprise. "And what may this valuable piece of information be?" he inquired, with a smile.

Rufus shipped his oars steadily, gravely, with purpose. "I saw you cross the quicksand last night," he said.

The Tidal Wave and Other Stories | 39

"Indeed!" Knight's voice was of the most casual quality. He was feeling for his cigarette-case.

Rufus continued heavily, fatefully, gathering force with every word, as a loosened rock beginning to roll down a mountain side. "The light was bad. It was a tomfool thing to do. And Columbine was with you."

Knight raised his shoulders ever so slightly. "Or rather—I was with her. Miss Columbine knows the lie of the quicksand. I—do not."

Rufus went on as if he had not spoken. "There's danger all along that beach as far as the Spear Point. Adam will tell you the same. When it's a spring tide there's times when there's such a swell that it's round the Point and over the pool like a tidal wave. You'll hear the bell-buoy tolling when there's a swell like that. We call it the Death Current hereabouts, because there's nothing could live in it, and the bell always tolls. And once it comes up like that the way to the cliff-path is under water in less than thirty seconds. And the quicksand is the only chance left." He paused; it was as if the rock halted for a moment on the edge of the precipice before plunging finally into the abyss of silence below. "When there's a ground swell," he said, "the quicksand will pull a man down quicker than hell. And there's no one—not Adam himself—can tell the lay of it for certain when the light is bad."

His mouth closed upon the words like the snap of a strong spring. Knight waited for more, but none came. Whatever the thought behind the warning that he had just uttered it was evident that Rufus had no intention of giving it expression. He had uttered the girl's name with no more emotion than that of his father, but it seemed to Knight that by that very fact he had managed to convey a warning more potent than any that had followed. Otherwise he would scarcely have taken the trouble to mention her. The possibility of subtlety in this great, slow-speaking giant piqued him to a keener interest. He resolved to probe a little deeper.

"Miss Columbine is a very reliable guide," he remarked. "If you and Adam have been her instructors in shore-craft, she does you credit."

His remark went into utter silence. Rufus, with huge hands loosely clasped between his knees, appeared to be engrossed in watching the progress of the boat as she drifted gently on the rising tide. His face was utterly blank of expression, unless a certain grim fixity could be described as such.

Knight became slightly exasperated. Was the fellow no more than the fool Columbine believed him to be after all? He determined to settle this question once and for all at a single stroke.

"I suppose she has all you fellows at Spear Point at her feet?" he said, with an easy smile. "But I hope you are all too large-minded to grudge a poor artist the biggest find that has ever come his way."

There was a pause, but the burning blue eyes were no longer fixed upon the sparkling ripples through which they had travelled. They were turned upon Knight's face, searching, piercing, intent. Before he spoke again, Knight's doubt as to the existence of a brain behind the massive brow was fully set at rest.

"There is another thing I have to say," said Rufus.

Knight's smile broadened encouragingly. "By all means let us hear it!" he said.

Rufus proceeded. "You speak of Columbine as if she were just a bit of amber or such-like as you'd found on the shore and picked up and put in your pocket. You speak as if she's your property to do what you like with. That's just what she is not. You're making love to her. I know it. I seen it. And it's got to stop."

He spoke with blunt force; his hands were suddenly locked upon each other in a hard grip.

Knight lifted his shoulders; his smile had become whimsical. He had drawn the fellow at last. "I thought you'd seen something," he remarked, "by your way. But who could help making love to a girl with a face like that? It would take a heart of stone to resist it. Why, even you"—and his look challenged Rufus with careless derision—"even you have fallen to that temptation before now, or I'm much mistaken. But I gather that your attentions did not meet with a very favourable response."

He was baiting the animal now, taunting him, with the semi-humorous malice of the mischievous schoolboy. He had no particular grudge against Rufus, but he had a lively desire to see him squirm.

But this desire was not to be gratified. Rufus met the thrust without the faintest hint of feeling.

"What you think," he said, in his weighty fashion, "has nothing to do with me. What you do is all that matters. And I tell you straight"—a blue flame suddenly leapt up like a volcanic light in the sombre eyes—"that no man that hasn't honest intentions by her is going to make love to Columbine."

"Great Jove!" mocked Knight, with his careless laugh. "And who told you, most worthy swain, what my intentions were?"

Rufus leaned towards him slowly, with something of the action of a crouching beast. "No one told me," he said in a voice that was deeply menacing. "But—I know."

Knight made a gesture of supreme indifference. "You are on an entirely wrong scent," he observed. "But you seem to be enjoying it." He paused to take out a cigarette. "Have a smoke!" he suggested after a moment, proffering his case.

Rufus did not so much as see it. His whole attitude was one of strain, as if he barely held himself back from springing at the other's throat.

Knight, however, was elaborately unconscious of any tension. He smiled and closed his cigarette case. Then with the utmost deliberation he searched for his matches, found them, and lighted his cigarette.

Having puffed forth the first deep breath with luxurious enjoyment, he spoke again. "It is a little difficult to get a man of your stamp to comprehend the fact that an artist—a true artist—is not one to be greatly drawn by the grosser things of life, more especially when he is in ardent pursuit of that elusive flame called inspiration. But you would hardly grasp a condition in which the body—and the impulses of the body—are in complete subjection to the aspirations of the mind. You"—he blew forth a cloud of smoke—"are probably incapable of realizing that the worship of beauty can be of so purely artistic a nature as to be practically free from the physical element, certainly independent of it. I am taking you out of your depth, I know, but it is hard to make myself clear to an untrained mind. I might try a homely simile and suggest to you that you go a-fishing, not for love of the fish, but because it is your profession; but that does not wholly illustrate my meaning, for I love everything in the way of beauty that comes my way. I follow beauty like a guiding star. And sometimes—but seldom, oh, very seldom"—a sudden odd thrill sounded in his voice as if by accident some hidden string had been struck and set vibrating—"I fulfil my desire—I realise my dream—I grasp and hold a spark of the Divine." He paused again, his face to the gold of the dawn and in his eyes the far-off rapture of one who watches some soaring flight of fancy. Then abruptly, lightly, he resumed his normal, half-quizzing demeanour. "Doubtless I weary you," he said. "But you mustn't run away with the idea that I am in love because I feel myself inspired. It may sound callous to you, but if Miss Columbine were to lose her exquisite beauty (which heaven forbid!) I should never voluntarily look upon her again. That I take it, is the test of love, which, we are told, is blind to all defects."

He ceased to speak, and carelessly, yet with obvious enjoyment, he sent forth another cloud of smoke into the crystal air of the morning.

He was not looking at Rufus. It was abundantly evident that he had not realised how near to open violence the young fisherman had been. His nonchalant explanation was plainly all-sufficing in his own opinion, and during the very marked silence that followed he displayed no faintest hint of anxiety or even interest as to the fashion of its reception.

The boat was rocking lightly on the swell; the sea all around was flooded with gold. The great jagged outline of the Spear Point looked like the castle of a dream. The haze of the newly risen sun had touched with magic all the world. Knight's eyes were half-closed. He had the look of a man at peace with himself.

And Rufus relaxed. The tension went out of his attitude; the volcanic fires died down. For half a minute or more he sat absolutely passive. Then slowly, with massive deliberation, he moved, unshipped the oars, and bent himself to pull. In another ten seconds the boat was rushing through the water under the compulsion of his powerful strokes, heading straight for the boats of the fishing fleet that dotted the bay....

It must have been fully a quarter of an hour later that Knight, having finished his cigarette, came out of his reverie.

"And so, you see," he remarked in the tone of one pleasantly rounding off a conversation, "until my picture is painted I remain the slave of my dream. I wonder if I have succeeded at all in making myself intelligible."

His eyes opened lazily and met Rufus's sombre gaze; they held a laughing challenge, the easy challenge of the practised fencer who condescends to try a bout with ignorance.

Stolidly Rufus met the look. If he realised the challenge he did not accept it. He had barred himself in once more behind an impenetrable wall of unresponsiveness. His gaze was once more obscure and bovine. All hint of violence was gone from his bearing. Only solid force remained—the force that drove the boat strongly, unerringly, through the golden-crested waves.

"If you're going to do a picture of Columbine," he said slowly, "I hope it'll be a good one."

"It will probably be—great," said Knight, and flicked some ash from his sleeve with the complacent air of a man who has accomplished his purpose.

CHAPTER VI
THE MIDSUMMER MOON

It was very late that night, just as the first long rays of a full moon streamed across a dreaming sea, that the door that led out of the conservatory at The Ship softly opened, and a slim figure, clad in a long, dark garment, flitted forth. Neither to right nor left did it glance, but, closing the door without sound, slipped out over the grass almost as if it moved on wings, and so down to the beach-path that wound steeply to the shore.

The tide was rising with the moon; the roar of it swelled and sank like the mighty breathing of a giant. The waters shone in the gathering light in a vast silver shimmer almost too dazzling for the eye to endure. In another hour it would be as light as day. A few dim clouds were floating over the stars, filmy wisps that had escaped from the ragged edges of a dark curtain that had veiled the sun before its time. The breeze that had blown them free wandered far overhead; below, especially on the shore, it was almost tropically warm, and no breath of air seemed to stir.

Swiftly went the flitting figure, like a brown moth drawn by the glitter of the moonlight. There was no other living thing in sight.

All the lights of Spear Point village had gone out long since. Rufus's cottage, with its slip of garden on the shelf of the cliff, was no more than a faint blur of white against the towering sandstone behind. No light had shone there all the evening, for the daylight had not died till ten, and he was often in bed at that hour. The fishing fleet would be out again with the dawn if the weather held, or even earlier; and the hours of sleep were precious.

Down on the rocks on the edge of the sleeping pool a grey shadow lurked amidst darker shadows. A faint scent of cigarette smoke hung about the silver beach—a drifting suggestion intangible as the magic of the night.

Could it have been this faint, floating fragrance that drew the flitting brown moth by way of the quicksand, swiftly, swiftly, along the moonlit shore travelling with mysterious certainty, irresistibly attracted? There was no pause in its rapid progress, though the course it followed was tortuous. It pursued, with absolute confidence, an invisible, winding path. And ever the roar of the sea grew louder and louder.

Across the pool, carved in the blackness of the outstretched curving scimitar of rock, there was a ledge, washed smooth by every tide, but a foot or more above the water when the tide was out. It was inaccessible save by way of the pool itself, and yet it had the look of a pathway cut in the face of the Spear Point Rock. The moonlight gleamed upon its wet surface. In the very centre of the great curving rock there was a deeper darkness that might have been a cave.

It must have been after midnight when the little brown figure that had flitted so securely through the quicksand came with its noiseless feet over the tumble of rocks that lay about the pool, and the shadow that lurked in the shadows rose up and became a man.

They met on the edge of the pool, but there was about the lesser form a hesitancy of movement, a shyness, almost a wildness, that seemed as if it would end in flight.

But the man remained quite motionless, and in a moment or two the impulse passed or was controlled. Two quivering hands came forth to him as if in supplication.

"So you are waiting!" a low voice said.

He took the hands, bending to her. The moonlight made his eyes gleam with a strange intensity.

"I have been waiting a long time," he said.

Even then she made a small, fluttering movement backward, as if she would evade him. And then with a sharp sob she conquered her reluctance again. She gave herself into his arms.

He held her closely, passionately. He kissed her face, her neck, her bosom, as if he would devour the sweetness of her in a few mad moments of utter abandonment.

But in a little he checked himself. "You are so late, sweetheart. The tide won't wait for us. There will be time for this—afterwards."

She lay burning and quivering against his heart. "There is tomorrow," she whispered, clinging to him.

He kissed her again. "Yes, there is tomorrow. But who can tell what may happen then? There will never be such a night as this again, sweet. See the light against that rock! It is a marvel of black and white, and I swear that the pool is green. There is magic abroad tonight. Let me catch it! Let me catch it! Afterwards!—when the tide comes up—we will drink our fill of love."

He spoke as if urged by strong excitement, and having spoken his arms relaxed. But she clung to him still.

"Oh, darling, I am frightened—I am frightened! I couldn't come sooner. I had a feeling—of being watched. I nearly—very nearly—didn't come at all. And now I am here—I feel—I feel—afraid."

He bent his face to hers again. His hand rested lightly, reassuringly upon her head. "No, no! There is nothing to frighten you, my passion-flower. If you had only come to me sooner it would have made it easier for you. But now there is no time." The soothing note in his voice sounded oddly strained, as though an undernote of fever throbbed below it. "You're not going to fail me," he urged softly. "Think how much it means to you—to me! And there is only half an hour left, dear. Give me that half-hour to catch the magic! Then—when the tide comes up"—his voice sank, he whispered deeply into her ear—"I will teach you the greatest magic this old world knows."

She thrilled at his words, thrilled through her trembling. She lifted her face to the moonlight. "I love you!" she said. "Oh, I love you!"

"And you will do this one thing for me?" he urged.

She threw her arms wide. "I would die for you," she told him passionately.

A moment she stood so, then with a swift movement that had in it something of fierce surrender she sprang away from him on to the flat rock above the pool where but two nights before the gates of love's wonderland had first opened to her.

Here for a second she stood, motionless it seemed. And then strangely, amazingly, she moved again. The brown garment slipped from her, and like a streak of light, she was gone, and the still pool received her with a rippling splash as of fairy laughter.

The man on the brink drew a short, hard breath, and put his hand to his eyes as if dazed. And from beyond the Spear Point there sounded the deep tolling of the bell-buoy as it rocked on the rising tide.

CHAPTER VII
THE DEATH CURRENT

The pool was still again, still as a sheet of glass, reflecting the midnight glory of the moon. It was climbing high in the sky, and the cloud-wreaths were mounting towards it as incense smoke from an altar. The thick, black curtain that hung in the west was growing like a monstrous shadow, threatening to overspread the whole earth.

Down on the silver beach, crouched on one of the rocks that bordered the shining pool, Knight worked with fevered intensity to catch the magic of the hour. The light was wonderful. The pool shone strangely, deeply green; the rocks about it might have been delicately carved in ivory. And across the pool, clear-cut against the utter darkness of the Spear Point Rock, stood Aphrodite the Beautiful, clad in some green translucent draperies, her black hair loose about her, her white arms outstretched to the moonlight, her face—exquisite as a flower—upturned to meet the glory. She was like a dream too wonderful to be true, save for the passion that lived in her eyes. That was vivid, that was poignant—the fire of sacrifice burning inwardly.

The man worked on as one driven by a ruthless force. His teeth were clenched upon his lower lip. His hands were shaking, and yet he knew that what he did was too superb for criticism. It was the work of genius—the driving force within that would not let him pause to listen to the wild urgings of his heart. That might come after. But this—this power that compelled was supreme. While it gripped him he was not his own master. He was, as he himself had said, a slave.

And while he worked at its behest, watching the wonderful thing that inspiration was weaving by his hand, scarcely conscious of effort, though the perspiration was streaming down his face, he whispered over and over between his clenched teeth the title of the picture that was to astonish the world—"The Goddess Veiled in Foam."

There was no foam as yet on the pool, but he remembered how two nights before he had seen the breaking of the first wave that had turned it into a seething cauldron of surf. That was what he wanted now—just the first great wave washing over her exquisite feet and flinging its garment of spray like a flimsy veil over her perfect form. He wanted that as he wanted nothing else on earth. And then—then—he would catch his dream, he would chain for ever the fairy vision that might never be granted again.

There came a boom like a distant gunshot on the other side of the Spear Point Rock, and again, but very far away, there sounded the tolling of the bell beyond the reef. The man's heart gave a great leap. It was coming!

In the same moment the girl's voice came to him across the pool, mingling with the rushing of great waters.

"The tide is coming up fast. It won't be safe much longer."

"Don't move! Don't move!" he cried back almost frantically. "It is absolutely safe. I will swim across and help you if you are afraid. But wait—wait just a few moments more!"

She did not urge him. Her surrender had been too complete. Perhaps his promise reassured her, or perhaps she did not fully realise the danger. She waited motionless and the man worked on.

Again there came that sound that was like the report of a distant gun, and the roaring of the sea swelled to tumult.

"Don't move! Don't move!" he cried again.

But she could not have heard him in the overwhelming rush of the sea.

There came a sudden dimness. A cloud had drifted over the moon, and Knight looked up and cursed it with furious impatience. It passed, and he saw her again—his vision, the goddess of his dream, still as the rock behind her, yet splendidly alive. He bent himself again to his work. Would that wave never come to veil her in sparkling raiment of foam?

Ah! At last! The peace of the pool was shattered. A shining wave, curved, green, transparent, gleamed round the corner, ran, swift as a flame, along the rock, and broke with a thunderous roar in a torrent of snow-white surf. In a moment the pool was a seething tumult of water, and in that moment Knight saw his goddess as the artist in him had yearned to see her, her beauty half-veiled and half-revealed in a shimmering robe of foam.

The vision vanished. Another cloud had drifted over the moon. Only the swirling water remained.

Again he lifted his head to curse the fate that baffled him, and as he did so a hand came suddenly from the darkness behind and gripped him by the shoulder. A voice that was like the angry bellow of a bull roared in his ear.

What it said he did not hear; so amazed was he by the utter unexpectedness of the attack. Before he had time to realise what was happening, he was shaken with furious force and flung aside. He fell—and his precious work fell with him—on the very edge of that swirling pool....

Seconds later, when the moon gleamed out again, he was still frantically groping for it on the stones. The roar of the sea was terrible and imminent, like the roar of a destroying monster racing upon its prey, and from the caves there came a hollow groaning as of chained spirits under the earth.

The light flashed away again just as he spied his treasure on the brink of the dashing water. He sprang to save it, intent upon naught else; but in that instant there came a roar such as he had not heard before—a sound so compelling, so nerve-shattering, that even he was arrested, entrapped as it were by a horror of crashing elements that made him wonder if all the fiends in hell were fighting for his soul. And, as he paused, the swirl of a great wave caught him in the darkness like the blow of a concrete thing, nearly flinging him backwards. He staggered, for the first time stricken with fear, and then in the howling uproar of that dreadful place there came to him like a searchlight wheeling inwards the thought of the girl. The water receded from him, leaving him drenched, almost dazed, but a voice within—an urgent, insistent voice—clamoured that his safety was at stake, his life a matter of mere moments if he lingered. This was the Death Current of which Rufus had warned him only that afternoon. Had not the bell-buoy been tolling to deaf ears for some time past? The Death Current that came like a tidal wave! And nothing could live in it. The girl—surely the girl had been washed off her ledge and overwhelmed in the flood before it had reached him. Possibly Rufus would manage to save her, for that it was Rufus who had so savagely sprung upon him he had no doubt; but he himself was powerless. If he saved his own life it would be by a miracle. Had not the fellow warned him that retreat by way of the cliff-path would be cut off in thirty seconds when the tide raced up like that? And if he failed to reach that, only the quicksand was left—the quicksand that dragged a man down quicker than hell!

He set his teeth and turned his face to the cliff. A light was shining half-way up it—that must come from the window of Rufus's cottage. He took it as a beacon, and began to stumble through the howling darkness towards it. He knew the cliff-path. He had come down it only that night to make sure that there was no one spying upon them. The cottage had been shut and dark then, the little garden empty. He had concluded that Rufus had gone early to rest after a long day with the nets, and had passed on securely to wait for Columbine on the edge of their magic pool. But what he did not know was exactly where the cliff-path ran out on to the beach. The opening was close to the Caves and sheltered by rocks. Could he find it in this infernal darkness? Could he ever make his way to it in time? With the waves crashing behind him he struggled desperately towards the blackness of the cliffs.

The rocks under his feet were wet and slippery. He fought his way over them, feeling as if a hundred demons were in league to hold him back. The swirl of the incoming tide sounded in his ears like a monstrous chant of death. Again and again he slipped and fell, and yet again he dragged himself up, grimly determined to fight the desperate battle to the last gasp. The thought of Columbine had gone wholly from him, even as the thought of his lost treasure. Only the elemental desire of life gripped him, vital and urgent, forcing him to the greatest physical effort he had ever made. He went like a goaded animal, savage, stubborn, fiercely surmounting every obstacle, driven not so much by fear as by a furious determination to frustrate the fate that menaced him.

It must have been nearly a minute later that the moon shone forth again, throwing gleaming streaks of brightness upon the mighty breakers that had swallowed the magic pool. They were riding in past the Spear Point in majestic and unending procession, and the rocks that surrounded the pool were already deeply covered. The surf of one great wave was rushing over the beach to the Caves, and the spray of it blew over Knight, drenching him from head to foot. Desperately, by that passing gleam of moonlight, he searched for the opening of the path, the foam of the oncoming procession already swirling about his feet. He spied it suddenly at length, and in the same instant something within him—could it have been his heart?—dropped abruptly like a loosened weight to the very depths of his being. The way of escape in that direction was already cut off. In the darkness he had not taken a straight course, and it was too late.

Wildly he turned—like a hunted animal seeking refuge. With great leaps and gigantic effort, he made for the open beach. He reached it, reached the loose dry sand so soon to be covered by the roaring tumult of great waters. His eyes glared out over the level stretch that intervened between the Spear Point Rock and the harbour quay. The tide would not be over it yet.

He flung his last defiance to the fate that relentlessly hunted him as he took the only alternative, and set himself to traverse the way of the quicksand—that dragged a man down quicker than hell.

CHAPTER VIII
THE BOON

Someone was mounting the steep cliff-path that led to Rufus's cottage—a man, square-built and powerful, who carried a burden. The moon shone dimly upon his progress through a veil of drifting cloud. He was streaming with water at every step, but he moved as if his drenched clothing were in no way a hindrance—steadily, strongly, with stubborn fixity of purpose. The burden he carried hung limply in his arms, and over his shoulder there drifted a heavy mass of wet, black hair.

He came at length on his firm, bare feet to the little gate that led to the lonely cottage, and, without pausing, passed through. The cottage door was ajar. He pushed it back and entered, closing it, even as he did so, with a backward fling of the heel. Then, in the tiny living-room, by the light of the lamp that shone in the window, he laid his burden down.

White and cold, she lay with closed eyes upon the little sofa, motionless and beautiful as a statue recumbent upon a tomb, her drenched draperies clinging about her. He stood for a second looking upon her; then, still with the absolute steadiness of set purpose, he turned and went into the inner room.

He came back with a blanket, and stooping, he lifted the limp form and, with a certain deftness that seemed a part of his immovable resolution, he wrapped it in the rough grey folds.

It was while he was doing this that a sudden sigh came from between the parted lips, and the closed eyes flashed open.

They gazed upon him in bewilderment, but he continued his ministrations with grim persistence and an almost bovine expression of countenance. Only when two hands came quivering out of the enveloping blanket and pushed him desperately away did he desist. He straightened himself then and turned away.

"You'll be—all right," he said in his deep voice.

Then Columbine started up on her elbow, clutching wildly at the blanket, drawing it close about her. The cold stillness of her was gone, as though a sudden flame had scorched her. Her face, her neck, her whole body were burning, burning.

"What—what happened?" she gasped. "You—why have you brought me—here?"

He did not look at her.

"It was the nearest place," he said. "The Death Current caught you, and you were stunned. I got you out."

"You—got me—out!" she repeated, saying the words slowly as if she were teaching herself a lesson.

He nodded his great head.

"Yes. I came up in time. I saw what would happen. There's often a tidal wave about now. I thought you knew that—thought Adam would have told you. He"—his voice suddenly went a tone deeper—"knew it. I told him this morning."

"Ah!" She uttered the word upon a swift intake of breath; her startled eyes suddenly dilated. "Where is he?" she said.

The man's huge frame stiffened at the question; she saw his hands clench. But he kept his head turned from her; she could not see his face. There followed a pause that seemed to her fevered imagination to have something deadly in it. Then: "I hope he's gone where he belongs," said Rufus, with terrible deliberation.

Her cry of agony cut across his last word like the severing of a taut string. She leapt to her feet, in that moment of anguish supremely forgetful of self.

"Rufus!" she cried, and wildly gripped his arm, "You've never—left him—to be—killed!"

She felt his muscles harden in grim resistance to her grasp. She saw that his averted face was set like a stone mask.

"It's none of my business," he said, speaking through rigid lips.

She turned from him with a gasp of horror and sprang for the door. But in an instant he wheeled, thrust out a great arm, and caught her. His fingers closed upon her bare shoulder.

"Columbine!" he said.

She resisted him frantically, bending now this way, now that. But he held her in spite of it, held her, and slowly brought her nearer to him.

"Stand still!" he said.

His voice came upon her like a blow. She flinched at the sound of it—flinched and obeyed.

"Let me go!" she gasped out. "He—may be drowning—at this moment!"

"Let him drown!" said Rufus.

She lifted her tortured face in frenzied protest, but it died upon her lips. For in that moment she met his eyes, and the blazing blue of them made her feel as though spirit had been poured upon her flame, consuming her. Words failed her utterly. She stood palpitating in his hold, not breathing—a wild thing trapped.

Slowly he bent towards her. "Let him drown!" he said again. "Do you think I'm going to let you throw your life away for a cur like that?"

There was uncloaked ferocity in the question. His hold was merciless.

"I saved you," he said. "It wasn't especially easy. But I did it. For the matter of that, I'd have gone through hell for you. And do you think I'm going to let you go again—now?"

She did not answer him. Only her lips moved stiffly, as though they formed words she could not utter. She could not take her eyes from his, though his looks seared her through and through.

He went on, deeply, with gathering force. "He'd have let you be swept away. He didn't care. All he wanted was to get you for his picture. That was all he made love to you for. He'd have sacrificed you to the devil for that. You don't believe me, maybe, but I know—I know!"

There was savage certainty in the reiterated words, and the girl recoiled from them, her face like death. But he held her still, implacably, relentlessly.

"That's all he wants of you," he said. "To use you for his purpose, and then—to throw you aside. Why"—and he suddenly showed his clenched teeth—"he dared—damn him!—he dared to tell me so!"

"He—told you!" Her lips spoke the words at last, but they seemed to come from a long way off.

"Yes." With suppressed violence he answered her. "He didn't put it that way—being a gentleman! But he took care to make me understand that he only wanted you for the sake of his accursed picture. That's the only thing that counts with him, and he's the sort not to care what he does to get it. He wouldn't have got you—like this—if he hadn't made you love him first. I know that too—as well as if you'd told me."

The passion in his voice was rising, and it was as if the heat of it rekindled her animation. With a jerky movement she flung up both her hands, grasping tensely the arms that held her so rigidly.

"Yes, I love him!" she said, and her voice rang wildly. "I love him! I don't care what he is! Rufus—Rufus—oh, for the love of Heaven, don't let him drown!" The words rushed out desperately; it was as if her whole nature, all her pride, all her courage, were flung into that frantic appeal. She clung to the man with straining entreaty. "Oh, go down and save him!" she begged. "I'll do anything for you in return—anything you like to ask! Only do this one thing for me! He may have escaped the tide. If so, he'll try the quicksand, and he don't know the lie of it! Rufus, you wouldn't want—your worst enemy—to die like that!"

She broke off, wildly sobbing, yet still clinging to him in agonised entreaty. The man's face, with its crude ferocity, the untamed glitter of its fiery eyes, was still bent to hers, but she no longer shrank from it. The power that moved her was too immense to be swayed by lesser things. His attitude no longer affected her, one way or another. It had ceased to count, so that she only wrenched from him this one great boon.

And Rufus must have realised the fact, for he stood up sharply and backed against the door, releasing her.

"You don't know what you're saying," he said gruffly.

"I do—I do!" With anguished reiteration she answered him. "I'm not the sort that offers and then doesn't pay. Oh, don't waste time talking! Every moment may be his last. Go down—go down to the shore! You're so strong. Save him—save him!"

She beat her clasped hands against his broad chest, till abruptly he put up his own again and held them still.

"Columbine!" For the second time he uttered her name, and for the second time the command in his voice caught and compelled her. "Just you listen a minute!" he said, and as he spoke his look swept her with a mastery that dominated even her agony. "If I go and save the cur, you've done with him for ever—you swear that?"

"Yes!" she cried. "Yes! Only go—only go!"

But he remained square and resolute against the door. "And you'll stay here—you swear to stay here till I come back?"

"Yes!" she cried again.

He bent to her once more; his gaze possessed her. "And—afterwards?" he said, his voice deep and very low.

Her eyes had been raised to his; they closed suddenly and sharply, as if to shut him out. "I will give you—all I have," she said, and shivered, violently, uncontrollably.

The next instant his hands were gone from hers, and she was free.

Trembling, she sank upon the sofa, hiding her face; and even as she did so the banging of the cottage door told her he was gone.

Thereafter she sat crouched for a long, long time in the paralysis of a great fear.

CHAPTER IX
THE VISION

Down on the howling shore the great waves were hurling themselves in vast cataracts of snow-white surf that shone, dimly radiant, in the fitful moonlight. The sky was covered with broken clouds, and a rising storm-wind blew in gusts along the cliffs. The peace of the night was utterly shattered, the shining glory had departed. A wild and desolate grandeur had succeeded it.

"Shouldn't wonder if there was some trouble tonight," said Adam, awaking to the tumult.

"Lor' bless you!" said Mrs. Peck sensibly. "Wait till it comes."

The hint of impatience that marked her speech was not without reason, for a gale was to Adam as the sound of a gun to a sporting-dog. It invariably aroused him, even from the deepest slumber, to a state of alert expectation that to a woman as hard-working as Mrs. Peck was most exceptionally trying. When Adam scented disaster at sea there was no peace for either. As she was wont to remark, being the wife of the lifeboat coxswain wasn't all jam, not by any manner of means it wasn't. She knew now, by the way Adam turned, and checked his breathing to listen, that the final disturbance was not far off.

She herself feigned sleep, possibly in the hope of provoking him to consideration for her weariness; but she knew the effort to be quite futile even as she made it. Adam the coxswain was considerate only for those who might be in peril. At the next heavy gust that rattled the windows he flung the bedclothes back without the smallest thought for his companion's comfort, and tumbled on to his feet.

"Just going to have a look round," he said. "I'll lay the fire in the kitchen, and you be ready to light it in a jiffy if wanted!"

That was so like Adam. He could think of nothing but possible victims of the storm. Mrs. Peck sniffed, and gathered the bedclothes back about her in expressive silence. It was quite useless to argue with Adam when he got the jumps. Experience had taught her that long since. She could only resume her broken rest and hope that it might not be again disturbed.

Adam pulled on his clothes with his usual brisk deftness of movement and went downstairs. The rising storm was calling him, and he could not be deaf to the call. He had belonged to the lifeboat ever since he had come to man's estate, and never a storm arose but he held himself ready for service.

His first, almost instinctive, action was to take the key of the lifeboat house from its nail in the kitchen. Then, whistling cheerily below his breath, he set about laying the fire. The kettles were already filled. Mrs. Peck always saw to that before retiring. There was milk in the pantry, brandy in the cupboard. According to invariable custom, all was in readiness for any possible emergency, and having satisfied himself that this was the case, he thrust his bare feet into boots and went to the door.

It had begun to rain. Great drops pattered down upon him as he emerged, and he turned back to clap his sou'wester upon his head. Then, without further preparation, he sallied forth.

As he went down the road that ran to the quay a terrible streak of lightning reft the dark sky, and the wild crash of thunder that followed drowned even the roaring babel of the sea.

It did not check his progress; he was never one to be easily daunted. It was contrary to his very nature to seek shelter in a storm. He went swinging on to the very edge of the quay, and there stood facing the violence of the waves, the fierce turmoil of striving elements.

The tide was extraordinarily high—such a tide as he believed he had never seen before in summer. He stood in the pouring rain and looked first one way, then the other, with a quick birdlike scrutiny, but as far as his eyes could pierce he saw only an empty desolation of waters. There seemed none in need of his help that night.

"I wonder if Rufus is awake," he speculated to the angry tumult.

Nearly three miles out from the Spear Point there was a lighthouse with a revolving light. That light shone towards him now, casting a weird radiance across the tossing water, and as if in accompaniment to the warning gleam he heard the deep toll of the bell-buoy that rocked upon the swell.

Adam turned about. "I'll go and knock up Rufus," he decided. "It'd be a shame to miss a night like this."

Again the lightning rent the sky, and the whole great outline of the Spear Point was revealed in one awful second of intolerable radiance. Adam's keen eye chanced to be upon it, and he saw it in such detail as the strongest sunlight could never have achieved. The brightness dazzled, almost shocked him, but there was something besides the brightness that sent an odd sensation through him—a curious, sick feeling as if he had suddenly received a blow between the shoulders. For in that fraction of time he had seen something which reason, clamouring against the evidence of his senses, declared to be the impossible. He had seen a human figure—the figure of his son—clinging to the naked face of the rock, hanging between sea and sky where scarcely a bird could have found foothold, while something—a grey, indistinguishable burden—hung limp across his shoulder, weighing him down.

The thunder was still rolling around him when with a great shake Adam pulled himself together.

"I'm dreaming!" he told himself angrily. "A man couldn't ever climb the Spear Point, let alone live on a ledge that wouldn't harbour a sea-gull if he did. I'll go round to Rufus. I'll go round and knock him up."

With the words he tramped off through the rushing rain, and leaving the quay, struck upwards along the cliff in the direction of the narrow path that ran down to Rufus's dwelling above the Spear Point Caves.

Despite the spareness of his frame, he climbed the ascent with a rapidity that made him gasp. The wind also was against him, blowing in strong gusts, and the raging of the sea below was as the roaring of a thousand torrents. The great waves boomed against the cliff far beyond the summer watermark. They had long since covered the quicksand, and he thought he felt the ground shake with the shock of them.

He reached at length the gap in the cliff that led down to the cottage, and here he paused; for the descent was sharp, and the light that still filtered through the dense storm-clouds was very dim. But in a few seconds another great flash lit up the whole wild scene. He saw again the Spear Point Rock standing out, scimitar-like, in the sea. The water was dashing all around it. It stood up, grim and unapproachable, the great waves flinging their mighty clouds of spray over its stark summit. But—possibly because he viewed it from above instead of from below—he saw naught beside that grand and futile struggle of the elements.

Reassured, he started in the rain and darkness down the twisting path that led to his old home. He knew every foot of the way, but even so, he stumbled once or twice in the gloom.

The roaring of the sea sounded terribly near when finally he reached the little garden-gate and caught the ray of the lamp in the window.

Evidently it had awakened Rufus also. Almost unconsciously he quickened his pace as he went up the path.

He reached the door and fumbled for the latch; but ere he found it, it was flung open, and a strange and tragic figure met him on the threshold.

"Ah!" cried a woman's voice. "It is you! Where—where is Rufus?"

Adam's keen and birdlike eyes nearly leapt from his head. "Why—Columbine?" he said.

She was dressed in Rufus's suit of navy serge. It hung about her in clumsy folds, and over her shoulders and about her snow-white throat her glorious hair streamed like a black veil, still wet and shining in the lamplight.

She flung out her hands to him in piteous appeal. "Oh, Adam!" she said. "Have you seen them? Have you seen Rufus? He went—he went an hour ago—to save Mr. Knight from the quicksand!"

Adam's quick brain leapt to instant activity. The girl's presence baffled him, but it was no time for explanation. In some way she had discovered Knight in danger, and had rushed to Rufus for help. Then—then—that vision of his from the quay—that flash of revelation—had been no dream, after all! He had seen Rufus indeed—and probably for the last time in his life.

He stood, struck dumb for the moment, recalling every detail of the clinging figure that had hung above the leaping waves. Then the tragedy in Columbine's face made him pull himself together once more. He took her trembling hands.

"It's no good, my girl," he said. "I seen him. Yes, I seen him. I didn't believe my eyes, but I know now it was true. He was hanging on to a bit of rock half-way up the Spear Point, and t'other chap was lying across his shoulder. They've both been washed away by this, for the water's still coming up. There's not the ghost of a chance for 'em. I say it 'cos I know—not the ghost of a chance!"

A wild cry broke from the girl's lips. She wrenched her hands free and beat them upon her breast. Then suddenly a burst of wild tears came to her. She leaned against the cottage wall and sobbed in an agony that possessed her, soul and body.

Adam stood and looked at her. There was something terrible about the abandonment of her grief. It made him feel that his own was almost insignificant beside it. He had never seen any woman weep like that before. The anguish of it went through his heart.

He moved at length, laid a very gentle hand upon her shaking shoulder.

"My girl—my girl!" he said. "Don't take on so! I never thought as you cared a ha'p'orth for poor Rufus, though o' course I always knew as he loved you like mad."

She bowed herself lower under his hand. "And now I've killed him!" she gasped forth inarticulately. "I've killed him!"

"No, no, no!" protested Adam. "That ain't reasonable. Come, now—you're distraught! You don't know what you're saying. My Rufus is a fine chap. He'd take most any risk to save a life. He's got a big heart in him, and he don't stop to count the cost."

She uncovered her face sharply and looked at him, so that he clearly saw the ravages that her distress had wrought. "That wasn't what made him go," she said. "He wouldn't have gone but for me. It was I as made him go. But I thought he'd be in time. I hoped he'd be in time." Her voice rose wildly; she wrung her hands. "Oh, can't you do anything? Can't you take out the lifeboat? There must be some way—surely there must be some way—of saving them!"

But Adam shook his head. "He's past our help," he said. "There's no boat could live among them rocks in such a tide as this. We couldn't get anywhere near. No—no, there's nothing we can do. The lad's gone—my Rufus—finest chap along the shore, if he was my son. Never thought as he'd go before me—never thought—never thought!"

The loud roll of the waves filled the bitter silence that followed, but the battering of the rain upon the cottage roof was decreasing. The storm was no longer overhead.

Adam leaned on the back of a chair with his head in his hands. All the wiry activity seemed to have gone out of him. He looked old and broken.

The girl stood motionless behind him. A strange impassivity had succeeded her last fruitless appeal, as though through excess of suffering her faculties were numbed, animation itself were suspended. She leaned against the wall, staring with wide, tragic eyes at the flame of the lamp that stood in the window. Her arms hung stiffly at her sides, and the hands were clenched. She seemed to be gazing upon unutterable things.

There was nothing to be done—nothing to be done! Till the waves had spent their fury, till that raging sea went down, they were as helpless as babes to stay the hand of Fate. No boat could live in that fearful turmoil of water. Adam had said it, and she knew that what he said was true, knew by the utter dejection of his attitude, the completeness of his despair. She had never seen Adam in despair before; probably no one had ever seen him as he was now. He was a man to strain every nerve while the faintest ray of hope remained. He had faced many a furious storm, saved many a life that had been given up for lost by other men. But now he could do nothing, and he crouched there—an old and broken man—for the first time realising his helplessness.

A long time passed. The only sound within the cottage was the ticking of a grandfather-clock in a corner, while without the great sound of the breaking seas filled all the world. The storm above had passed. Now the thunder-blast no longer shook the cottage. A faint greyness had begun to show beyond the lamp in the window. The dawn was drawing near.

As one awaking from a trance of terrible visions, the girl drew a deep breath and spoke:

"Adam!"

He did not stir. He had not stirred for the greater part of an hour.

She made a curiously jerky movement, as if she wrenched herself free from some constricting hold. She went to the bowed, despairing figure.

"Adam, the day is breaking. The tide must be on the turn. Shan't we go?"

He stood up with the gesture of an old man. "What's the good?" he said. "Do you think I want to see my boy's dead body left behind by the sea?"

She shivered at the question. "But we can't stay here," she urged. "Aunt Liza, you know—she'll be wondering."

"Ah!" He passed his hand over his eyes. He was swaying a little as he stood. She supported his elbow, for he seemed to have lost control of his limbs. He stared at her in a dazed way. "You'd better go and tell your Aunt Liza," he said. "I think I'll stay here a bit longer. Maybe my boy'll come and talk to me if I'm alone. We're partners, you know, and we lived here a good many years alone together. He wouldn't leave me—not for the long voyage—without a word. Yes, you go, my dear, you go! I'll stay here and wait for him."

She saw that no persuasion of hers would move him, and it seemed useless to remain. An intolerable restlessness urged her, moreover, to be gone. The awful inertia of the past two hours had turned into a fevered desire for action. It was the swing of the pendulum, and she felt that if she did not respond to it she would go mad.

Her knees were still trembling under her, but she controlled them and turned to the door. As she lifted the latch she looked back and saw Adam drop heavily into the chair upon which he had leaned for so long. His attitude was one of almost stubborn patience, but it was evident that her presence had ceased to count with him. He was waiting—she saw it clearly in every line of him—waiting to bid his boy Godspeed ere he fared forth finally on the long voyage from which there is no return.

A sharp sob rose in her throat. She caught her hand to it, forcing it back. Then, barefooted, she stepped out into the grey dimness that veiled all things, and left the door of Rufus's cottage open behind her.

CHAPTER X
THE LONG VOYAGE

She never remembered afterwards how she accomplished the homeward journey. The rough stones cut her feet again and again, but she never felt the pain. She went as one who has an urgent mission to perform, though what that mission was she scarcely knew.

The night—that night of dreadful tragedy—had changed her. Columbine, the passionate, the impulsive had turned into a being that was foreign to herself. All the happy girlhood had been stamped out of her as by the cruel pressure of a hot iron. She had ceased to feel the agony of it; somehow she did not think that she ever could feel pain again. The nerve tissues had been destroyed and all vitality was gone. The creature that passed like a swift shadow through the twilight of the dawn was an old and withered woman who had lived beyond her allotted time.

She reached the old Ship Inn, meeting no one. She entered by the door of the conservatory through which she had flitted æons and æons before to meet her lover. She went to her room and changed into her own clothes. The suit that had belonged to Rufus so long ago she laid away with an odd reverence, still scarcely knowing what she did, driven as it were by a mechanism that worked without any volition of hers.

Then she went to the glass and began to coil up her hair. It was dank and heavy yet with the seawater, but she wound it about her head without noticing. The light was growing, and she peered at herself with a detached sort of curiosity, till something in her own eyes frightened her, and she turned away.

She went to the window and opened it wide. The sound of the sea yet filled the world, but it was not so insistent as it had been. The waves, though mountainous still, were gradually receding from the shore. It was as though the dawn had come just in time to prevent the powers of darkness from triumphing.

She heard someone moving in the house and turned back into the room. Aunt Liza must be told.

Through the spectral dawnlight she went down the stairs and took her way to the kitchen. The door stood half open; she heard the cheery crackling of the newly lighted fire before she entered. And hearing it, she was aware of a great coldness that clung like a chain, fettering her every movement.

Someone moved as she pushed open the door. An enormous shadow leaped upon the wall like a fantastic monster of the deep. She recoiled for a second, then, as if drawn against her will, she entered.

By the ruddy glow of the fire she saw a man's broad-chested figure, she saw the gleam of tawny hair above a thick bull-neck. He was bending slightly over the fire at her entrance, but, hearing her, he turned. And in that moment every numbed nerve in Columbine's body was pierced into quivering life.

She stood as one transfixed, and he stood motionless also in the flickering light of the flames, gazing at her with eyes of awful blue that were as burning spirit. But he spoke not a word—not a word. How could a dead man speak?

And as they stood thus, facing each other, the floor between them began suddenly to heave, became a mass of seething billows that rocked her, caught her, engulfed her. She went down into them, and as the tossing darkness received her, her last thought was that Rufus had come back indeed—not to say farewell, but to take her with him on the long voyage from which there is no return....

CHAPTER XI
DEEP WATERS

Wild white roses that grew in the sandy stubble above the shore, little orange-scented roses that straggled through the grass—they called to something that ran in Columbine's blood, they spoke to her of the South. She was sure that she would find those roses all about her feet when she came to the end of the long voyage. She would see their golden hearts wide open to the sun. For their fragrance haunted her day by day as she floated down the long glassy stretches and rocked on the waveless swells.

Sometimes she had a curious fancy that she was lying dead, and they had strewn the sweet flowers all about her. She hoped that they might not be buried with her; they were too beautiful for that.

At other times she thought of them as a bridal wreath, purer than the purest orange-blossom that ever decked a bride. Once, too—this was when she was nearing the end of the voyage—there came to her a magic whiff of wet bog-myrtle that made her fancy that she must be a bride indeed.

At last, just when it seemed to her that her boat was gently grounding upon the sand where the little white roses grew, she opened her eyes widely, wonderingly, and realised that the voyage was over.

She was lying in her own little room at The Ship, and Mrs. Peck, with motherly kindness writ large on her comely, plump face, was bending over her with a cup of steaming broth in her hand.

Columbine gazed at her with a bewildered sense of having slept too long.

Mrs. Peck nodded at her cheerily. "There, my dear! You're better, I can see. A fine time you've given us. I thought as I should never see your bright eyes again."

Columbine put forth a trembling hand with a curious feeling that it did not belong to her at all. "Have I been ill?" she said.

Mrs. Peck nodded again cheerily. "Why, it's more than a week you've been lying here, and how I have worried about you! Prostration following severe shock was what the doctor called it, but it looked to me more like a touch of brain fever. But there, you're better! Drink this like a good girl, and you'll feel better still!"

Meekly, with the docility of great weakness, Columbine swallowed the proffered nourishment. She wanted to recall all that had happened, but her brain felt too clogged to serve her. She could only lie and gaze and gaze at a little vase of wild white roses that faced her upon the mantelpiece. Somehow those roses seemed to her to play an oddly important part in her awakening.

"Where did they come from?" she suddenly asked.

Mrs. Peck glanced up indifferently. "They're just those little common things that grow with the pinks on the cliff," she said.

But that did not satisfy Columbine. "Who brought them in?" she said. "Who gathered them?"

Mrs. Peck hesitated momentarily, almost as if she did not want to answer. Then, half defiantly, "Why, Rufus, to be sure," she said.

"Rufus!" A great hot wave of crimson suddenly suffused Columbine's face—a pitiless, burning blush that spread tingling over her whole body.

She lay very still while it lasted, and Mrs. Peck set down the cup and, rising energetically, began to tidy the room.

At length, faintly, the girl spoke again: "Aunt Liza!"

Mrs. Peck turned. There was a curious look in her eyes, a look half stern and yet half compassionate. "There, my dear, that'll do," she said. "I think you've talked enough. The doctor said as I was to keep you very quiet, especially when you began to get back your senses. Shut your eyes, do, and go to sleep!"

But Columbine's eyes remained open. "I'm not sleepy," she said. "And I must speak to you. I want to know—I must know"—she faltered painfully, but forced herself to continue—"Rufus—did he—did he really come back—that night?"

Mrs. Peck's compassion perceptibly diminished and her severity increased. "Oh, if you want the whole story," she said, "you'd better have it and have done; that is, so far as I know it myself. There are certain ins and outs that I don't know even yet, for Rufus can be very secretive if he likes. Well then, yes, he did come back, and he brought Mr. Knight with him. They were washed up by a great wave that dropped 'em high and dry near the quay. Mr. Knight was half drowned, and Rufus left him at Sam Jefferson's cottage and came on here for brandy and hot milk and such. He wasn't a penny the worse himself, but I suppose you thought it was his ghost. You behaved like as if you did, anyway. That's all I can tell you. Mr. Knight he got better in a day or two, and he's gone, said he'd had enough of it, and I don't blame him neither. Now that'll do for the present. By and by, when you're stronger, maybe I'll ask you to tell me something. But the doctor says as I'm not to let you talk at present."

Mrs. Peck took up the empty cup with the words, and turned with decision to the door.

Columbine did not attempt to detain her. She had read the doubt in the good woman's eyes, and she was thankful at that moment for the reprieve that the doctor's fiat had secured her.

She lay for a long, long time without moving after Mrs. Peck's departure. Her brain felt unutterably weary, but it was clear, and she was able to face the situation in all its grimness. Mr. Knight had gone. Mr. Knight had had enough of it. Had he really left without a word? Was she, then, so little to him as that? She, who had clung to him, had offered him unconditionally and without stint all that was hers!

She remembered how he had said that it would not last, that love was moonshine, love would pass. And how passionately—and withal how fruitlessly!—had she revolted against that pronouncement of his! She had declared that such was not love, and he—he had warned her against loving too well, giving too freely. With cruel distinctness it all came back to her. She felt again those hot kisses upon brow and lips and throat. Though he had warned her against giving, he had not been slow to take. He had revelled in the abandonment of that first free love of hers. He had drained her of all that she held most precious that he might drink his fill. And all for what? Again she burned from head to foot, and, groaning, hid her face. All for the making of a picture that should bring him world-wide fame! His love for her had been naught but small change flung liberally enough that he might purchase therewith the desire of his artist's soul. It had been just a means to an end. No more than that! No more than that!

Time passed, but she knew naught of its passing. She was in a place of bitterness very far removed from the ordinary things of life. She shed no tears. The misery and shame that burned her soul were beyond all expression or alleviation. She could have laughed over the irony of it all more easily than she could have wept.

That she—the proud and dainty, for whom no one had been good enough—should have fallen thus easily to the careless attraction of a man to whom she was nothing, nothing but a piece of prettiness to be bought as cheaply as possible and treasured not at all. Some whim of inspiration had moved him. He had obeyed his Muse. And he had been ready—he had been ready—even to offer her life in sacrifice to his idol. She did not count with him in the smallest degree. He had never cared—he had never cared!

She lifted her face at last. The torture was eating into her soul. It was more than she could bear. All the tender words he had spoken, the caresses he had lavished upon her, were as burning darts that pierced her whichever way she turned. Her surrender had been so free, so absolute, and in return he had left her in the dark. He had gone his careless way without a single thought for all the fierce devotion she had poured out to him. It had only appealed to him while the mood lasted. And now he had had enough of it. He had gone.

The murmur of the summer sea came to her as she lay, and she thought of the Death Current. Why—ah, why—had it been cheated of its prey? She shivered violently as the memory of that awful struggle in deep waters came to her. She had been saved, how she scarcely realised, though deep within her she knew—she knew!

Her burning eyes fell upon the little wild white roses on the shelf. Why had he brought them to her? Why had he chosen them? She felt as if they held a message for her, but it was a message she did not dare to read. And then again she quivered as the dread memory of that night swept over her anew, and the eyes of flaming blue that had looked into hers.

Somewhere—somewhere outside herself, it seemed to her—a voice was speaking, very articulate and persistent, and she could not shut out the words it uttered. She lacked the strength.

"I always knew," it said, and it averred it over and over again, "as he loved you like mad."

Love! Love! But what was Love? Was any man capable of it? Was it ever anything more than brutal passion or callous amusement? And hearts were broken and lives were ruined to bring men sport.

She clenched her hands, still gazing at the wild white roses with their orange scent of purity. Why had he sent them? What had moved him to gather them? He who had bargained with her, had wrung from her submission to his will as it were at the sword's point! He who had forced her to promise herself to him! What was love—or the making of love—to such as he?

The sweetness of the flowers seemed to pierce her. Ah, if they had only been Knight's gift, how different—how different—had been all things.

But they had come from Rufus. And so somehow their message passed her by. The blackness of utter misery, utter hopelessness, closed in like a prison-cell around her soul.

CHAPTER XII
THE SAFE HAVEN

In the days that followed, Mrs. Peck's honest soul was both vexed and anxious concerning her charge. She found Columbine extraordinarily reticent. As she herself put it, it was impossible to get any sense out of her.

In compliance with the doctor's order and by the exercise of extreme self-restraint, she refrained from questioning her upon the matter of her behaviour on the night of the great tide. That Columbine would have enlightened her had she done so was exceedingly doubtful. But there was no doubt that something very unusual had taken place. The little white roses that Rufus presented as a daily offering would have told her that, apart from any other indications. She would have questioned Rufus, but something held her back; and Adam, when urged thereto, flatly refused to interfere.

Adam, rejuvenated and jubilant, went whistling about his work as of yore. His boy had come back to him in the flesh, and he was more than satisfied to leave things as they were.

"Leave 'em alone, Missus!" was his counsel "Rufus he knows what he's about. He'll steer a straight course, and he'll bring her into harbour sooner or later. You leave it to him, and be thankful that curly-topped chap has sheered off at last!"

Mrs. Peck had no choice but to obey, but her anxiety regarding Columbine did not diminish. The girl was so listless, so unlike herself, so miserable. It was many days before she summoned the energy to dress, and even then she displayed an almost painful reluctance to go downstairs. She seemed to live in continual dread of some approaching ordeal.

"I believe it's Rufus she's afraid of," was Mrs. Peck's verdict.

But Adam scouted the idea as absurd. "What will you think of next, woman? Why, any one can see as he's quiet and well-behaved enough for any lass. She's missing the curly-topped chap a bit maybe. But she'll get over that. Give her time! Give her time!"

So Mrs. Peck gave her time and urged her not at all. She was not very friendly with Columbine in those days. She disapproved of her, and her manner said as much. She kept all suspicions to herself, but she could not behave as if nothing had happened.

"There's wild blood in her," she said darkly. "I mistrust her."

And Columbine was fully aware of the fact, but she was too wretched to resent it. In any case, she would never have turned to Mrs. Peck for comfort.

She came downstairs at last one summer evening when Mrs. Peck was busy in the kitchen and no one was about. She had made no mention of her intention; perhaps she wanted to be unhampered by observation. It had been a soft, showery day, and there was the promise of more rain in the sky.

She moved wearily, but not without purpose; and soon she was walking with a hood drawn over her head in the direction of the cliff-edge where grew the sweet bog-myrtle and the little roses.

She met no one by the way. It was nearing the hour for the evening meal, nearing the hour when Mrs. Peck usually entered her room with the daily offering of flowers that filled it with orange fragrance. Mrs. Peck was not very fond of that particular task, though she never expressed her reluctance. Well, she would not have it to accomplish tonight.

A bare-legged, blue-jerseyed figure was moving in a bent attitude along the slope that overlooked Rufus's cottage and the Spear Point. The girl stood a moment gazing out over the curving reef as if she had not seen it. The pool was smooth as a mirror, and reflecting the drifting clouds. The tide was out. But, stay! It must be on the turn, for as she stood, there came the deep, tolling note of the bell-buoy. It sounded like a knell.

As it struck solemnly over the water, the man straightened himself, and in a moment he saw her.

He did not move to meet her, merely stood motionless, nearly knee-deep in the bog-myrtle, and waited for her, the white roses in one great, clenched hand. And she, as if compelled, moved towards him, till at last she reached and stood before him, white, mute, passive as a prisoner in iron fetters.

It was the man who spoke, with an odd jerkiness of tone and demeanour that might have indicated embarrassment or even possibly some deeper emotion. "So you've come along at last!" he said.

She nodded. For an instant her dark eyes were raised, but they flashed downwards again immediately, almost before they had met his own.

Abruptly he thrust out to her the flowers he held. "I was getting these for you."

She took them in a trembling hand. She bent her face over them to hide the piteous quivering of her lips. "Why—do you get them?" she whispered almost inarticulately.

He did not answer for a moment. Then: "Come down to my place!" he said. "It's but a step."

She made a swift gesture that had in it something of recoil, but the next moment, without a word, she began to walk down the slope.

He trod through the growth beside her, barefooted, unfaltering. His blue eyes looked straight before him; they were unwavering and resolute as the man himself.

They reached the cottage. He made her enter it before him, and he followed, but he did not close the door. Instead, he stopped and deliberately hooked it back.

Then, with the low call of the sea filling the humble little room, he turned round to the girl, who stood with her head bent, awaiting his pleasure.

"Columbine," he said, and the name came with an unaccustomed softness from his lips, "I've something to say to you. You've been hiding yourself from me. I know. I know. And you needn't. Them flowers—I gathered 'em and I sent 'em up to you every day, because I wanted you to understand as you've nothing to fear from me. I wanted you to know as everything is all right, and I mean well by you. I didn't know how to tell you, and then I saw the roses growing outside the door, and I thought as maybe they'd do it for me. They made me think of you somehow. They were so white—and pure."

"Ah!" The word was a wrung sound, half cry, half sob. His roses fell suddenly and scattered upon the floor between them. Columbine's hands covered her face.

She stood for a second or two in tense silence, then under her breath she spoke. "You don't believe—that—of me!"

"I do, then," asserted Rufus, in his deep voice a note that was almost aggressive.

She lifted her face suddenly, even fiercely, showing him the shamed blush that burned there. "You didn't believe it—that night!" she said.

His eyes met hers with a certain stubbornness. "All right. I didn't," he said.

Her look became a challenge. "Then why—how—have you come to change your mind?"

He faced her steadily. "Maybe I know you better than I knew you then," he said slowly.

She made a sharp gesture as if pierced by an intolerable pain. "And that—that has made a difference to your—your intentions!"

He moved also at that. His red brows came together. "You're quite wrong," he said, his voice very low. "That night—I know—I was beyond myself, I was mad. But since then I've come to my senses. And—I love you too much to harm you. That's the truth. I'd love you anyway—whatever you were. It's just my nature to."

His hands clenched with the words; he spoke with strong effort; but his eyes looked deeply into hers, and they held no passion. They were still and quiet as the summer sea below them.

Columbine stood facing him as if at bay, but she must have felt the influence of his restraint, for she showed no fear. "There's no such thing as love," she said bitterly. "You dress it up and call it that. But all the time it's something quite different. And I tell you this"—recklessly she flung the words—"that if it hadn't been for that tidal wave I'd be just what you took me for that night, what Aunt Liza thinks I am this minute. I wasn't keeping back—anything, and"—she uttered a sudden wild laugh—"if I've kept my virtue, I've lost my innocence. I know—I know now—just what the thing you call love is worth! And nothing will ever make me forget it!"

She stopped, quivering from head to foot, passionate protest in every line.

But the blue eyes that watched her never wavered. The man's face was rock-like in its steadfast calm. He did not speak for a full minute after the utterance of her wild words. Then very steadily, very forcibly, he answered her. "I'll tell you, shall I, what the thing I call love is like?" He turned with a sweep of the arm and pointed out to the harbour beyond the quay. "It's just like that. It's a wall to keep off the storms. It's a safe haven where nothing hurtful can reach you. You're not bound to give yourself to it, but once given you're safe."

"Not bound!" Sharply she broke in upon him. "Not bound—when you made me promise—"

He dropped his arm to his side. "I set you free from that promise," he said.

Those few words, sombrely spoken, checked her wild outburst as surely as a hand upon her mouth. She stood gazing at him for a space in utter amazement, but gradually under his unchanging regard her look began to fail. She turned at length with a little gasp, and sat down on the old horsehair sofa, huddling herself together as if she desired to withdraw herself from his observation.

He did not stir, and a long, long silence fell between them, broken only by the ticking of the grandfather-clock in the corner and the everlasting murmur of the sea.

The deep, warning note of the bell-buoy floated presently through the summer silence, and as if in answer to a voice Rufus moved at last and spoke. "You'd better go, lass. They'll be wondering about you. But don't be afraid of me after this! I swear—before God—I'll give you no cause!"

She started a little at the sound of his voice, but she made no movement to go. Her face was hidden in her hands. She rocked herself to and fro, to and fro, as if in pain.

He stood looking down at her with troubled eyes, but after a while, as she did not speak, he moved to her side and stood there. At last, slowly and massively, he stooped and touched her.

"Columbine!"

She made no direct response, only suddenly, as if his action had released in her such a flood of emotion as was utterly beyond her control, she broke into violent weeping, her head bowed low upon her knees.

"My dear!" he said.

And then—how it came about neither of them ever knew—he was on his knees beside her, holding her close in his great arms, and she was sobbing out her agony upon his breast.

It lasted for many minutes that storm of weeping. All the torment of humiliation and grief, which till then had found no relief, was poured out in that burning torrent of tears. She clung to him convulsively as though she even yet struggled in the deep waters, and he held her through it all with that sustaining strength that had borne her up safely against the Death Current on that night of dreadful storm.

Possibly the firm upholding of his arms brought back the memory of that former terrible struggle, for it was of that that she first spoke when speech became possible.

"Oh, why didn't you leave me to die? Why—why—why?"

He answered her in a voice that seemed to rise from the depths of the broad chest that supported her.

"I wanted you."

She buried her face deeper that he might not see the cruel burning of it. "So did he—then."

"Not he!" The deep voice held unutterable contempt. "He wanted to make his fortune out of you, that's all. He didn't care whether you lived or died, the damn' cur!"

She shrank at the fierce words, and was instantly aware of the jealous closing of his arms about her.

"You aren't going to break your heart for a dirty swab like that," he said, with more of insistence than interrogation in his voice. "Look you here, Columbine! You're too honest to care for a beast like that. Why—though I pulled him out of the quicksand and saved him from the sea—I'd have wrung his neck if he'd stayed another day. I would that."

She started at the fiery declaration, and raised her head. "Oh, it was you who sent him away, then?"

Her look held almost desperate entreaty for a moment, but he met it with the utmost grimness and it quickly died.

"I didn't then," he said, with rough simplicity. "He made up his mind without any help from me. He knew he couldn't face you again. It's not a mite of good trying to deceive yourself now you know the truth. He's gone, and he won't come back. Columbine, don't tell me as you want him to!"

His expression for the moment was formidable. She caught an ominous gleam in the stern eyes, but almost immediately they softened. He uttered a sigh that ended in a groan. "Now I'm being a brute to you, when there's nothing that I wouldn't do for your sake." His voice shook a little. "You won't believe it, but it's true—it's true."

"Why shouldn't I believe it?" she said swiftly. She had begun to tremble in his hold.

He looked at her with an odd wistfulness. "Because I'm too big an oaf—to make you understand," he said.

"And that is why you have set me free?" she questioned.

He bent his head, almost as if the sudden question embarrassed him. "Yes, that," he said after a moment. "And because I care too much about you to—marry you against your will."

"And you call that love?" she said.

He made a slight gesture of surprise. "It is love," he said simply.

His arms were still around her, but she had only to move to be free. She did not move, save that she quivered like a vibrating wire, quivered and hid her face.

"Rufus!" she said.

"Yes?" His head was bent above hers, but he could only see her black hair, so completely was her face averted from him.

Her voice came, tensely whispering. "What if I were—willing to marry you?"

Something of her agitation had entered into him. A great quiver went through him also. But—"You're not," he said quietly, with conviction.

A trembling hand strayed upwards, feeling over his neck and throat, groping for his face. "Rufus"—again came the tense whisper—"how do you know that?"

He took the wandering hand and pressed it softly against his cheek. "Because you don't love me, Columbine," he said.

"Ah!" A low sob escaped her; she lifted her head suddenly; the tears were running down her face. "But—but—you could teach me, Rufus. You could teach me what love—true love—is. I want the real thing—the real thing. Will you give it to me? I want it—more than anything else in the world." She drew nearer to him with the words, like a frozen creature seeking warmth, and in a moment her arms were slipping round his neck. "You are so true—so strong!" she sobbed. "I want to forget—I want to forget that I ever loved—any one but you."

His arms were close about her again. He pressed her so hard against his heart that she felt its strong beating against her own. His eyes gazed straight into hers, and in them she saw again that deep, deep blue as of flaming spirit.

"You mean it?" he said.

Breathlessly she answered him. "Yes, I mean it."

"Then"—he bent his great head to her, and for the fraction of a moment she saw the meteor-like flash of his smile—"yes, I'll teach you, Columbine," he said.

With the words he kissed her on the lips, kissed her closely, kissed her lingeringly, and in that kiss her torn heart found its first balm of healing.

"Well, what did I say?" crowed Adam a little later. "Didn't I tell you if you left 'em alone he'd steer her safe into harbour? Wasn't I right, missus? Wasn't I right?"

"I'm not gainsaying it," said Mrs. Peck, with a touch of severity. "And I'm sure I hope as all will turn out for the best."

"Turn out for the best? Why, o' course it will!" said Adam, with cheery confidence. "My son Rufus he may be slow, but he's no fool. And he's a good man, too, missus, a long sight better than that curly-topped chap. Him and me's partners, so I ought to know."

"To be sure you ought," said Mrs. Peck tolerantly. "And it's to be hoped that Columbine knows it as well."

And in the solitude of her own room Columbine bent her dainty head and kissed with reverence the little wild white roses that spoke to her of the purity of a good man's love.

THE MAGIC CIRCLE

The persistent chirping of a sparrow made it almost harder to bear. Lady Brooke finally rose abruptly from the table, her black brows drawn close together, and swept to the window to scare the intruder away.

"I really have not the smallest idea what your objections can be," she observed, pausing with her back to the room.

"A little exercise of your imagination might be of some assistance to you," returned her husband dryly, not troubling to raise his eyes from his paper.

He was leaning back in a chair in an attitude of unstudied ease. It was characteristic of Sir Roland Brooke to make himself physically comfortable at least, whatever his mental atmosphere. He seldom raised his voice, and never swore. Yet there was about him a certain amount of force that made itself felt more by his silence than his speech.

His young wife, though she shrugged her shoulders and looked contemptuous, did not venture upon open defiance.

"I am to decline the invitation, then?" she asked presently, without turning.

"Certainly!" Sir Roland again made leisurely reply as he scanned the page before him.

"And give as an excuse that you are too staunch a Tory to approve of such an innovation as the waltz?"

"You may give any excuse that you consider suitable," he returned with unruffled composure.

"I know of none," she answered, with a quick vehemence that trembled on the edge of rebellion.

Sir Roland turned very slowly in his chair and regarded the delicate outline of his wife's figure against the window-frame.

"Then, my dear," he said very deliberately, "let me recommend you once more to have recourse to your ever romantic imagination!"

She quivered, and clenched her hands, as if goaded beyond endurance. "You do not treat me fairly," she murmured under her breath.

Sir Roland continued to look at her with the air of a naturalist examining an interesting specimen of his cult. He said nothing till, driven by his scrutiny, she turned and faced him.

"What is your complaint?" he asked then.

She hesitated for an instant. There was doubt—even a hint of fear—upon her beautiful face. Then, with a certain recklessness, she spoke:

"I have been accustomed to freedom of action all my life. I never dreamed, when I married you, that I should be called upon to sacrifice this."

Her voice quivered. She would not meet his eyes. Sir Roland sat and passively regarded her. His face expressed no more than a detached and waning interest.

"I am sorry," he said finally, "that the romance of your marriage has ceased to attract you. But I was not aware that its hold upon you was ever very strong."

Lady Brooke made a quick movement, and broke into a light laugh.

"It certainly did not fall upon very fruitful ground," she said. "It is scarcely surprising that it did not flourish."

Sir Roland made no response. The interest had faded entirely from his face. He looked supremely bored.

Lady Brooke moved towards the door.

"It seems to be your pleasure to thwart me at every turn," she said. "A labourer's wife has more variety in her existence than I."

"Infinitely more," said Sir Roland, returning to his paper. "A labourer's wife, my dear, has an occasional beating to chasten her spirit, and she is considerably the better for it."

His wife stood still, very erect and queenly.

"Not only the better, but the happier," she said very bitterly. "Even a dog would rather be beaten than kicked to one side."

Sir Roland lowered his paper again with startling suddenness.

"Is that your point of view?" he said. "Then I fear I have been neglecting my duty most outrageously. However, it is an omission easily remedied. Let me hear no more of this masquerade, Lady Brooke! You have my orders, and if you transgress them you will be punished in a fashion scarcely to your liking. Is that clearly understood?"

He looked straight up at her with cold, smiling eyes that yet seemed to convey a steely warning.

She shivered very slightly as she encountered them. "You make a mockery of everything," she said, her voice very low.

Sir Roland uttered a quiet laugh.

"I am nevertheless a man of my word, Naomi," he said. "If you wish to test me, you have your opportunity."

He immersed himself finally in his paper as he ended, and she, with a smile of proud contempt, turned and passed from the room.

She had married him out of pique, it was true, but life with him had never seemed intolerable until he had shown her that he knew it.

She took her invitation with her, and in her own room sat down to read it once again. It was from a near neighbour, Lady Blythebury, an acquaintance with whom she was more intimate than was Sir Roland. Lady Blythebury was a very lively person indeed. She had been on the stage in her young days, and she had decidedly advanced ideas on the subject of social entertainment. As a hostess, she was notorious for her originality and energy, and though some of the county families disapproved of her, she always knew how to secure as many guests as she desired. Lady Brooke had known her previous to her own marriage, and she clung to this friendship, notwithstanding Sir Roland's very obvious lack of sympathy.

He knew Lord Blythebury in the hunting-field. Their properties adjoined, and it was inevitable that certain courtesies should be exchanged. But he refused so steadily to fall a captive to Lady Blythebury's bow and spear, that he very speedily aroused her aversion. He soon realised that her influence over his wife was very far from benevolent towards himself, but, save that he persisted in declining all social invitations to Blythebury, he made no attempt to counteract the evil. In fact, it was not his custom to coerce her. He denied her very little, though with regard to that little he was as adamant.

But to Naomi his non-interference was many a time more galling than his interdiction. It was but seldom that she attempted to oppose him, and, save that Lady Blythebury's masquerade had been discussed between them for weeks, she would not have greatly cared for his refusal to attend it. When Sir Roland asserted himself, it was her habit to yield without argument.

But now, for the first time, she asked herself if he were not presuming upon her wifely submission. He would think more of her if she resisted him, whispered her hurt pride, recalling the courteous indifference which it was his custom to mete out to her. But dared she do this thing?

She took up the invitation again and read it. It was to be a fancy-dress ball, and all were to wear masks. The waltz which she had learned to dance from Lady Blythebury herself and which was only just coming into vogue in England, was to be one of the greatest features of the evening. There would be no foolish formality, Lady Blythebury had assured her. The masks would preclude that. Altogether the whole entertainment promised to be of so entrancing a nature that she had permitted herself to look forward to it with considerable pleasure. But she might have guessed that Sir Roland would refuse to go, she reflected, as she sat in her dainty room with the invitation before her. Did he ever attend any function that was not so stiff and dull that she invariably pined to depart from the moment of arrival?

Again she read the invitation, recalling Lady Blythebury's gay words when last they had talked the matter over.

"If only Una could come without the lion for once!" she had said.

And she herself had almost echoed the wish. Sir Roland always spoilt everything.

Well!—She took up her pen. She supposed she must refuse. A moment it hovered above the paper. Then, very slowly, it descended and began to write.

The chatter of many voices and the rhythm of dancing feet, the strains of a string-band in the distance, and, piercing all, the clear, high notes of a flute, filled the spring night with wonderful sound. Lady Blythebury had turned her husband's house into a fairy palace of delight. She stood in the doorway of the ballroom, her florid face beaming above her Elizabethan ruffles, looking in upon the gay and ever-shifting scene which she had called into being.

"I feel as if I had stepped into an Arabian Night," she laughed to one of her guests, who stood beside her. He was dressed as a court jester, and carried a wand which he flourished dramatically. He wore a close-fitting black mask.

"There is certainly magic abroad," he declared, in a rich, Irish brogue that Lady Blythebury smiled to hear. For she also was Irish to the backbone.

"You know something of the art yourself, Captain Sullivan?" she asked.

She knew the man for a friend of her husband's. He was more or less disreputable, she believed, but he was none the less welcome on that account. It was just such men as he who knew how to make things a success. She relied upon the disreputable more than she would have admitted.

"Egad, I'm no novice in most things!" declared the court jester, waving his wand bombastically. "But it's the magic of a pretty woman that I'm after at the present moment. These masks, Lady Blythebury, are uncommon inconvenient. It's yourself that knows better than to wear one. Sure, beauty should never go veiled."

Lady Blythebury laughed indulgently. Though she knew it for what it was, the fellow's blarney was good to hear.

"Ah, go and dance!" she said. "I've heard all that before. It never means anything. Go and dance with the little lady over there in the pink domino! I give you my word that she is pretty. Her name is Una, but she is minus the lion on this occasion. I shall tell you no more than that."

"Egad! It's more than enough!" said the court jester, as he bowed and moved away.

The lady indicated stood alone in the curtained embrasure of a bay-window. She was watching the dancers with an absorbed air, and did not notice his approach.

He drew near, walking with a free swagger in time to the haunting waltz-music. Reaching her, he stopped and executed a sweeping bow, his hand upon his heart.

"May I have the pleasure—"

She looked up with a start. Her eyes shone through her mask with a momentary irresolution as she bent in response to his bow.

With scarcely a pause he offered her his arm.

"You dance the waltz?"

She hesitated for a second; then, with an affirmatory murmur, accepted the proffered arm. The bold stare with which he met her look had in it something of compulsion.

He led her instantly away from her retreat, and in a moment his hand was upon her waist. He guided her into the gay stream of dancers without a word.

They began to waltz—a dream—waltz in which she seemed to float without effort, without conscious volition. Instinctively she responded to his touch, keenly, vibrantly aware of the arm that supported her, of the dark, free eyes that persistently sought her own.

"Faith!" he suddenly said in his soft, Irish voice. "To find Una without the lion is a piece of good fortune I had scarcely prayed for. And what was the persuasion that you used at all to keep the monster in his den?"

She glanced up, half-startled by his speech. What did this man know about her?

"If you mean my husband," she said at last, "I did not persuade him. He never wished or intended to come."

Her companion laughed as one well pleased.

"Very generous of him!" he commented, in a tone that sent the blood to her cheeks.

He guided her dexterously among the dancers. The girl's breath came quickly, unevenly, but her feet never faltered.

"If I were the lion," said her partner daringly, "by the powers, I'd play the part! I wouldn't be a tame beast, egad! If Una went out to a fancy ball, my faith, I would go too!"

Lady Brooke uttered a little, excited laugh. The words caught her interest.

"And suppose Una went without your leave?" she said.

The Irishman looked at her with a humorous twist at one corner of his mouth.

"I'm thinking that I'd still go too," he said.

"But if you didn't know?" She asked the question with a curious vehemence. Her instinct told her that, however he might profess to trifle, here at least was a man.

"That wouldn't happen," he said, with conviction, "if I were the lion."

The music was quickening to the *finale,* and she felt the strong arm grow tense about her.

"Come!" he said. "We will go into the garden."

She went with him because it seemed that she must, but deep in her heart there lurked a certain misgiving. There was an almost arrogant air of power about this man. She wondered what Sir Roland would say if he knew, and comforted herself almost immediately with the reflection that he never could know. He had gone to Scotland, and she did not expect him back for several weeks.

So she turned aside with this stranger, and passed out upon his arm into the dusk of the soft spring night.

"You know these gardens well?" he questioned.

She came out of her meditations.

"Not really well. Lady Blythebury and I are friends, but we do not visit very often."

"And that but secretly," he laughed, "when the lion is absent?" She did not answer him, and he continued after a moment: "'Pon my life, the very mention of him seems to cast a cloud. Let us draw a magic circle, and exclude him!" He waved his wand. "You knew that I was a magician?"

There was a hint of something more than banter in his voice. They had reached the end of the terrace, and were slowly descending the steps. But at his last words, Lady Brooke stood suddenly still.

"I only believe in one sort of magic," she said, "and that is beyond the reach of all but fools."

Her voice quivered with an almost passionate disdain. She was suddenly aware of an intense burning misery that seemed to gnaw into her very soul. Why had she come out with this buffoon, she wondered? Why had she come to the masquerade at all? She was utterly out of sympathy with its festive gaiety. A great and overmastering desire for solitude descended upon her. She turned almost angrily to go.

But in the same instant the jester's hand caught her own.

"Even so, lady," he said. "But the magic of fools has led to paradise before now."

She laughed out bitterly:

"A fool's paradise!"

"Is ever green," he said whimsically. "Faith, it's no place at all for cynics. Shall we go hand in hand to find it then—in case you miss the way?"

She laughed again at the quaint adroitness of his speech. But her lips were curiously unsteady, and she found the darkness very comforting. There was no moon, and the sky was veiled. She suffered the strong clasp of his fingers about her own without protest. What did it matter—for just one night?

"Where are we going?" she asked.

"Wait till we get there!" murmured her companion. "We are just within the magic circle. Una has escaped from the lion."

She felt turf beneath her feet, and once or twice the brushing of twigs against her hand. She began to have a faint suspicion as to whither he was leading her. But she would not ask a second time. She had yielded to his guidance, and though her heart fluttered strangely she would not seem to doubt. The dread of Sir Roland's displeasure had receded to the back of her mind. Surely there was indeed magic abroad that night! It seemed diffused in the very air she breathed. In silence they moved along the dim grass path. From far away there came to them fitfully the sound of music, remote and wonderful, like straying echoes of paradise. A soft wind stirred above them, lingering secretly among opening leaves. There was a scent of violets almost intoxicatingly sweet.

The silence seemed magnetic. It held them like a spell. Through it, vague and intangible as the night at first, but gradually taking definite shape, strange thoughts began to rise in the girl's heart.

She had consented to this adventure from sheer lack of purpose. But whither was it leading her? She was a married woman, with her shackles heavy upon her. Yet she walked that night with a stranger, as one who owned her freedom. The silence between them was intimate and wonderful, the silence which only kindred spirits can ever know. It possessed her magically, making her past life seem dim and shadowy, and the present only real.

And yet she knew that she was not free. She trespassed on forbidden ground. She tasted the forbidden fruit, and found it tragically sweet.

Suddenly and softly he spoke:

"Does the magic begin to work?"

She started and tried to stop. Surely it were wiser to go back while she had the will! But he drew her forward still. The mist overhead was faintly silver. The moon was rising.

"We will go to the heart of the tangle," he said. "There is nothing to fear. The lion himself could not frighten you here."

Again she yielded to him. There was a suspicion of raillery in his voice that strangely reassured her. The grasp of his hand was very close.

"We are in the maze," she said at last, breaking her silence. "Are you sure of the way?"

He answered her instantly with complete self-assurance.

"Like the heart of a woman, it's hard, that it is, to find. But I think I have the key. And if not, by the saints, I'm near enough now to break through."

The words thrilled her inexplicably. Truly the magic was swift and potent. A few more steps, and she was aware of a widening of the hedge. They were emerging into the centre of the maze.

"Ah," said the jester, "I thought I should win through!"

He led her forward into the shadow of a great tree. The mist was passing very slowly from the sky. By the silvery light that filtered down from the hidden moon Naomi made out the strong outline of his shoulders as he stood before her, and the vague darkness of his mask.

She put up her free hand and removed her own. The breeze had died down. The atmosphere was hushed and airless.

"Do you know the way back?" she asked him, in a voice that sounded unnatural even to herself.

"Do you want to go back, then?" he queried keenly.

There was something in his tone—a subtle something that she had not detected before. She began to tremble. For the first time, actual fear took hold of her.

"You must know the way back!" she exclaimed. "This is folly! They will be wondering where we are."

"Faith, Lady Una! It is the fool's paradise," he told her coolly. "They will not wonder. They know too well that there is no way back."

His manner terrified her. Its very quietness seemed a menace. Desperately she tore herself from his hold, and turned to escape. But it was as though she fled in a nightmare. Whichever way she turned she met only the impenetrable ramparts of the hedge that surrounded her. She could find neither entrance nor exit. It was as though the way by which she had come had been closed behind her.

But the brightness above was growing. She whispered to herself that she would soon be able to see, that she could not be a prisoner for long.

Suddenly she heard her captor close to her, and, turning in terror, she found him erect and dominating against the hedge. With a tremendous effort she controlled her rising panic to plead with him.

"Indeed, I must go back!" she said, her voice unsteady, but very urgent. "I have already stayed too long. You cannot wish to keep me here against my will?"

She saw him shrug his shoulders slightly.

"There is no way back," he said, "or, if there is, I do not know it."

There was no dismay in his voice, but neither was there exultation. He simply stated the fact with absolute composure. Her heart gave a wild throb of misgiving. Was the man wholly sane?

Again she caught wildly at her failing courage, and drew herself up to her full height. Perhaps she might awe him, even yet.

"Sir," she said, "I am Sir Roland Brooke's wife. And I—"

"Egad!" he broke in banteringly, "that was yesterday. You are free to-day. I have brought you out of bondage. We have found paradise together, and, my pretty Lady Una, there is no way back."

"But there is, there is!" she cried desperately. "And I must find it! I tell you I am Sir Roland Brooke's wife. I belong to him. No one can keep me from him!"

It was as though she beat upon an iron door.

"There is no way out of the magic circle," said the jester inexorably.

A white shaft of light illumined the mist above them, revealing the girl's pale face, making sinister the man's masked one. He seemed to be smiling. He bent towards her.

"You seem amazingly fond of your chains," he said softly. "And yet, from what I have heard, Sir Roland is no gentle tyrant. How is it, pretty one? What makes you cling to your bondage so?"

"He is my husband!" she said, through white lips.

"Faith, that is no answer," he declared. "Own, now, that you hate him, that you loathe his presence and shudder at his touch! I told you I was a magician, Lady Una; but you wouldn't believe me at all."

She confronted him with a sudden fury that marvellously reinforced her failing courage.

"You lie, sir!" she cried, stamping passionately upon the soft earth. "I do none of these things. I have never hated him. I have never shrunk from his touch. We have not understood each other, perhaps, but that is a different matter, and no concern of yours."

"He has not made you happy," said the jester persistently. "You will never go back to him now that you are free!"

"I will go back to him!" she cried stormily. "How dare you say such a thing to me? How dare you?"

He came nearer to her.

"Listen!" he said. "It is deliverance that I am offering you. I ask nothing at all in return, simply to make you happy, and to teach you the blessed magic which now you scorn. Faith! It's the greatest game in the world, Lady Una; and it only takes two players, dear, only two players!"

There was a subtle, caressing quality in his voice. His masked face was bending close to hers. She felt trapped and helpless, but she forced herself to stand her ground.

"You insult me!" she said, her voice quivering, but striving to be calm.

"Never a bit!" he declared. "Since I am the truest friend you have!"

She drew away from him with a gesture of repulsion.

"You insult me!" she said again. "I have my husband, and I need no other."

He laughed sneeringly, the insinuating banter all gone from his manner.

"You know he is nothing to you," he said. "He neglects you. He bullies you. You married him because you wanted to be a married woman. Be honest, now! You never loved him. You do not know what love is!"

"It is false!" she cried. "I will not listen to you. Let me go!"

He took a sudden step forward.

"You refuse deliverance?" he questioned harshly.

She did not retreat this time, but faced him proudly.

"I do!"

"Listen!" he said again, and his voice was stern. "Sir Roland Brooke has returned home. He knows that you have disobeyed him. He knows that you are here with me. You will not dare to face him. You have gone too far to return."

She gasped hysterically, and tottered for an instant, but recovered herself.

"I will—I will go back!" she said.

"He will beat you like a labourer's wife," warned the jester. "He may do worse."

She was swaying as she stood.

"He will do—as he sees fit," she said.

He stooped a little lower.

"I would make you happy, Lady Una," he whispered. "I would protect you—shelter you—love you!"

She flung out her hands with a wild and desperate gesture. The magnetism of his presence had become horrible to her.

"I am going to him—now," she said.

Behind him she saw, in the brightening moonlight, the opening which she had vainly sought a few minutes before. She sprang for it, darting past him like a frightened bird seeking refuge, and in another moment she was lost in the green labyrinths.

The moonlight had become clear and strong, casting black shadows all about her. Twice, in her frantic efforts to escape, she ran back into the centre of the maze. The jester had gone, but she imagined him lurking behind every corner, and she impotently recalled his words: "There is no way out of the magic circle."

At last, panting and exhausted, she knew that she was unwinding the puzzle. Often as its intricacies baffled her, she kept her head, rectifying each mistake and pressing on, till the wider curve told her that she was very near the entrance. She came upon it finally quite suddenly, and found herself, to her astonishment, close to the terrace steps.

She mounted them with trembling limbs, and paused a moment to summon her composure. Then, outwardly calm, she traversed the terrace and entered the house.

Lady Blythebury was dancing, and she felt she could not wait. She scribbled a few hasty words of farewell, and gave them to a servant as she entered her carriage. Hers was the first departure, and no one noted it.

She sank back at length, thankfully, in the darkness, and closed her eyes. Whatever lay before her, she had escaped from the nightmare horror of the shadowy garden.

But as the brief drive neared its end, her anxiety revived. Had Sir Roland indeed returned and discovered her absence? Was it possible?

Her face was white and haggard as she entered the hall at last. Her eyes were hunted.

The servant who opened to her looked at her oddly for a moment.

"What is it?" she said nervously.

"Sir Roland has returned, my lady," he said. "He arrived two hours ago, and went straight to his room, saying he would not disturb your ladyship."

She turned away in silence, and mounted the stairs. Did he know? Had he guessed? Was it that that had brought him back?

She entered her room, and dismissed the maid she found awaiting her.

Swiftly she threw off the pink domino, and began to loosen her hair with stiff, fumbling fingers, then shook it about her shoulders, and sank quivering upon a couch. She could not go to bed. The terror that possessed her was too intense, too overmastering.

Ah! What was that? Every pulse in her body leaped and stood still at sound of a low knock at the door. Who could it be? gasped her fainting heart. Not Sir Roland, surely! He never came to her room now.

Softly the door opened. It was Sir Roland and none other—Sir Roland wearing an old velvet smoking—jacket, composed as ever, his grey eyes very level and inscrutable.

He paused for a single instant upon the threshold, then came noiselessly in and closed the door.

Naomi sat motionless and speechless. She lacked the strength to rise. Her hands were pressed upon her heart. She thought its beating would suffocate her.

He came quietly across the room to her, not seeming to notice her agitation.

"I should not have disturbed you at this hour if I had not been sure that you were awake," he said.

Reaching her, he bent and touched her white cheek.

"Why, child, how cold you are!" he said.

She started violently back, and then, as a sudden memory assailed her, she caught his hand and held it for an instant.

"It is nothing," she said with an effort. "You—you startled me."

"You are nervous tonight," said Sir Roland.

She shrank under his look.

"You see, I did not expect you," she murmured.

"Evidently not." Sir Roland stood gravely considering her. "I came back," he said, after a moment, "because it occurred to me that you might be lonely after all, in spite of your assurance to the contrary. I did not ask you to accompany me, Naomi. I did not think you would care to do so. But I regretted it later, and I have come back to remedy the omission. Will you come with me to Scotland?"

His tone was quiet and somewhat formal, but there was in it a kindliness that sent the blood pulsing through her veins in a wave of relief even greater than her astonishment at his words. He did not know, then. That was her one all-possessing thought. He could not know, or he had not spoken to her thus.

She sat slowly forward, drawing her hair about her shoulders like a cloak. She felt for the moment an overpowering weakness, and she could not look up.

"I will come, of course," she said at last, her voice very low, "if you wish it."

Sir Roland did not respond at once. Then, as his silence was beginning to disquiet her again, he laid a steady hand upon the shadowing hair.

"My dear," he said gently, "have you no wishes upon the subject?"

Again she started at his touch, and again, as if to rectify the start, drew ever so slightly nearer to him. It was many, many days since she had heard that tone from him.

"My wishes are yours," she told him faintly.

His hand was caressing her softly, very softly. Again he was silent for a while, and into her heart there began to creep a new feeling that made her gradually forget the immensity of her relief. She sat motionless, save that her head drooped a little lower, ever a little lower.

"Naomi," he said, at last, "I have been thinking a good deal lately. We seem to have been wandering round and round in a circle. I have been wondering if we could not by any means find a way out?"

She made a sharp, involuntary movement. What was this that he was saying to her?

"I don't quite understand," she murmured.

His hand pressed a little upon her, and she knew that he was bending down.

"You are not happy," he said, with grave conviction.

She could not contradict him.

"It is my own fault," she managed to say, without lifting her head.

"I do not think so," he returned, "at least, not entirely. I know that there have frequently been times when you have regretted your marriage. For that you were not to blame." He paused an instant. "Naomi," he said, a new note in his voice, "I think I am right in believing that, notwithstanding this regret, you do not in your heart wish to leave me?"

She quivered, and hid her face in silence.

He waited a few seconds, and finally went on as if she had answered in the affirmative.

"That being so, I have a foundation on which to build. I would not ask of you anything which you feel unable to grant. But there is only one way for us to get out of the circle that I can see. Will you take it with me, Naomi? Shall we go away together, and leave this miserable estrangement behind us?"

His voice was low and tender. Yet she felt instinctively that he had not found it easy to expose his most sacred reserve thus. She moved convulsively, trying to answer him, trying for several unworthy moments to accept in silence the shelter his generosity had offered her. But her efforts failed, for she had not been moulded for deception; and this new weapon of his had cut her to the heart. Heavy, shaking sobs overcame her.

"Hush!" he said. "Hush! I never dreamed you felt it so."

"Ah, you don't know me!" she whispered. "I—I am not what you think me. I have disobeyed you, deceived you, cheated you!" Humbled to the earth, she made piteous, halting confession before her tyrant. "I was at the masquerade tonight. I waltzed—and afterwards went into the maze—in the dark—with a stranger—who made love to me. I never—meant you—to know."

Silence succeeded her words, and, as she waited for him to rise and spurn her, she wondered how she had ever brought herself to utter them. But she would not have recalled them even then. He moved at last, but not as she had anticipated. He gathered the tumbled hair back from her face, and, bending over her, he spoke. Even in her agony of apprehension she noted the curious huskiness of his voice.

"And yet you told me," he said. "Why?"

She could not answer him, nor could she raise her face. He was not angry, she knew now; but yet she felt that she could not meet his eyes.

There was a short silence, then he spoke again, close to her ear:

"You need not have told me, Naomi."

The words amazed her. With a great start of bewilderment she lifted her head and looked at him. He put his hands upon her shoulders. She thought she saw a smile hovering about his lips, but it was of a species she had never seen there before.

"Because," he explained gently, "I knew."

She stared at him in wonder, scarcely breathing, the tears all gone from her eyes.

"You—knew!" she said slowly, at last.

"Yes, I knew," he said. He looked deep into her eyes for seconds, and then she felt him drawing her irresistibly to him. She yielded herself as driftwood yields to a racing flood, no longer caring for the interpretation of the riddle, scarcely remembering its existence; heard him laugh above her head—a brief, exultant laugh—as he clasped her. And then came his lips upon her own....

"You see, dear," he said later, a quiver that was not all laughter in his voice, "it is not so remarkably wonderful, after all, that I should know all about it, when you come to consider that I was there—there with you in the magic circle all the time."

"You were there!" she echoed, turning in his arms. "But how was it I never knew? Why did I not see you?"

"Faith, sweetheart, I think you did!" said Sir Roland. Then, at her quick cry of amazed understanding: "I wanted to teach you a lesson, but, sure, I'm thinking it's myself that learned one, after all." And, as she clung to him, still hardly believing: "We have found our paradise together, my Lady Una," he whispered softly. "And, love, there is no way back."

THE LOOKER-ON

I

"Oh, I'm going to be Lady Jane Grey," said Charlie Cleveland, balancing himself on the deck-rail in front of his friends, Mrs. Langdale and Mollie Erle, with considerable agility. "And, Mollie, I say, will you lend me a black silk skirt? I saw you were wearing one last night."

He spoke with complete seriousness. It was this boy's way to infuse into all his actions an enthusiasm that deprived the most trifling of the commonplace element. He was the gayest passenger on board—the very life of the boat. Yet he had few accomplishments to recommend him, his abundant spirits alone attaining for him the popularity he everywhere enjoyed.

Molly Erle, who with Mrs. Langdale was returning home after spending the winter with some friends at Calcutta, regarded him with a toleration not wholly devoid of contempt. He apparently deemed it necessary to pay her a good deal of attention, and Molly was strongly determined to keep him at a distance—a matter, by the way, that had its difficulties in face of young Cleveland's romping lack of ceremony.

"Yes, you may have the skirt," she said with a generosity not wholly spontaneous, as he waited expectantly for a reply to his request.

"Ah, good!" he said effusively. "That is a great weight off my mind. And may I have Number Ten on your programme?"

"Are you going to dance?" asked Mrs. Langdale, with a half-suppressed laugh.

He turned upon her, grinning openly.

"No. Fisher says I mustn't. I'm going to sit out, dear Mrs. Langdale—a modest wall-flower for once. I hope you will all be very kind to me. Have you made a note of Number Ten, Molly—I mean, Miss Erle? No? But you will, though. Ah! Thanks, awfully! Here comes Fisher! I wish you would persuade him to do Guildford Dudley. I can't."

He bounced off the rail and departed, laughing.

Molly looked after him with slight disapprobation on her pretty face. He was such a thoroughly nice boy. She wished with almost unreasonable intensity that he possessed more of that sterling quality, solidity, for which his travelling companion, Fisher, was chiefly noteworthy.

Captain Fisher approached them with a casual air as if he had drifted their way by accident. He was one of those oppressively quiet men who possess the unhappy knack of appearing wholly out of touch with all social surroundings. There was a reticence about him which almost all took for surliness, but which was in reality merely a somewhat unattractive mixture of awkwardness and laziness.

He was in the Royal Engineers, and believed to be a very clever man in his profession. But there was never anything in the least bright or original in his conversation. Yet, for some vague reason, Molly credited him with the ability to do great deeds, and was particularly gracious to him.

Mrs. Langdale, who was lively herself, infinitely preferred Charlie Cleveland's boisterous company, and on the present occasion she rose to follow him with great promptitude.

"I must find out how he has managed the rest of his costume," she said to Molly. "It is sure to be strikingly original—like himself."

The contempt deepened a little on Molly's face, contempt and regret—an odd mixture.

"He is very funny, no doubt," she said; "but I think one gets a little tired of his perpetual gaiety. I don't think we should find him so delightful if a storm came on. I haven't much faith in those people who can never take anything really seriously. I believe he would die laughing."

"All the better," declared Mrs. Langdale, who loved Charlie's impetuous ways with maternal tolerance. "It is always better to laugh than cry, my dear; though it isn't always easier by any means."

She departed with the words, laughing a little to herself at Molly's critical mood; and Captain Fisher went and sat stolidly down beside Molly, who turned to him with an instant smile of welcome. She was the only lady on board who was never bored by this man's quiet society. She liked him thoroughly, finding the contrast between him and his volatile friend a great relief.

Fisher never talked frivolities; indeed, he seldom talked at all. Yet to Molly the hour he spent beside her on that sunny day in the Mediterranean passed as pleasantly and easily as she could have desired.

Captain Fisher might seem heavy to others, but never to her—a fact of which secretly she was rather proud.

II

"Come up on deck!" whispered Charlie in an eager undertone. "There's no one there, and the night is divine."

Molly Erie looked at the strange figure in fancy-dress beside her and laughed aloud. She had not allowed Charlie a *tête-à-tête* for many days, but she felt that he could scarcely attempt to be sentimental in that costume.

She went with him, therefore, thinking what a pretty girl he would have made.

Charlie led her to the deck-rail. His ridiculous figure was less obtrusively absurd in the dim light. His laughing voice, lowered half-confidently, half-reverently, sounded less inconsequent than was its wont.

Suddenly he turned to her and spoke with wholly unexpected vehemence.

"I can't keep it in," he said. "You've got to know it. Molly, I love you most awfully. You do know it, I believe, without being told. Why do you always run away and hide when I try to speak?"

He spoke quickly, jerkily. She glanced at him with a nervous movement as she drew back. He was not laughing for once, yet she fancied there was the shadow of a smile quivering about his face. Possibly it was an illusion. The dim light made everything indefinite. But the suspicion roused in her in full strength her prejudice against him. She drew back deliberately, and her anger grew from scorn to cruelty during the moments that intervened between his question and her answer.

"You have chosen a very appropriate occasion," she remarked icily at length. "Do you imagine yourself irresistible when playing the fool, I wonder?"

He faced round on her.

"I have taken the only opportunity I could get," he said. "I am a slave of circumstance. If I had come to you in rational costume you would not have consented to sit out with me."

There was a ring of laughter in his explanation. He did not take her anger seriously, then. Molly quivered with indignation. She would speedily show him his mistake.

"You think, then," she said, "that this buffoonery is too amusing to be foregone? I am afraid I do not agree with you."

She paused. Charlie had given a great start of surprise. She could see the astonishment on his boyish face under the white mantilla he wore.

"Oh, look here!" he exclaimed impetuously. "You have got the wrong side of everything. It isn't buffoonery. I don't play with sacred things. I'm in earnest, Molly. Can't you see it? What do you take me for?"

She heard the note of honesty in his voice and shifted her batteries.

"You may be—for a moment," she said, scorn vibrating in every word she uttered. "But you will soon get over it, you know. By to-morrow, or even sooner, all danger will be over."

"Stop!" exclaimed Charlie. For the first time in all her dealings with him he spoke sternly, as a man might speak, and Molly started at his tone. "You are making a mistake," he said more quietly. "I am not the superficial ass you take me for."

"I have only your word for that," she returned, striking without pity because for a second he had startled her out of her contemptuous attitude.

He looked at her in silence, and again her indignation arose full-armed against him. How dared he—this clown in woman's clothes—speak to her at such a moment of that which she rightly held to be the holiest thing on earth?

"How can you expect me to believe you?" she demanded. "You tell me you are in earnest. But you know as well as I do that that is a mere figure of speech. You are never in earnest. You play all day long. You will do it all your life. You never do anything worth mentioning. Other people do the work. You simply skim the surface of things. You are merely a looker-on."

"A very intelligent looker-on, though," said Charlie, in a tone she did not wholly understand.

"And if I don't do anything worth doing, it is possibly lack of opportunity, isn't it? I can do many things, from driving engines to playing skittles. Take a man for what he is, not for what he does! It is the only fair estimate. Otherwise the blatant fools get all the honey."

Molly uttered a scornful little laugh.

"This is paltry," she exclaimed. "A man's actions are the actual man. He can make his own opportunities. No, Mr. Cleveland. You will never convince me of your intrinsic worth by talking."

She paused, as it were, involuntarily. Again that startled feeling of uncertainty was at her heart. There was a momentary silence. Then Charlie made her an odd, jerky bow, and without a single word further turned and left her.

Quaint as was his attire, ungainly as were his movements, there was in his withdrawal a touch of dignity, even a hint of the sublime; and Molly could not understand it.

She paced the length of the deck and sat down to regain her composure. The interview had left her considerably ruffled, even ill at ease.

III

She had been sitting there for some moments when suddenly, with a great throb that seemed to vibrate through the whole length of the great vessel from end to end, the engines ceased. The music in the large saloon, where the first-class passengers were dancing, came to an abrupt stop. There was a pause, a thrilling, intense pause; and then the confusion of voices.

A man ran quickly by her to the bridge, where she could dimly discern the first-officer on watch. She sprang up, dreading she knew not what, and at the same instant Charlie—she knew it was he by the flutter of the ridiculous garb he wore—leapt off the bridge like a hurricane, and tore past her.

He was gone in a second, almost before she had had time to realise his flying presence; and the next moment passengers were streaming up on deck, asking questions, uttering surmises, on the verge of panic, yet trying to ignore the anxiety that tugged at their resolution.

Molly joined the crowd. She was frightened too, badly frightened; but it is always better to face fear in company. So at least says human instinct.

The passengers collected in a restless mass on the upper deck. The captain was seen going swiftly to the bridge. After a brief word with him the first-officer came down to them. He was a pleasant, easy-tempered man, and did not appear in the least dismayed.

"It's all right," he said, raising his voice. "Please don't be alarmed! There has been a little accident in the engine-room. The captain hopes you won't let it interfere with your dancing."

He placed himself in the thick of the strangely dressed crowd. His clean-shaven face was perfectly unconcerned.

"I'll come and join you, if I may," he said. "The captain allows me to knock off. Will you admit a non-fancy-dresser?"

He led the way below, calling for the orchestra as he went. The frightened crowd turned and followed as if in this one man who spoke with the voice of authority protection could be found. But they hung back from dancing, and after a pause the first-officer seized a banjo and proceeded to entertain them with comic songs. He kept it up for a while, and then Mrs.

Langdale went nobly to his assistance and sang some Irish songs. One or two other volunteers presented themselves, and the evening's entertainment developed into a concert.

The tension relaxed considerably as the time slipped by, but it did not wholly pass. It was noticed that the doctor was absent.

A reluctance to disperse for the night was very manifestly obvious.

About two hours after the first alarm the great ship thrilled as if in answer to some monster touch. The languid roll ceased. The engines started again firmly, regularly, with gradually rising speed. In less than a minute all was as it had been.

A look of intense relief shot across the first-officer's quiet face.

"That means 'All's well,'" he said, raising his voice a little. "Let us congratulate ourselves and turn in!"

"There has been danger, then, Mr. Gresley?" queried Mrs. Granville, a lady who liked to know everything in detail.

Mr. Gresley laughed with an indifference perfectly unaffected. "I believe the engineers thought so," he said. "I must refer you to them for particulars. Anyhow, it's all right now. I am going to tell the steward to bring coffee."

He got up leisurely and strolled away.

There was a slight commotion on the other side of the door as he opened it, a giggle that sounded rather hysterical. A moment later Lady Jane Grey; her head-gear gone, her shorn curls looking absurdly frivolous, walked mincingly into the saloon and subsided upon the nearest seat. She was attended by Captain Fisher, who looked anxious.

"Such a misfortune!" she remarked, in a squeaky voice that sounded, somehow, a horrible strain. "I have been shut up in the Tower and have only just escaped. I trust I am not too late for my execution. I'm afraid I have kept you all waiting."

All the heaviness of misgiving passed out of the atmosphere in a burst of merriment.

"Where on earth have you been hiding?" shouted Major Granville. "I believe you have been playing the fool with us, you rascal."

"I!" cried Charlie. "My dear sir, what are you thinking of? If you were to breathe such a suspicion as that to the captain he would clap me in irons for the rest of the voyage."

"You have been in the engine-room for all that," said Mrs. Langdale, whose powers of observation were very keen. "Look at your skirt!"

Charlie glanced at the garment in question. It was certainly the worse for wear. There were some curious patches in the front that had the appearance of oil stains.

"That'll be all right!" he said cheerfully. "I had a fright and tumbled upstairs. Skirts are beastly awkward things to run away in, aren't they, Mrs. Langdale? Well, good-night all! I'm going to bed."

He got up with the words, grinned at everyone collectively, picked up the injured skirt with exaggerated care, and stepped out of the saloon.

Mrs. Langdale looked after him, half-laughing, yet with a touch of concern.

"He looks queer," she remarked to Molly, who was standing by her. "Quite white and shaky. I believe something has happened to him. He has hurt himself in some way."

But Molly was feeling peculiarly indignant at that moment, though not on account of her ruined skirt.

"He's a silly poltroon!" she said with emphasis, and walked stiffly away.

Charlie Cleveland had recovered from his serious fit even sooner than she had thought possible; and, though she had made it sufficiently clear to him that as a serious suitor he was utterly unwelcome, she was intensely angry with him for having so swiftly resumed his customary gay spirits.

IV

"Come! What happened last evening? We want to know," said Major Granville, in his slightly overbearing manner. "I saw you with the second engineer this morning, Fisher. I'm sure you have ferreted it out."

"I am not at liberty to pass on my information," responded Fisher stolidly. "You wouldn't understand it if I did, Major. There was danger and there was steam. Two of the engineers had their arms scalded, and one of the stokers was badly hurt. I can't tell you any more than that."

"Do you go so far as to say that the ship herself was in danger?" asked Major Granville. He was talking loudly, as was his wont, across the smoking saloon.

"I should say so," said Fisher, without lifting his eyes from the magazine he was deliberately studying.

"Where is young Cleveland this morning?" asked the Major abruptly.

Fisher shrugged his shoulders.

"He was in his bunk when I saw him last. Heaven knows what he may be up to by now."

Charlie Cleveland strolled in at this juncture. He had his right arm in a sling.

"Hullo!" he said. "How are you all? I'm on the sick-list to-day. I sprained my wrist when I fell up the steps yesterday."

Fisher glanced at him for a moment over the top of his magazine and resumed his reading in silence.

"Look here, my friend!" he said. "You were in the thick of this engine business. I am sure of it."

"I was," said Charlie readily. "But for me you would all be at the bottom of the sea by this time."

He threw himself into a chair with a broad grin at Major Granville's contemptuous countenance and took up a book.

Major Granville looked intensely disgusted. It was scarcely credible that a passenger could have penetrated to the engine-room and interfered with the machinery there, yet he more than half believed that this outrageous thing had actually occurred. He got up after a brief silence and stalked stiffly from the saloon.

Charlie banged down his book with a yell of laughter.

"Didn't I tell you, Fisher?" he cried. "He's gone to have a good, square, face-to-face talk with the captain. But he won't get anything out of him. I've been there first."

He went up on deck and found a party of quoit-players. Molly Erle was among them. Charlie stood and watched, yelling advice and encouragement.

"Looking on as usual?" the girl said to him presently, with a bitter little smile, as she found herself near him.

He nodded.

"I'm really afraid to speak to you to-day," he said. "Your skirt will never again bear the light of day."

"What happened?" she said briefly.

The game was over, and they strolled away together across the deck.

"I'll tell you," he said, with ill-suppressed gaiety in his voice. "We should all have been blown out of the water last night if it hadn't been for me. Forgetful of my finery, I went and—looked on. The magic result was that I saved the situation, and—incidentally, of course—the ship."

He stopped.

"You don't believe me?" he said abruptly.

Her lip curled a little.

"Do you really expect to be believed?" she said.

"I don't know," he said; "I thought it was the usual thing to do between friends."

"I was not aware—" began Molly.

He broke in with a most disarming smile.

"Oh, please," he said. "I don't deserve that—anyhow. I'm awfully sorry about the skirt. I hope you'll let me bear the cost of the damage. I've got into hot water all round. Nobody will believe I'm seriously sorry, though it's a fact for all that. Don't be hard on me, Molly, I say!"

There was a note of genuine pleading in the last words that induced her to relent a little.

"Oh, well, I'll forgive you for the skirt," she said. "I suppose boys can't help being mischievous, though you are nearly old enough to know better."

She looked at him as she said it. His face was comically penitent. Somehow she could not quarrel with the lurking smile in his merry eyes. He was certainly a boy. He would never be anything else. But Molly did not realise this, and she was still too young herself to have appreciated the gift of perpetual youth had she been aware of its existence.

"That's right!" said Charlie cheerily. "And perhaps"—he spoke cautiously, with a half-deprecatory glance at her bright face—"perhaps—in time, you know—you will be able to forgive me for something else as well."

"I think the less we say about that the better," remarked Molly, tilting her chin a little.

"All right!" said Charlie equably. "Only, you know"—his voice was suddenly grave—"I was—and am—in earnest."

Molly laughed.

"So far as in you lies, I suppose?" she said indifferently. "I wonder if you ever really did anything worth doing in your life, Mr. Cleveland."

"I wish you would call me Charlie!" he said impulsively. "Yes. I proposed to you last night. Wasn't that worth doing?"

She drew her brows together in a quick frown, but she made no reply. Fisher was drifting towards them. She turned deliberately, her head very high, and strolled to meet him.

Charlie glanced over his shoulder, stood a moment irresolute, then walked away more soberly than usual towards the bridge, where he was a constant and welcome visitor.

V

"There are plenty of fine chaps in the world who aren't to be recognised as such at first sight," drawled Bertie Richmond to his young cousin, Molly Erle, who was sitting with her feet on the fender on a very cold winter evening.

"I'm sure of that," said Mrs. Richmond from the other side of the fire, with a tender glance at her husband's loosely knit figure. "I never thought there was an inch of heroism in you, Bertie darling, till that day when we went punting and we got upset. How brave you were! I've never forgotten it. It was the beginning of everything."

"It sounds as if it were nearer being the end," remarked Molly, who systematically avoided all sentiment. "I don't believe myself that any man can be actually heroic and yet not betray it somehow."

"You're wrong," said Bertie.

"I don't think so," said Molly. She could be quite as obstinate as most women, and this was a point upon which she was very decided.

"I'll prove it," said Bertie, with quiet determination. "There's a chap coming with the crowd of sportsmen to-morrow who is the bravest and, I think, the best fellow I ever met. I shan't tell you who he is. I'll leave you to find out—if you can. But I don't believe you will."

"I am quite sure I can tell the difference between a looker-on, a mere loafer, and a man who does," said Molly, with absolute confidence.

"Bet you you don't!" murmured Bertie Richmond, smiling at the ceiling. "I know the woman's theory so jolly well."

Molly smiled also.

"I'll take your bet, whatever it is, Bertie," she said.

Bertie shook his head.

"No, I don't bet on a dead cert," he said comfortably. "I'll even tell you the fellow's heroic deeds, and then you'll never spot him. I met him first in South Africa. He saved my life twice. Once he carried me nearly a mile under fire, and got wounded in the process. Another time he sat all night under fire holding a fellow's artery. Since then he has been knocking about in odd corners, doing splendid things in the dark, as it were, for he is horribly

102 | The Tidal Wave and Other Stories

modest. The last I heard of him was from my friend Captain Raglan. He travelled on Raglan's ship from Calcutta, One night in the Mediterranean something went wrong in the engine-room. Two of the boat's engineers were badly scalded. They managed to get away, but a wretched stoker was too hurt to escape, and this fellow—this hero of mine—went down into a perfect inferno and got him out. Not only that, he went back afterwards with one of the engineers to direct him, and worked like a bull till the mischief was put right. There was danger of an explosion every moment, but he never lost his nerve for an instant. When it was over everyone concerned was sworn to secrecy, and not a passenger on board that boat knew what had actually taken place. As I said before, he is not the sort of chap anyone would credit with that sort of heroism. I shan't tell you what he is like in other respects."

"I probably know," said Molly. "I came home on Captain Raglan's ship in the autumn."

"What! You were on board?" exclaimed Bertie. "What a rum go! You will meet one or two old friends, then. And the hero is probably known to you already, though I'm sure you have never taken him for such."

"Oh, you're quite wrong!" laughed Molly. "I have known him and detected his splendid qualities for quite a long while. He is nice, isn't he? I am glad he is coming."

She took up her book with slightly heightened colour, and began to turn over its pages.

Bertie Richmond stared at her in silence for some moments.

"Well!" he said at last. "You have got sharper insight than any woman I know."

"Thanks!" said Molly, with an indifferent laugh. "But you are not so awfully great on that point yourself, are you, Bertie? I should say you are scarcely a competent judge."

Mrs. Richmond protested on Bertie's behalf, but without effect. Molly was slightly vexed with him for imagining that she could be so dull.

VI

The great country house was invaded by a host of guests on the following day. Portmanteaux and gun-cases were continually in evidence. The place was filled to overflowing.

Mrs. Langdale, who was Mrs. Richmond's greatest friend, arrived in excellent spirits, and was delighted to find Molly Erle a fellow-guest.

"And actually," she said, "Charlie Cleveland and Captain Fisher are going to swell the throng of sportsmen. We shall imagine ourselves back in our old board-ship days. Charlie was talking about them and of all the fun we had only last Saturday. Yes, I have seen him several times lately. He has been staying in town, waiting for something to turn up, he says. Funny boy! He is just as gay as ever. And Captain Fisher, whom he dragged to my flat to tea, is every bit as heavy and uninteresting, poor dear!"

"I don't call Captain Fisher uninteresting," remarked Molly. "At least, I never found him so in the old days."

"My dear, he is heavy as lead!" declared Mrs. Langdale. "I believe he only opened his mouth once to speak, and then it was to ask for five lumps of sugar instead of three. A most wearing person to entertain. I will never have him at my table without Charlie to raise the gloom. He and Charlie seemed to have decided to join forces for the present. They spent Christmas together with Captain Fisher's people. I don't know if they are as sober as he is. If so, poor dear Charlie must have felt distinctly out of his element. But his spirits are wonderful. I believe he would make a tombstone laugh."

"It will be nice to see him again," said Molly tolerantly. "It is three months now since we dispersed."

She made the remark with another thought in her mind. Surely by this Charlie would have forgotten the folly that had caused her annoyance in the old days! Constancy was the very last quality with which she credited him. Or so at least she thought.

She went for a walk on the rocky shore that afternoon, meeting the steely north-east blast with a good deal of resolution, if scant enjoyment. Something in the immediate future she found vaguely disquieting, something connected with Charlie Cleveland.

She did not believe that her estimate of this young man was in any way wide of the mark. And yet the thought of meeting him again had in it a disturbing element for which she could not account. It worried her a good deal that wild afternoon in January. Perhaps a suspicion that she had once done young Cleveland an injustice strengthened the unwelcome sense of regret, for it felt like regret in her mind.

Yet as she turned homeward along the windy shore one comforting reflection came to her and remained with her. She was at least unfeignedly glad that Captain Fisher was going to be there. She liked those silent, strong men who did all the hard work and then stood aside to let the tide of praise and admiration flood past.

Right well did her cousin's description fit this quiet hero, she told herself with flushed cheeks.

She remembered how he had spoken of him as "doing splendid things in the dark, as it were," as being "horribly modest." Fisher's heavy personality came before her with the memory. She could detect the heroism behind the grave exterior with which this man baffled all others.

If Charlie had been a hero, too, instead of a frivolous imp of mischief!

A sigh rose in her heart. Somehow, even though she told herself she had no interest in the matter, Molly wished that he were something more valuable than the flippant looker-on she took him to be. How could any man, who was worth anything, bear to be only that, she wondered?

She found a large party gathered in the hall at tea on her return. A laugh she knew fell on her ears as she entered, and an instant later she was aware of Charlie springing to meet her, his brown face aglow with the smile of welcome.

"How awfully good to meet you here, Molly!" he said, with that audacious use of her Christian name against which no protest of hers seemed to take any effect.

She shook hands with him and she tried to do it coldly, but his warm grasp was close and lingering. She realised with something of a shock that he really was as glad as he professed to be to see her again.

She went forward to the group around the fire and shook hands with all she knew.

Captain Fisher was the last to receive this attention. He was standing in the background. He moved forward half a pace to greet her. In his own peculiar, dumb fashion he also seemed pleased to meet her there.

He had an untasted cup of tea in his hand which he hastened to pass on to her.

"I shouldn't accept it if I were you," laughed Mrs. Langdale. "I saw ten lumps of sugar go into it just now."

Fisher raised his eyebrows, but made no verbal protest. He never spoke if a gesture would do as well.

Molly accepted the cup of tea with a gracious smile, and Fisher found her a chair and sat silently down beside her.

Molly had plenty to say at all times. Her companion did not embarrass her by his lack of responsiveness as he embarrassed most people. She had a feeling that his reticence did not spring from inattention.

"I am going to let you have the Silent Fish, as Charlie calls him, for partner at dinner," her hostess said to her later. "You are a positive marvel, Molly. He becomes quite genial under your influence."

Fisher brightened considerably when he found himself allotted to Molly. He even conversed a little, and went so far as to seek her out in the drawing-room later.

Charlie, who was making tracks in the same direction, turned sharply away when he saw it, and went off to the billiard-room where several of the rest were collected playing pool. He was in uproarious spirits, and the whole gathering was speedily infected thereby.

The evening ended in a boisterous abandonment to childish games, and the party broke up at midnight, exhausted but still merry. Charlie, after an animated sponge-fight with half-a-dozen other sportsmen, finally effaced himself by bolting into Fisher's bedroom and locking himself in.

To Fisher, who was smoking peacefully by the fire, he made hurried apology, to which Fisher gruffly responded by requesting him to get out.

But Charlie, after listening to the babel dying away down the corridor, turned round with a smile and established himself at comfortable length on Fisher's bed.

"I want to talk to you, dear old fellow," he tenderly remarked. "Can you spare me a few moments of your valuable time?"

"Two minutes," said Fisher with brevity.

"By Jove! What generosity!" ejaculated Charlie, his hands clasped behind his head, his eyes on the ceiling. "It's rather a delicate matter. However, here goes! Do you seriously mean business, or don't you? Are you in sober earnest, or aren't you? Are you badly smitten, or are you only just beginning to hover round the candle? Pardon my mixture of similes! The meaning remains intact."

Silence followed his somewhat involved speech. After a pause Captain Fisher got up slowly, and turned round to face the boy on his bed.

"Whatever your meaning may be, I don't fathom it," he said curtly.

Charlie rolled on to his side to look at him.

"Dense as a London fog," he murmured.

"You'd better go," said Fisher, dropping his cigarette into the fire and beginning to undress.

Charlie sat up and watched him with an air of interest. Fisher took no more notice of him. There was no waste of ceremony between these two.

Charlie got up at last and laid sudden hands on his friend's square shoulders.

"I think it wouldn't hurt you to give me a straight answer, old boy," he said, a flicker of something that was not mischief in his eyes.

Fisher faced him instantly.

"What is it you want to know?" he inquired bluntly.

"This only," Charlie said, with perfect steadiness. "Are you going in for Miss Erle in solid earnest or are you not? I want to know your intentions, that's all."

"I can't enlighten you, then," returned Fisher.

Charlie laughed without effort.

"Cautious old duffer!" he said. "Well, tell me this! I've no right to ask it. Only somehow I've got to know. You care for her, don't you?"

Fisher looked at him keenly for a moment. "Why do you ask?" he said.

"Oh, it's infernal impertinence, of course. I admit that," said Charlie, his tanned face growing suddenly red. "I suspected it, you see, ages ago—on board ship, in fact. Is it true, then?"

Fisher turned abruptly from him, and began to wind his watch with extreme care. He spoke at length with his back turned on Charlie, who was waiting with extraordinary patience for his answer.

"Yes," he said deliberately. "It is true."

"Go on and prosper!" said Charlie with a gay laugh. "You have my blessing, old chap. Thanks for telling me!"

He moved up to Fisher and thrust out an immense brown paw.

"Take a friend's advice, man!" he said. "Ask her soon!"

Then he bounced out of the room with his usual brisk energy, and shut the door noisily behind him.

VII

Was it by happy accident or by some kind friend's deliberate provision that Fisher found himself walking alone with Molly Erle to church on the following Sunday? Across the frosty park the voices of the other churchgoers sounded fitfully distinct.

Charlie Cleveland and another boy called Archie Croft, as hare-brained as himself, were making Mrs. Langdale slide along the slippery drive. Mrs.

Langdale's laughter could be plainly heard. Molly thought her, privately, rather childish to suffer herself to be thus carried away.

Her companion was sauntering very slowly at her side.

"I think we are late," Molly presently remarked, in a suggestive tone.

"Are we?" said Fisher. "Does it matter?"

"Yes," said Molly with decision. "I don't like going in after the service has begun."

"We won't," said Fisher.

She looked at him in some surprise and found him gravely watching her.

"I don't think we ought to do that," she remarked, smiling a little.

"I'll go with you to-night," said Fisher, "if you will come with me now."

They had come to a path that branched off towards the shore. He stopped with an air of determination.

Molly stopped too, looking irresolute. Her heart was beating very fast. She wished he would turn his eyes away.

Suddenly he took his hand from his pocket and held it out to her.

"Come with me, Miss Erle!" he said, in a quiet tone.

She hesitated momentarily, then as he waited she put her hand in his.

She glanced up at him as she did so, her face a glow of colour.

"How far, Captain Fisher?" she said faintly.

"All the way," said Fisher, with a sudden smile that illuminated his sombre countenance like a searchlight on a dark sea.

Molly laughed softly.

"How far is that?" she said.

He drew the little hand to his breast and put his free arm round her.

"Further than we can see, Molly," he said, and his quiet voice suddenly thrilled. "Side by side through eternity."

Thus, with no word of love, did Fisher the Silent take to himself the priceless gift of love. And the girl he wooed loved him the better for that which he left unuttered.

They returned home late for lunch, entering sheepishly, and sitting down as far apart as the length of the table would allow.

Charlie fell upon Fisher with merciless promptitude.

"You base defaulter!" he cried. "I'll see you march in front next time. I was never more scandalised in my life than when I realised that you and Molly had done a slope."

Fisher shrugged the shoulder nearest to him and offered no explanation of his and Molly's defection.

Charlie kept up a running fire of chaff for some time, to which Fisher, as was his wont, showed himself to be perfectly indifferent. Lunch over, Molly disappeared. Charlie saw her go and turned instantly to Fisher.

"Come and have a single on the asphalt court!" he said. "I haven't tried it yet. I want to."

Fisher was reluctant, but yielded to persuasion.

They went off together, Charlie with an affectionate arm round his friend's shoulders.

"I am to congratulate, I suppose?" he asked, as they crossed the garden to the tennis-court.

Fisher looked at him gravely, a hint of suspicion in his eyes.

"You may, if it gives you any pleasure to do so, my boy," he said.

"Ah, that's good!" said Charlie. "You're a jolly good fellow, old chap. You'll make her awfully happy."

"I shall do my best," Fisher said.

Charlie passed instantly to less serious matters, but the critical look did not pass entirely from Fisher's face. He seemed to be watching for something, for some card that Charlie did not appear disposed to play.

Throughout the hard set that followed, his vigilance did not relax; but Charlie played with all his customary zest. Tennis was to him for the time being the only thing worth doing on the face of the earth. In his enthusiasm he speedily stripped off his coat and rolled his sleeves to the shoulder as if it had been the hottest summer day.

At the end of the set, which Charlie won, a couple of spectators who had come up unseen applauded their energy, and Charlie, swinging round in flushed triumph, raced up for a word with his host and Molly Erie.

"I can't stuff over a fire all the afternoon," he said. "But the light is getting bad, isn't it? Fisher and I will have to knock off. Are you two going for a walk? We'll come, too, if you are, eh, Fisher?"

He turned towards Fisher, who had come up, and held out his hand for the other's racquet.

Molly uttered a sudden startled exclamation.

"Why, Charlie," she ejaculated, "what have you done to your arm? What is the matter with it?"

Charlie jumped at her startled tone and tore down his shirt-sleeve hastily.

"An old wound," he said, with a shame-faced laugh.

She put her gloved hand swiftly on his to stay his operations.

"No, tell me!" she said. "What is it—really? How was it done?"

"You will never get him to tell you that," laughed Bertie Richmond. "You had better ask Fisher."

"Oh, rats!" cried Charlie vehemently. "Fisher, I'll break your head with this racquet if you give my show away. Come along! I believe the moon has contracted a romantic habit of rising over the sea when the sun sets. Let's go and——"

"I'll tell you, Molly," broke in Bertie, linking a firm arm in Charlie's to keep him quiet. "He can't break his host's head, you know. It's a scald, eh, Charlie? He got it in the engine-room of the *Andover* one night in the autumn. You were on board, you know. Help me to hold him, Fisher! He's getting restive. But I thought you knew all about it, Molly. You told me so."

"Oh, I didn't know—this!" the girl said. "How could I? I never guessed—this!"

Her three listeners were all surprised by the tragic note in her voice. There was a momentary silence. Then Charlie made a fierce attempt to wrest himself free.

"You infernal idiots!" he exclaimed violently. "Fisher, if you interfere with me any more I—I'll punch your head! Bertie, don't be such a fool!"

He shook them off with an angry effort. Fisher laughed quietly.

"You can't always hide your light, my dear fellow," he observed. "If you will do impossible things, you will have to put up with the penalty of being occasionally found out."

"Silly ass!" commented Bertie. "Anyone would think that to save a few hundred human lives was a thing to be ashamed of. It was the same thing in South Africa; always slinking off into the background when the work was done, till everyone took you for nothing but a looker-on—a chap who ought to wear the V.C., if ever there was one," he ended, thrusting an arm through Charlie's, as the latter, having put on his coat, turned once more towards them.

"Oh, you are utterly wrong," the boy said forcibly, almost angrily. "If you judge a man by what he does on impulse you might decorate the biggest blackguard in the world with the V.C."

"You're made of impulse, my dear lad," Bertie remarked, walking off with him. "You're a mass of impulse. That's why you do such idiotic things."

Charlie yielded, chafing, to the friendly hand.

"I should like to kick you, Bertie," he said.

But he went no further than that. Bertie Richmond was his very good friend, and he was Bertie's. Neither of them was likely to forget that fact.

VIII

"Oh, Charlie, here you are! I *am* glad!"

Molly entered the smoking-room with an air of resolution. She had just returned from evening church with Fisher. They were late, and the latter had gone off to dress forthwith.

But Molly had glanced into the smoking-room, and, seeing Charlie alone there, as she had half hoped but scarcely expected, she entered.

Charlie sprang up instantly, his brown face exceedingly alert.

"Come to the fire!" he said hospitably.

Molly went, but did not sit down. She stood facing him on the hearth-rug. Her young face was very troubled.

"I want to tell you," she said steadily, "how sorry—and grieved—I am for all the hard things I have said and thought of you. I would like to retract them all. I was quite wrong. I took you for an idler—a buffoon almost. I know better now. And I—I should like you to forgive me."

Her voice suddenly faltered. Her eyes were full of tears she could neither repress nor conceal.

Charlie, however, seemed to notice nothing strained in the atmosphere. He broke into a gay laugh and held out his hand.

"Oh, that's all right," he said briskly. "Shake hands and forget what those asses said about me! You were quite right, you know. I am a buffoon. There isn't an inch of heroism anywhere about me. You took my measure long ago, didn't you? To change the subject, I'm most awfully pleased to hear that you and old Fisher have come to an understanding. Congratulate you most heartily. There's solid worth in that chap. He goes straight ahead and never plays the fool."

He looked straight at her as he spoke. Not by the flicker of an eyelid did he seem to recall the fact that he had once asked on his own behalf that which he apparently so heartily approved of her bestowing upon another.

Yet Molly, torn with remorse over what was irrevocable, did a most outrageous thing.

"Charlie!" she cried, with a deep ringing passion that would not be suppressed. "Why have I been deceived like this? Why didn't you tell me? How could you let me imagine anything so false?" She flung out her other hand to him and he took it; but still he laughed.

"Oh, come, Molly!" he protested. "I did tell you, you know. I told you the day after it happened. Don't you remember? I had to account for the skirt."

She wrenched her hands away from him. The thrill of laughter in his voice seemed to jar all her nerves. She was, moreover, wearied with the emotions of the day.

"Oh, don't you see," she cried passionately, "how different it might have been? If you had told me—if you had made me understand! I could have cared—I did care—only you seemed to me—unworthy. How could I know? What chance had I?"

She bowed her head suddenly, and burst into a storm of bitter weeping.

Charlie turned white to his lips. He stood perfectly motionless till the anguished sobbing goaded him beyond endurance. Then he flung round with a jerk.

"Stop, for Heaven's sake!" he exclaimed harshly. "I can't bear it. It's too much—too much."

He moved close to her, his face twitching, and took her shaking shoulders between his hands.

"Molly!" he said almost violently. "You don't know what you said just now. You didn't mean it. It has always been Fisher—always, from the very beginning."

She did not contradict him. She did not even answer him. She was sobbing as in passionate despair.

And it was that moment which Fisher chose for poking his head into the smoking-room in search of Charlie, whom he expected to find dozing over the fire, ignorant of the fact that it was close upon dinner-time.

Charlie leapt round at the opening of the door, but Fisher had taken stock of the situation. He entered with that in his face which the boy had never seen there before—a look that it was impossible to ignore.

Charlie met Fisher half-way across the room.

"Come into the billiard-room!" he said hurriedly.

He seized Fisher's arms with muscular fingers.

"Not here," he whispered urgently. "She is tired—upset. There is nothing really the matter."

But Fisher resisted the impulsive grip.

"I will talk to you presently," he said. "You clear out!"

He pushed past Charlie and went straight to the girl. His jaw was set with a determination that would have astonished most of his friends.

"What is it, Molly?" he said, halting close beside her. "What is wrong, child?"

But Molly could not tell him. She turned towards him indeed, laying an imploring hand on his arm; but she kept her face hidden and uttered no word.

It was Charlie who plunged recklessly into the opening breach— plunged with a wholesale gallantry, regardless of everything but the moment's emergency.

"It's my doing, Fisher," he declared, his voice shaking a little. "I've been making an ass of myself. It was, partly your fault, too—yours and Bertie's. Let her go! I'll explain."

He was excited and he spoke quickly, but his eyes were very steady.

"Molly," he said, "you go upstairs! You've got to dress, you know, and you'll be late. I'll make it all right. Don't you worry yourself!"

Molly lifted a perfectly white face and looked at Fisher. She met his eyes, struggled with herself a moment, then with quivering lips turned slowly away. He did not try to stop her. He realised that Charlie must be disposed of before he attempted to extract an explanation from her.

Charlie sprang to the door, shut it hastily after her, and turned the key.

"Now!" he said, and, wheeling, marched straight back to Fisher and halted before him. "You want an explanation. You shall have one. You gave my show away this afternoon. You made her imagine that in taking me for an ordinary—or perhaps I should say a rather extraordinary—fool she had done me an injustice. She came in her sweetness and told me she was sorry. And I—forgot myself, and said things that made her cry. That is the whole matter."

"What did you say to her?" demanded Fisher.

"I'm not going to tell you."

"You shall tell me!" said Fisher.

He took a step forward, all the hidden force in him risen to the surface.

Charlie faced him for a second with his head flung defiantly back, then, as Fisher laid a powerful hand on his shoulder, he stuck his hands in his pockets and smiled a little.

"No, old chap," he said. "I'll apologise to you, if you like. But you haven't any right to ask for more."

"I have a right to know why what you said upset her," Fisher said.

Charlie shook his head.

"Not the smallest," he said. "But I should have thought your imagination might have accomplished that much. Surely you needn't grudge the tears of pity a woman wastes over a man she has had to disappoint?"

He spoke with his eyes on Fisher's face. He was not afraid of Fisher, yet his look of relief was unmistakable as the hand on his shoulder relaxed.

"You care for her, then?" Fisher said.

Charlie flung impetuously away from him.

"Oh, need we discuss the thing any further?" he said. "I'm on the wrong side of the hedge, and that's enough. I hope you won't say any more to her about it. You will only distress her."

He walked to the end of the room and came slowly back to Fisher, whose eyes were sternly fixed upon him. He thrust out his hand impulsively.

"Forgive me, old chap!" he said. "After all, I've got the hardest part."

Fisher's face softened.

"I'm sorry, boy," he said, and took the proffered hand.

"I'll clear out to-morrow," Charlie said. "You'll forget this foolery of mine?" gripping Fisher's hand hard for a moment.

Fisher did not answer him. He struck him instead a sounding blow on the shoulder, and Charlie turned away satisfied. He had played a difficult game with considerable skill. That it had been a losing game did not at the moment enter into his calculations. He had not played for his own stakes.

IX

"Jove! It's a wild night," said Archie Croft comfortably, as he stretched out his legs to the smoking-room fire. "What's become of Charlie? He doesn't usually retire early."

"I don't believe he has retired," said Bertie Richmond sleepily. "I saw him go out something over an hour ago."

"Out?" said Croft. "What on earth for?"

"Up to some fool trick or other, no doubt," said Fisher from the smoking-room sofa.

"Hullo, Fisher! I thought you were asleep," said Bertie. "You ought to be. It's after midnight. Time we all turned in if we mean to start early with the guns to-morrow."

Croft stretched himself and rose leisurely.

"It's a positively murderous night!" he remarked, strolling to the window. "There must be a tremendous sea."

He drew aside the blind, staring at the blackness that seemed to press against the pane. A moment later, with a sharp exclamation, he ripped back the blind and flung the window wide open. An icy spout of rain and snow whirled into the room. Richmond turned round to expostulate, but was met by a face of such wild excitement that his protest remained unuttered.

"I saw a rocket!" Croft declared.

"Oh, rats!" murmured Fisher.

"It isn't rats!" he said indignantly. "It's a ship down among those infernal rocks. I'm off to see what's doing."

"Hi! Wait a minute!" exclaimed his host, starting up. "You are perfectly certain, are you, Croft? No humbug? I heard no report."

"Who could hear anything in a gale like this?" returned Croft impatiently. "Yes, of course, I am certain. Are you coming?"

"I must send a man on horseback to the life-boat station," said Bertie, starting towards the door. "It's two miles round the headland. They may not know there is anything up."

He was out of the room with the words. The rest of the men in the smoking-room followed. Fisher remained to shut the window. He stood a couple of seconds before it, facing the hurricane. The night was like pitch. The angry roar of the sea half-a-mile away surged up on the tearing gale like the voice of a devouring monster. He turned away into the cosy room and followed the others.

The whole party went out into the raging night. They groped their way after Bertie to the stables. A groom was dispatched on horseback to the lifeboat station. Lanterns were then procured, and, with the blast full in their teeth, they fought their way to the shore.

Here were darkness and desolation unspeakable. The tide was high. Great waves, flashing white through the darkness, came smiting through the rocks as if they would rend the very surface of the earth apart. The clouds scurrying overhead uncovered a star or two and instantly drew together in impenetrable darkness.

Down by the sea-wall that protected the little village nestling between the cliffs and the sea they found a knot of men and women. A short distance away in the boiling tumult there shone a shifting light, but between it and the shore the storm-god held undisputed possession.

"That's her!" explained one of the men to Bertie Richmond. "She's sunk right down in them rocks, sir. It's a little schooner. I see her masts a-stickin' up just now."

The man was one of his own gardeners. He yelled his information into Bertie's ear with great enjoyment.

"Have you sent to the lifeboat chaps?" shouted Bertie.

"Young gentleman went an hour ago," came the answer. "But they are off on another job to Mulworth, t'other side of the station. He wanted us to go out in a fishing-boat. But no one 'ud go. He be gone for a bit o' rope now. You see, sir, them rocks 'ud dash a boat to pieces like a bit o' eggshell. There's only three chaps aboard as far as we could see awhile ago. And not a hundred yards off us. But it's a hundred yards of death, as you might say. No boat could live through it. It ain't worth the trying."

A hundred yards of death and only three little human lives to be gained by the awful risk of braving that hundred yards!

Bertie turned away, feeling sick, yet silently agreeing. Who could hope to pass unharmed through that raging darkness, that tossing nightmare of great waters? Yet the thought of those three lives beating outward in agony and terror while he and his friends stood helplessly by took him by the throat.

Suddenly through a lull of the tempest there came a great shout.

The clouds had drifted asunder and a few stars shone vaguely down on the wild scene. The dim light showed the doomed vessel wedged among the rocks that stuck up, black and threatening, through the racing foam.

Nearer at hand, huddled on the stout sea-wall, stood the little group of watchers, their faces all turned outwards towards the two masts of the little schooner, which remained faintly discernible through the shifting gloom.

It was not more than a hundred yards away, Bertie realised. Yet the impossibility of rescue was as apparent as if it had been a hundred miles from land. He fancied he could see a couple of figures half-way up one of the masts, but the light was elusive. He could not be certain of this.

Suddenly a hand gripped his elbow, and he found Archie Croft beside him, yelling excitedly.

"Don't let him go!" he bawled. "It's madness—sheer madness!"

Bertie turned sharply. Close to him, his head bare, and clothed still in evening dress, stood Charlie Cleveland. A coil of rope lay at his feet. He had knotted one end firmly round his body.

"Listen, you fellows!" he cried. "I'm going to have a shot at it. Pay out the rope as I go. Count up to five hundred, and if it is limp, pull it in again. If it holds, make it fast! Got me?"

He turned at once to a flight of iron steps that led off the wall down into the awful, seething water. But someone, Fisher, sprang suddenly after him and held him back. Charlie wheeled instantly. The light of a lantern striking on his face revealed it, unafraid, even laughing.

"You silly ass!" he cried. "Hang on to the rope instead of behaving like a fellow's grandmother!"

"You shan't do it!" Fisher said, holding him fast. "It is certain death!"

"All right," Charlie yelled back. "I choose death, then. I prefer it to sitting still and seeing others die. My life is my own. I choose to risk it."

He looked at Fisher closely for a moment, then, with one immense effort, he wrenched himself away. He went leaping down the steps as a boy going for a summer-morning dip.

Fisher turned round and met Bertie Richmond hurrying to help him.

"Let him go!" Fisher said briefly.

Thereafter came a terrible interval of waiting. The sky was clearing, but the tempest did not abate. The rope ran out with jerks and pauses. Fisher stood and counted at the head of the steps, his eyes on the tumult that had swallowed up the slight active figure of the one man among them all who had elected to risk his life against those overwhelming odds.

"He must be dashed to pieces!" Bertie Richmond gasped to himself, with a shudder.

The rope ceased to run. Fisher had counted four hundred and fifty. He counted on resolutely to five hundred, then turned and raised his hand to the men who held the coil. They hauled at the rope. It was limp. Hand over hand they dragged it in through the foam. Fisher peered downwards. It came so rapidly that he thought it must have parted among the rocks. Then he saw a dark object bobbing strangely among the waves. He went down the steps, that quivered and trembled like cardboard under his feet.

Clinging to the iron rail, he reached out a hand and guided the rope to him. A great sea broke over him and nearly swept him off. He saved himself by hanging with both hands on to the rope. Thus he was dragged up the steps to safety, and behind him, buffeted, bleeding, helpless, came two limp bodies lashed fast together.

They cut the two asunder by the light of the lanterns, and one of them, Charlie, staggered to his feet.

"I've got to go back!" he gasped. "You pulled too soon. There are two others."

He dashed the blood from his face, seized a pocket flask someone held out to him, and drained it at a long gulp.

"That's better!" he said. "That you, Fisher? Good-bye, old chap!"

The first pale light of a rising moon burst suddenly through the cloud drift.

"I'll go myself," Fisher abruptly said.

Even in that roar of sound they heard the boyish laugh that rang out upon the words.

"No, no, no!" shouted Charlie. "Bless you, dear fellow! But this is my job—alone. You've got to stay behind—you're wanted."

He stood a few seconds poising himself on the steps, drawing deep breaths in preparation for the coming struggle. The moonlight smote upon him. He lifted his face to it, and seemed to hesitate. Then suddenly he turned to Fisher and laid impetuous hands upon his shoulders.

"Lookers-on see most of the game," he said. "And I've been one from the first, though I own I thought at one time I should like to take a hand. Go on and prosper, old boy! You've played a winning game all along, you know. You're a better chap than I am, and it's you she really cares for—always has been. That's how I came to know what I'd got to do. I find it's easy—thank God!—it's very easy."

And with that he plunged down again into the breakers. The tide was on the turn. The worst fury was over. The awful darkness had lifted.

Those who mutely watched him fancied they heard him laugh as he met the crested waves.

X

Molly had spent a night of feverish restlessness. It was with a feeling of relief that she answered a tap that came at her door in the early dusk of the January morning; but she gave a start of surprise when she saw Mrs. Langdale enter.

She started up on her elbow.

"Oh, what is it? It has been a fearful night. Has something dreadful happened?" she cried.

Mrs. Langdale's usually merry face was pale and quiet. She went quickly to the girl's side and took her hands into a tight clasp.

"My dear," she said, "Gerald Fisher asked me to come and tell you. There has been a wreck in the night. A vessel ran on to the rocks. There were three men on board. They could not reach them with an ordinary boat, and the life-boat was not available."

"Go on!" gasped Molly, her eyes on her friend's face.

Mrs. Langdale went on, with an effort.

"Charlie Cleveland—dear fellow—went out to them with a rope. He reached them, brought one safely back, returned for the others—and—and—" Her voice failed. Her hands tightened upon Molly's; they were very cold. "He managed to get to them again," she whispered, "but—the rope wasn't long enough. He unlashed himself and bound them together. They pulled them ashore—both living. But—he—was lost!"

The composure suddenly forsook Mrs. Langdale's face. She hid it on Molly's pillow.

"Oh, Molly, that darling boy!" she cried, with a burst of tears. "And they say he went to his death—laughing."

"He would," Molly said, in a strange voice. "I always knew he would."

She lay back again. Her face was suddenly pinched and grey, but she felt not the smallest desire to cry.

"I wonder why!" she presently said. "How I wonder why!"

Mrs. Langdale recovered herself with an effort. The frozen voice seemed to give her strength.

"Have we any right to ask that?" she whispered. "No one on this side can ever know."

"Oh, I think you are wrong," Molly said. "We can't be meant to grope in outer darkness."

Mrs. Langdale whispered something about "those the gods love." She was too broken-down herself to be able to offer any solid comfort.

After a painful silence she got up and busied herself with reviving Molly's fire, which had almost gone out. She felt as she had felt only once before in her life, and that had been ten years previously, when her only child had died suddenly. She wished passionately that she were back in Calcutta with her husband. She hated the bleak English winter, the cruel English seas.

Molly lay quite still for some time, her young face drawn and stricken.

At length she got up and went to the window. It was a morning of bleak winds and shifting clouds. The sea was just visible, very far and dim and grey. She stood a long while gazing stonily out.

"Can I get you anything, darling?" said Mrs. Langdale's voice softly behind her.

"No, thank you," the girl said, without turning. "Please leave me; that's all!"

And Mrs. Langdale crept away through the hushed house to her own apartment, there to lay down her head and cry herself exhausted. Dear, gallant Charlie! Her heart ached for him. His irrepressible gaiety, his reckless generosity, these had become the attributes of a hero for ever in her eyes.

After a while her hostess came to her, pale and tearful, to beg her, if she possibly could, to show herself at the breakfast table. Captain Fisher had repeatedly asked for her, she said; and he seemed very uneasy.

Mrs. Langdale rose, washed her face, and made an effort to powder away the evidence of her grief. Then she went bravely down and faced the silent crowd in the breakfast room. No one was eating anything. The very air smote chill and cheerless as she entered. As if he had been lying in wait for her, Fisher pounced upon her on the threshold.

"I must speak to you for a moment," he said. "Come into the smoking-room!"

Mrs. Langdale accompanied him without a word.

"How is she?" he demanded, almost before they entered. "How did she take it?"

There was something about Fisher just then with which Mrs. Langdale was wholly unacquainted. He was alert, impatient, almost feverish. She answered him with brevity.

"I think she is stunned by the news."

He began to pace to and fro with heavy restlessness.

"Ask her to come to me if she is up!" he said at length. "Tell her—tell her not to be afraid! Say I am waiting for her. I must see her."

Mrs. Langdale hesitated.

"She asked me to leave her alone," she said irresolutely.

Fisher wheeled swiftly round.

"I don't think she will refuse to see me," he said. "At least try!"

There was entreaty in his voice, urgent entreaty, which Mrs. Langdale found herself unable to withstand.

She departed therefore on her thankless errand and Fisher flung himself down at the table with his face buried in his hands. In this room but a few short hours ago Charlie had faced and turned away his anger with all the courage and sweetness which, combined, had made of him the hero he was.

It seemed to Fisher, looking back upon the interview, that the boy had done a braver thing, had offered a sacrifice more splendid, there, in that room, than any he had done or offered a little later down on the howling shore.

There came a slight sound at the door and Fisher jerked himself upright. Molly had entered softly. She was standing, looking at him with a strange species of wonder on her white face. He rose instantly and went to meet her.

"I have something to give you, Molly," he said. She raised her eyes questioningly.

"It was brought to me," he said, controlling his voice to quietness with a strong effort, "after Mrs. Langdale went to tell you of—what had happened. I wish to give it to you myself. And—afterwards to ask you a question."

"What is it?" Molly asked, with a sudden sharp eagerness.

"A note," Fisher said, and gave her a folded paper. "It was found on his dressing-table, addressed to you. His servant brought it to me."

Molly's hand trembled as she took the missive.

Fisher turned away from her, and stood before the window in dead silence. There was a long, quiet pause. Then a sudden sound made him swing swiftly round and stride to the door to turn the key. The next moment he was stooping over Molly, who had sunk down on the hearth-rug and was sobbing terrible, anguished sobs.

He lifted her to a chair with no fuss of words, and knelt beside her, stroking her hair, comforting her, with something of a woman's tenderness.

Molly suffered him passively, and the first wild agony of her trouble spent itself unrestrained on his shoulder. Then she grew calmer, and presently begged him in a whisper to read the message which Charlie had left behind him.

For a moment Fisher hesitated; then, as she repeated her desire, he took up the scrawl and deliberately read it through. It had evidently been written immediately after his interview with the writer.

"Dear Molly," the note said, "It's all right with Fisher, so don't you worry yourself! I clear out to-morrow, so that there may be no awkwardness, but we haven't quarrelled, he and I. Forget all about this business! It's been a mistake from start to finish. I ought to have known that I was only fit to be a looker-on when I fell at the first fence. You put your money on Fisher and you'll never lose a halfpenny! I'm nothing but a humble spectator, and I wish you—and him also—the best of luck. If I might be permitted, to offer a little, serious, fatherly advice, it would be this:

"Don't let yourself get dazzled by the outside shine of any man's actions! A man isn't necessarily a hero because he doesn't run away. It is the true-hearted, steady-going chaps like Fisher who keep the world wagging. They are the solid material. The others are only a sort of trimming stuck on for effect and torn off when the time comes for something new. So marry the man you love, Molly, and forget that anyone else ever made a fool of himself for your sweet sake!

"Your friend for ever,

"Charlie."

Thus ended, with a simplicity sublime, the few words of fatherly advice which as a legacy this boy had left behind him.

Fisher laid the note reverently aside and spoke with a great gentleness.

"Tell me, dear," he said, "will it make it any easier for you if I go away? If so—you have only to say so."

The words cost him greater resolution than any he had ever uttered. Yet he said them without apparent effort.

Molly did not answer him for many seconds. Her head drooped a little lower.

"I have been—dazzled," she said at last, and there was a piteous quiver in her voice. "I do not know if I shall ever make you understand."

"You need never attempt it, Molly," he answered very steadily. "I make no claim upon you. Simply, I am yours to keep or to throw away. Which are you going to do?"

He paused for her answer. But she made none. Only in her trouble it seemed to him that she clung to his support.

He drew her a little closer to him.

"Molly," he said very tenderly, "do you want me, child? Shall I stay?"

And at length she answered him, realising that it was to this man, hero or no hero, she had given her heart.

"Yes, stay, Gerald!" she whispered earnestly. "I want you."

Perhaps he understood her better than she thought. Perhaps Charlie's last words to him had taught him a wisdom to which he had not otherwise attained. Or perhaps his love was large enough to cover and hide all that might be lacking in that which she offered to him.

But at least neither then nor later did he ever seek to know how deeply the glamour of another man's heroism had pierced her heart. She tried to whisper an explanation, but he hushed the words unuttered.

"It is all right, child," he said. "I am satisfied. It is only the lookers-on who are allowed to see all the cards. I think when we meet him again he will tell us that we played them right."

There was a deep quiver in his voice as he spoke, but there was no lack of confidence in his words. Looking upwards, Molly saw that his eyes were full of tears.

THE SECOND FIDDLE

A low whistle floated through the slumbrous silence and died softly away among the sand-dunes.

The man who sat in the little wooden summer-house that faced the sea raised his head from his hand and stared outwards. The signal had scarcely penetrated to his inner consciousness, but it had vaguely disturbed his train of thought. His eyes were dull and emotionless as he stared across the blue, smiling water to the long, straight line of the horizon. They were heavy also as if he had not slept for weeks, and there were deep lines about his clean-shaven mouth.

Before him on the rough, wooden table lay a letter—a letter that he knew by heart, yet carried always with him. The writing upon it was firm and regular, but unmistakably a woman's. It began: "Dear Hugh," and it ended: "Yours very sincerely," and it had been written to tell him that because he was crippled for life the writer could no longer entertain the idea of sharing hers with him.

There had been a ring enclosed with the letter, but this he had not kept. He had dropped it into the heart of a blazing fire on the day that he had first been able to move without assistance. He had not done it in anger. Simply the consciousness of possessing it had been a pain intolerable to him. So he had destroyed it; but the letter he had kept through all the dreary months that had followed that awful time. It was all that was left to him of one whom he had loved passionately, blindly, foolishly, and who had ceased to love him on the day, now nearly a year ago, when his friends had ceased to call him by the nickname of Hercules, that had been his from his boyhood.

And this was her wedding-day—a day of entrancing sunshine, of magic breezes, of perfect June.

He was picturing her to himself as he sat there, just as he had pictured her often—ah, often—in the old days.

From his place near the altar he watched her coming towards him up the great, white-decked church. Her eyes were shining with unclouded happiness. Behind her bridal veil he caught a glimpse of the exquisite beauty that chained his heart. Straight towards him the vision moved, and he—he braced himself to meet it.

A sharp pang of physical pain suddenly wrung his nerves, and in a moment the vision had passed from his eyes. He groaned and once more covered his face. Yes, it was her wedding-day. She was there before the altar in all the splendour of her youth and her loveliness. But he was alone with his suffering, his broken life, and the long, long, empty years stretching away before him.

He awoke to the soft splashing of the summer tide, out beyond the sand-dunes, and he heard again the clear, low whistle which before had disturbed his dream.

He remained motionless, and a dim, detached wonder crossed his mind. He had thought himself quite alone.

Again the whistle sounded. It seemed to come from immediately below him. Slowly and painfully he raised himself.

The next instant an enormous Newfoundland dog rushed panting into his retreat and proceeded to search every inch of the place with violent haste. The man on the bench sat still and watched him, but when the animal with a sudden, clumsy movement knocked his crutches on to the floor and out of his reach, he uttered an exclamation of annoyance.

The dog gave him a startled glance and continued his headlong investigation. He was very wet, and he left a trail of sea water wherever he went. Finally he bounded out as hurriedly as he had entered, and Hugh Durant was left a prisoner, the nearest of his crutches a full yard away.

He sat and stared at them with a heavy frown. His helplessness always oppressed him far more than the pain he had to endure. He cursed the dog under his breath.

"Oh, I am sorry!" a voice said suddenly some seconds later. "Let me get them for you!"

Durant looked round sharply. A brown-faced girl in a short, cotton dress stood in the doorway. Her head was bare and covered with short, black, curly hair that shone wet in the sunshine. Her eyes were very blue. For some reason she looked rather ashamed of herself.

She moved forward barefooted and picked up Durant's crutches.

"I'm sorry, sir," she said again. "I didn't know there was any one here till I heard Cæsar knock something down."

She dusted the tops of the crutches with her sleeve and propped them against the table.

"Thanks!" said Durant curtly. He was not feeling sociable—he could not feel sociable—on that day of all days in his life's record.

Yet, as if attracted by something, the girl lingered.

"It's lovely down on the shore," she said half shyly.

"No doubt," said Durant, and again his tone was curt to churlishness.

Then abruptly he felt that he had been unnecessarily surly, and wondered if he was getting querulous.

"Been bathing?" he asked, with a brief glance at her wet hair.

She gave him a quick, friendly smile.

"Yes, sir," she said; and added: "Cæsar and I."

"Fond of the sea, eh?" said Durant.

The soft eyes shone, and the man, who had been a sailor, told himself that they were deep-sea eyes.

"I love it," the girl said very earnestly.

Her intensity surprised him a little. He had not expected it in one who, to judge by her dress, must be a child of the humble fisher-folk. His interest began to awaken.

"You live near here?" he questioned.

She pointed a brown hand towards the sand-dunes.

"On the shore, sir," she said. "We hear the waves all night."

"So do I," said Durant, and his voice was suddenly sharp with a pain he could not try to silence. "All night and all day."

She did not seem to notice his tone.

"You live in the cottage on the cliff?" she asked.

He nodded.

"I came last week," he said. "I hadn't seen the sea for nearly a year. I wanted to be alone. And—so I am."

"All alone?" she queried quickly.

He nodded again.

"With my servant," he said. He repeated with a certain doggedness: "I wanted to be alone."

There was a pause. The girl was standing in the doorway. Her dog was basking in the sunshine not a yard away. She looked at the cripple with thoughtful eyes.

"I live alone, too," she said. "That is—Cæsar and I."

That successfully aroused Durant's curiosity.

"You!" he said incredulously.

She put up her hand with a quick movement and pushed the short curls back from her forehead.

"I am used to it," she said, with an odd womanly dignity. "I have been practically alone all my life."

Durant looked at her closely. She spoke in a very low voice, but there were rich notes in it that caught his attention.

"Isn't that very unusual for a girl of your age?" he said.

She smiled again without answering. A blue sunbonnet dangled on her arm. In the silence that followed she put it on. The great dog arose at the action, stretched himself, and went to her side. She laid her hand on his head.

"We play hide-and-seek, Cæsar and I," she said, "among the dunes."

Durant took his crutches and stumbled with difficulty to his feet. The lower part of his body was terribly crippled and weak. Only the broad shoulders of the man testified to the splendid strength that had once been his, and could never be his again as long as he lived. He saw the girl turn her head aside as he moved. The sunbonnet completely hid her face. A sharp spasm of pain set his own like a stone mask.

Suddenly she looked round.

"Will you—will you come and see me some day?" she asked him shyly.

Her tone was rather of request than invitation, and Durant was curiously touched. He had a feeling that she awaited his reply with eagerness.

He smiled for the first time.

"With pleasure," he said courteously, "if the path is easy and the distance not too great for my powers."

"It is quite close," she said readily, "hardly a stone's throw from here—a little wooden cottage—the first you come to."

"And you live quite alone?" Durant said.

"I like it best," she assured him.

"Will you tell me your name?" he asked.

"My name is Molly," she answered quietly.

"Nothing else?" said Durant with a puzzled frown.

"Nothing else, sir," she said, with her air of womanly dignity.

He made no outward comment, but inwardly he wondered. Was this odd little, dark-haired creature some nameless waif of the sea brought up on the charity of the fisher-folk, he asked himself.

She stood aside for him to pass, drawing Cæsar out of his way. He stopped a moment to pat the dog's head. And so standing, leaning upon his crutches, he suddenly and keenly looked into the olive-tinted face that the sunbonnet shadowed.

"Sorry for me, eh?" he said, and he uttered a laugh that was short and very bitter.

She bent down over the dog.

"Yes, I am sorry," she said, almost under her breath.

Bending lower, she picked up something that lay on the ground between them.

"You dropped this," she said.

He took it from her with a grim hardening of the mouth. It was the letter he had received from his *fiancée* a year ago. But his eyes never left the face of the girl before him.

"I wonder—" he said abruptly, and stopped.

There was a pause. The girl waited, her hand nervously caressing the Newfoundland's curls. She did not raise her eyes, but the lids fluttered strangely.

"I wonder," Durant said, and his voice was suddenly kind, "if I might ask you to do something for me."

She gave him a swift glance.

"Please do!" she murmured.

"This letter," he said, and he held it out to her.

"I should like it torn up—very small."

She took the envelope and hesitated. Durant was watching her. There was unmistakable mastery in his eyes.

"Go on!" he said briefly.

And with a quick, startled movement, she obeyed. The letter fluttered around them both in tiny fragments. Hugh Durant looked on with a hard, impassive face, as he might have looked on at an execution.

The girl's hands were shaking. She glanced at him once or twice uncertainly.

When the work of destruction was accomplished she made him a nervous curtsey and turned to go.

Durant's face softened a second time into a smile.

"Thank you—Molly," he said, and he put his hand to his hat though she was not looking at him.

And afterwards he stood among the fragments of his letter and watched till both the girl and the dog were out of sight.

Twenty-four hours later Hugh Durant stood on the sandy shore and tapped with his crutch on the large, flat stone that was set for a step on the threshold of the little, wooden cottage behind the sand dunes.

He had reached the place with much difficulty, persevering with a doggedness characteristic of him; and there were great drops on his forehead though the afternoon was cloudy and cool.

A quick step sounded in answer to his summons, and in a moment his hostess appeared at the open door.

"Why didn't you come straight in?" she said hospitably.

She was dressed in lilac print. Her sleeves were turned up to the elbows, and she wore a big apron with a bib. He noticed that her feet were no longer bare.

He took off his hat as he answered.

"Perhaps I might have been tempted to do so," he said, "if I had felt equal to mounting the step without assistance."

"Oh!" She pulled down her sleeves hastily. "Will you let me help you?" she suggested shyly.

Durant's eyes were slightly drawn with pain. Nevertheless they were very friendly as he made reply.

"Do you think you can?" he said.

She took his hat from him with an anxious smile, and then the crutch that he held towards her.

"Tell me exactly what to do!" she said in her sweet, low voice. "I am very strong."

"If I may put my arm on your shoulder," Durant said, "I think it can be managed. But say at once if it is too much for you!"

Her face was deeply flushed as she bent from the step to give him the help he needed.

"Bear harder!" she said, as he leant his weight upon her. "Bear much harder!"

There was an odd little quiver in her voice, but, slight as she was, she supported him with sturdy strength.

The door opened straight into the tiny cottage parlour. A large wicker chair, well cushioned, stood in readiness. As Durant lowered himself into it, he saw that the girl's eyes were brimming with tears.

"I've hurt you!" he exclaimed.

"No, no!" she said, and turned quickly away. "You didn't bear nearly hard enough."

He laughed a little, though his teeth were clenched.

"You're a very strong woman, Molly," he said.

"Oh, I am," she answered instantly. "Now shall you be all right while I go to fetch tea?"

"Of course," he said. "Pray don't make a stranger of me!"

She disappeared into the room at the back of the cottage, and he was left alone. The great dog came in with stately stride and lay down at his feet.

Durant sat and looked about him. There was little to attract the eye in the simple furnishing of the tiny room. There was a small bookcase in one corner, but it was covered by a red curtain. Two old-fashioned Dutch figures stood on the mantelpiece on each side of a cheap little clock that seemed to tick at him almost resentfully. The walls were tinted green and bore no pictures or decoration of any sort. There was a plain white tablecloth on the table, and in the middle stood a handleless jug filled with pink and white wild roses, freshly gathered. There was no carpet. The floor was strewn with beach sand.

All these details Durant took in with keen interest. Nothing could have exceeded the simplicity of this dwelling by the sea. There had obviously been no attempt at artistic arrangement. Cleanliness and a neatness almost severe were its only characteristics.

"I hope you like toasted scones, sir," said Molly's voice in the doorway.

He looked round to see her come forward with the tea-tray.

"Nothing better," he said lightly, "particularly if you have made them yourself."

She set down her tray and smiled at him. Her short, curling hair gave her an almost elfish look.

"I've been so busy getting ready," she said childishly. "I've never had a gentleman to tea before."

"That is a very great honour for me," said Durant.

Molly looked delighted.

"I think the honour is mine," she said in her shy voice. "I am just going to fetch the wooden chair out of the kitchen."

She departed hastily as if embarrassed, and Durant smiled to himself. It was wonderful how the oppression had been lifted from his spirit since his meeting with this lonely dweller on the shore.

When Molly reappeared, he saw that she had assumed a dignity worthy of the occasion. She sat down behind the brown teapot with a serious face. He waited for her to lead the conversation, and the result was complete silence for some seconds.

Then she said suddenly:

"Have you been sitting in the summer-house again?"

"No," said Durant.

"I am glad of that," said Molly.

"Why?" he asked.

She hesitated.

"Isn't it rather a lonely place?" she said.

He smiled faintly.

"You know I came here to be lonely, Molly," he said.

"Yes; you told me," said Molly, and he fancied that he heard her sigh.

"Are you never lonely?" he asked in a kindly tone.

"Often," she said. "Often."

She was pouring the tea as she spoke. Her head was slightly bent.

"And so you took pity on me?" said Durant.

She shook her head suddenly and vigorously.

"It wasn't that, sir," she said in a very low voice. "I—I wanted—someone—to speak to."

"I see," said Durant gently. He added after a moment: "Do you know, I am glad I chanced to be that someone."

She smiled at him over the teapot.

"You weren't pleased—at first," she said. "You were angry. I heard you saying—"

"What?" said Durant.

He looked across at her and laughed naturally, spontaneously, for the first time.

Molly had forgotten to be either embarrassed or dignified.

"I don't know what it was," she said; "I only know what it sounded like."

"And that made you want to speak to me?" said Durant.

The brown face opposite to him looked impish. Yet it seemed to him that there was sadness in her eyes.

"It didn't frighten me away," she said.

"It would need to be a very timid person to be frightened at me now," said Hugh Durant quietly.

She opened her eyes wide, and looked as if she were about to protest. Then, changing her mind, she remained silent.

"Yes," he said. "Please say it!"

She shook her head without speaking.

But he persisted. Something in her silence aroused his curiosity.

"Am I really formidable, Molly?" he asked.

She rose to take his empty cup, and paused for a moment at his side, looking down at him.

"I don't think you realise how strong you are," she said enigmatically.

He laughed rather drearily.

"I am gauging my weakness just at present," he said.

And then, glancing up, he saw quick pain in her eyes, and abruptly turned the conversation.

Later, when he took his leave, he stood on her step and looked out to the long, grey line of sea with a faint, dissatisfied frown on his face.

"You're not afraid—living here?" he asked her at the last moment.

"What is there to fear?" said Molly. "I have Cæsar, and there are other cottages not far away."

"Yes, I know," he said. "But at night—when it's dark—"

A sudden glory shone in the girl's pure eyes.

"Oh, no, sir," she said. "I am not afraid."

And he departed, hobbling with difficulty up the long, sandy slope.

At the top he paused and looked out over the grey, unquiet sea. The dissatisfaction on his face had given place to perplexity and a faint, dawning wonder that was like the birth of Hope.

During the long summer days that followed, that strange friendship, begun at the moment when Hugh Durant's life had touched its lowest point of suffering and misery, ripened into a curiously close intimacy.

The girl was his only visitor—the only friend who penetrated behind the barrier of loneliness that he had erected for himself. He had sought the place sick at heart and utterly weary of life, desiring only to be left alone. And yet, oddly enough, he did not resent the intrusion of this outsider, who had openly told him that she was sorry.

She visited him occasionally at his hermitage, but more frequently she would seek him out in his summer-house and take possession of him there with a winning enchantment that he made no effort to resist. Sometimes she brought him tea there; sometimes she persuaded him to return with her to her cottage on the shore.

The embarrassment had wholly passed from her manner. She was eager and ingenuous as a child. And yet there was something in her—a depth of feeling, a concentration half-revealed—that made him aware of her womanhood. She was never confidential with him, but yet he felt her confidence in every word she uttered.

And the life that had ebbed so low turned in the man's veins and began to flow with a steady, rising surge of which he was only vaguely conscious.

Molly had become his keenest interest. He had ceased to think with actual pain of the woman who had loved his strength, but had shrunk in horror from his weakness. His bitterness had seemed to disperse with the fragments of her torn letter. It was only a memory to him now—scarcely even that.

"This place has done me a lot of good," he said to Molly one day. "I have written to my friend Gregory Mountfort to come and see me. He is my doctor."

She looked up at him quickly. She was sitting on her doorstep and the August sunlight was on her hair. There were wonderful glints of gold among the dark curls.

"Shall you go away, then?" she asked.

"I may—soon," he said.

She was silent, bending over some work that she had taken up. The man looked down at the bowed head. The old look of perplexity, of wonder, was in his eyes.

"What shall you do?" he said abruptly.

She made a startled movement, but did not raise her eyes.

"I shall just—go on," she said, in a voice that was hardly audible.

"Not here," he said. "You will be lonely."

There was an unusual note of mastery in his voice. She glanced up, and met his eyes resolutely for a moment.

"I am used to loneliness," she said slowly.

"But you don't prefer it?" he said.

She bent her head again.

"Yes, I prefer it," she said.

There followed a pause. Then abruptly Durant asked a question.

"Are you still sorry for me?" he said.

"No," said Molly.

He bent slightly towards her. Movement had become much easier to him of late.

"Molly," he said very gently, "that is the kindest thing you have ever said."

She laughed in a queer, shaky note over her work.

He bent nearer.

"You have done a tremendous lot for me," he said, speaking very softly. "I wonder if I dare ask of you—one thing more?"

She did not answer. He put his hand on her shoulder.

"Molly," he said, "will you marry me?"

"No," said Molly under her breath.

"Ah!" he said. "Forgive me for asking!"

She looked up at him then with that in her eyes which he could not understand.

"Mr. Durant," she said, steadily, "I thank you very much, and it isn't—that. But I can only be your friend."

"Never anything more, Molly?" he said, and he smiled at her, very gently, very kindly, but without tenderness.

"No, sir," Molly said in the same steady tone. "Never anything more."

"Well," said Gregory Mountfort on the following day, "this place has done wonders for you, Hugh. You're a different man."

"I believe I am," said Hugh.

He spoke with his eyes upon a bouquet of poppies and corn that had been left at his door without any message early that morning. It was eloquent to him of a friendship that did not mean to be lightly extinguished, but his heart was heavy notwithstanding. He had begun to desire something greater than friendship.

"Physically," said Mountfort, "you are stronger than I ever expected to see you again. You don't suffer much pain now, do you?"

"No, not much," said Durant.

He turned to stare out of his open window at the sunlit sea. His eyes were full of weariness.

"Look here," the doctor said. "You're not an invalid any longer. I should leave this place if I were you. Go abroad! Go round the world! Don't stagnate any longer! It isn't worthy of you."

Hugh Durant shook his head.

"It's no good trying to float a stranded hulk, dear fellow," he said. "Don't attempt it! I am better off where I am."

"You ought to get married," his friend returned brusquely. "You weren't created for the lonely life."

"I shall never marry," Durant said quietly.

And Mountfort was disappointed. He wondered if he were still vexing his soul over the irrevocable.

He had motored down from town, and in the afternoon he carried his patient off for a thirty-mile spin. They went through the depths of the country, through tiny villages hidden among the hills, through long stretches of pine woods, over heather-covered uplands. But though it did him good, Durant was conscious of keenest pleasure when, returning, they ran into view of the sea. He felt that the shore and the sand-dunes were his own peculiar heritage.

Mountfort steered for the village scattered over the top of the cliff. Durant had persuaded him to remain for the night, and he had to send a telegram. They puffed up a steep, winding hill to the post-office, and the doctor got out.

"Back in thirty seconds," he said, as he walked away.

Hugh was in no hurry. It was a wonderfully calm evening. The sea looked like a sheet of silver, motionless, silent, immense. The tide was very low. The sand-dunes looked mere hummocks from that great height. Myriads of martens were circling about the edge of the cliff, which was protected by a crazy wooden railing. He sat and watched them without much interest. He was thinking chiefly of that one cottage on the shore a hundred feet below, which he knew so well.

He wondered if Molly had been to the summer-house to look for him; and then, chancing to glance up, he caught sight of her coming towards him from the roadside. At the same instant something jerked in the motor, and it began to move. It was facing up the hill, and the angle was a steep one. Very slowly at first the wheels revolved, and the car moved straight backwards as if pushed by an unseen hand.

Hugh realised the danger in a moment. The road curved sharply not a dozen yards behind him, and at that curve was the sheer precipice of the cliff. He was powerless to apply the brakes, and he could not even throw himself out. The sudden consciousness of this ran through him piercing as a sword-blade.

In every pulse of his being he felt the intense, the paralysing horror of violent death. For the first awful moment he could not even call for help. The sensation of falling headlong backwards gripped his throat and choked his utterance.

He made a wild, ineffectual movement with his hands. And then he heard a loud cry. A woman's figure flashed towards him. She seemed to swoop as the martens swooped along the face of the cliff. The car was running smoothly towards that awful edge. He felt that it was very near— horribly near; but he could not turn to look.

Even as the thought darted through his brain he saw Molly, wide-eyed, frenzied, clinging to the side of the car. She was in the act of springing on to it, and that knowledge loosened his tongue.

He yelled to her hoarsely to keep away. He even tried to thrust her hands off the woodwork. But she withstood him fiercely, with a strength that agonised and overcame. In a second she was on the step, where she swayed perilously, then fell forward on her hands and knees at his feet.

The car continued to run back. There came a sudden jerk, a crash of rending wood, a frightful pause. The railing had splintered. They were on the brink. Hugh bent and tried to take her in his arms.

He was strung to meet that awful plunge; he was face to face with death; but—was it by some miracle?—the car was stayed. There, on the very edge of destruction, with not an inch to spare, it stood suddenly motionless, as if checked by some mysterious, unseen force.

As complete understanding returned to him, Hugh saw that the woman at his feet had thrown herself upon the foot brake and was holding it pressed down with both her rigid hands.

"Yes; but who taught her where to look for the brake?" said Mountfort two hours later.

The excitement was over, but the subject fascinated Mountfort. The girl had sprung away and disappeared down one of the cliff paths directly Hugh had been extricated from danger. Mountfort was curious about her, but Hugh was uncommunicative. He had no answer ready to Mountfort's question. He scarcely seemed to hear it.

Barely a minute after its utterance he reached for his crutches and got upon his feet.

"I am going down to the shore," he said. "I shan't sleep otherwise. You'll excuse me, old fellow?"

Mountfort looked at him and nodded. He was very intimate with Hugh.

"Don't mind me!" he said.

And Hugh went out alone in the summer dusk.

The night was almost ghostly in its stillness. He went down the winding path that he knew so well without a halt. Far away the light of a steamer travelled over the quiet water. The sea murmured drowsily as the tide rose. It was not quite dark.

Outside her cottage-door he stopped and tapped upon the stone. The door stood open, and as he waited he heard a clear, low whistle behind him on the dunes. She was coming towards him, the great dog Cæsar bounding by her side. As she drew near he noticed again how slight she was, and marvelled at her strength.

She reached him in silence. The light was very dim. He put out his hand to her, but somehow he could not utter a word.

"I knew it must be you," she said. "I—I was waiting for you."

She put her hand into his; but still the man stood mute. No words would come to him.

She looked at him uncertainly, almost nervously. Then—

"What is it?" she asked, under her breath.

He spoke at last but not to utter the words she expected.

"I haven't come to say, 'Thank you,' Molly," he said. "I have come to ask why."

"Oh!" said Molly.

She was startled, confused, almost scared, by the mastery that underlay the gentleness of his tone. He kept her hand in his, standing there, facing her in the dimness; and, cripple as he was, she knew him for a strong man.

"I have come to ask," he said—"and I mean to know—why yesterday you refused to marry me."

She made a quick movement. His words astounded her. She felt inclined to run away. But he kept her prisoner.

"Don't be afraid of me, Molly!" he said half sadly. "You had a reason. What was it."

She bit her lip. Her eyes were full of sudden tears.

"Tell me!" he said.

And she answered, as if he compelled her:

"It was because—because you don't love me," she said with difficulty.

She felt his hand tighten upon hers.

"Ah!" he said. "And that was—the only reason?"

Molly was trembling.

"It was the only reason that mattered," she said in a choked voice.

He leant towards her in the dusk.

"Molly," he said. "Molly, I worship you!"

She heard the deep quiver in his voice, and it thrilled her from head to foot. She began to sob, and he drew her towards him.

"Wait!" she said, "Oh, wait! Come inside, and I'll tell you!"

He went in with her, leaning on her shoulder.

"Sit down!" whispered Molly. "I'm going to tell you something."

"Don't cry!" he said gently. "It may be something I know already."

"Oh, no, it isn't!" she said with conviction.

She stood before him in the twilight, her hands clasped tightly together.

"Do you remember a girl called Mary Fielding?" she said, with a piteous effort to control her voice. "She used to be the friend of—of—your *fiancée*, Lady Maud Belville, long ago, before you had your accident."

He nodded gravely.

"I remember her," he said.

"I don't suppose you ever noticed her much," the girl continued shakily. "She was uninteresting, and always in the background."

"I should know her anywhere," said Durant with confidence.

"No, no," she protested. "I'm sure you wouldn't. You—you never gave her a second thought, though she—was foolish enough—idiotic enough—to—to care whether you did or not."

"Was she?" he said softly. "Was she? And was that why she came to live among the sand-dunes and cut off her hair and wore print dresses—and—and made life taste sweet to me again?"

"Ah! You know now!" she said, with a sound that was like laughter through tears.

He held out his arms to her.

"My darling," he said. "I knew on the first day I saw you here."

She knelt down beside him with a quick, impulsive movement.

"You—knew!" she gasped incredulously.

He smiled at her with great tenderness.

"I knew," he said, "and I wondered—how I wondered—what you had come for!"

"I only came to be a friend," she broke in hastily, "to—to try to help you through your bad time."

"I guessed it must be that," he said softly over her bowed head, "when you said 'No' to me yesterday."

"But you didn't tell me you cared," protested Molly.

"No," he said. "I was so horribly afraid that you might take me out of pity, Molly."

"And I—I wasn't going to be second fiddle!" said Molly waywardly.

She resisted him a little as he turned her face upwards, but he had his way. There was a quiver of laughter in his voice when he spoke again.

"You could never be that," he said. "You were made to lead the orchestra. Still, tell me why you did it, darling! Make me understand!"

And Molly yielded at length with her arms about his neck.

"I loved you!" she said passionately. "I loved you!"

THE WOMAN OF HIS DREAM

PROLOGUE

It was growing very dark. The decks gleamed wet in the light of the swinging lamps. The wind howled across the sea like a monster in torment. It would be a fearful night.

The man who stood clutching at the slanting deck rail was drenched from head to foot, but, despite this fact, he had no thought of going below. Reginald Carey had been for many voyages on many seas, but the fascination of a storm in the bay attracted him irresistibly still. He had no sympathy with the uneasy crowd in the saloons. He even exulted in the wild tumult of wind and sea and blinding rain. He was as one spellbound in the grip of the tempest.

Curt and dry of speech, abrupt at times almost to rudeness, he was a man of whom most people stood in awe, and with whom very few were on terms of intimacy. Yet in the world of men he had made his mark.

By camp-fires and on the march, in prison and in hospital, Carey the journalist had become a byword for coolness and endurance. It was Carey, caustic of humour, uncompromising of attitude, who sauntered through a hail of bullets to fill a wounded man's water-tin; Carey who pushed his way among stampeding mules to rescue sorely needed medical stores; Carey who had limped beside footsore, jaded men, and whistled them out of their depression.

There were two fingers missing from Carey's left hand, and the limp had become permanent when he sailed home from South Africa at the end of the war, but he was the personal friend of half the army though there was not a single man who could boast that he knew him thoroughly well. For none knew exactly what this man, who scoffed so freely at disaster, carried in his heart.

As he leaned on the rail of the tossing vessel, gazing steadfastly into the howling darkness, his face was as serene as if he sailed a summer sea. The great waves that dashed their foam over him as he stood were powerless to raise fear in his soul! He stood as one apart—a lonely watcher whom no danger could appal.

It was growing late, but he took no count of time. More than once he had been hoarsely advised to go below, but he would not go. He believed himself to be the only passenger on deck, and he clung to his solitude. The bare thought of the stuffy saloon was abhorrent to him. He marvelled that no one else had developed the same distaste.

And with the thought he turned, breathless from the buffeting spray of a mighty wave, to find a woman standing near him on the swirling deck.

She stood poised lightly as a bird prepared for flight, her head bare, her face upturned to the storm. Her hands were fast gripped upon the rail, and the gleam of a gold ring caught Carey's eye. He saw that she was unconscious of his presence. The shifting, uncertain light had not revealed him. For a space he stood watching her, unperceived, wondering at the courage that upheld her. Her hair had blown loose in the wind, and lay in a black mass upon her neck. He could not see her features, but her bearing was superb.

And then at length, as if his quiet scrutiny had somehow touched in her a responsive chord, she turned her head and saw him. Their eyes met, and a curious thrill ran tingling through the man's veins. He had never seen this woman before, but as she looked at him, with wonderful dark eyes that seemed to hold a passionate exultation in their depths, he suddenly felt as if he had known her all his life. They were comrades. It was no hysterical panic that had driven her up from below. Like himself, she had been drawn by the magic of the storm.

Impulsively, almost involuntarily, he moved a pace towards her and stretched out a hand along the dripping rail.

She gave him her own instantly and confidently, responding to his action with absolute simplicity. It was a gesture of sympathy, of fellowship. She bore herself as a queen, but she did not condescend to him.

No words passed between them. Both realised the impossibility of speech in that shrieking tempest. Moreover, there was no need for speech. Earth's petty conventions had fallen away from them. They were as children standing hand in hand on the edge of the unknown, hearing the same thunderous music, bound by the same magic spell.

Carey wondered later how long a time elapsed whilst they stood thus, intently watching. It might have been for merely a few minutes, or it might have been for the greater part of an hour. He never knew.

The spell broke at length suddenly and terribly, with a grinding crash that flung them both sideways upon the slippery deck. He went down, still clinging instinctively to the rail, and the next instant, by its aid, he was on his feet again, dragging his companion up with him.

There followed a pause—a shuddering, expectant pause—while wind and sea raged all around them like beasts of prey. And through it there came the sound of the engine throbbing impotently spasmodically, like the heart of a dying man. Quite suddenly it ceased, and there was a frightful uproar of escaping steam. The deck on which they stood began to tilt slowly upwards.

Carey knew what had happened. They had struck a rock in that awful darkness, and they were going down with frightful rapidity into the seething, storm-tossed water.

He had never been shipwrecked before, but, as by instinct, he realised the madness of remaining where he was. A coil of rope lay almost at his feet, and he stooped and seized it. There had come a brief lull in the storm, but he knew that there was not a moment to spare. Still supporting his companion, he began to bind the rope around them both.

She looked up at him quickly, and he saw her lips move in protest. She even set her hands against his breast, as if to resist him. But he overcame her almost savagely. It was no moment for argument.

The slope of the deck was becoming every instant more acute. The wind was racing back across the sea. Above them—very far above them, it seemed—there was a confusion of figures, but the tumult of wind and waves drowned all other sound. Carey's feet began to slip on that awful slant. They were sinking rapidly, rapidly.

He knotted the rope and gathered himself together. An instant he hung on the rail, breathing deeply. Then with a jerk he relaxed his grip and leaped blindly into the howling darkness, hurling himself and the woman with him far into the raging sea.

It was suffocatingly hot. Carey raised his arms with a desperate movement. He felt as if he were swimming in hot vapour. And he had been swimming for a long time, too. He was deadly tired. A light flashed in his eyes, and very far above him—like an object viewed through the small end of a telescope—he saw a face. Vaguely he heard a voice speaking, but what it said was beyond his comprehension. It seemed to utter unintelligible things. For a while he laboured to understand, then the effort became too much for him. The light faded from his brain.

Later—much later, it seemed—he awoke to full consciousness, to find himself in a Breton fisherman's cottage, watched over by a kindly little French doctor who tended him as though he had been his brother.

"*Monsieur* is better, but much better," he was cheerily assured. "And for *madame* his wife he need have no inquietude. She is safe and well, and only concerns herself for *monsieur*."

This was reassuring, and Carey accepted it without comment or inquiry. He knew that there was a misunderstanding somewhere, but he was still too exhausted to trouble himself about so slight a matter. He thanked his kindly informant, and again he slept.

Two days later his interest in life revived. He began to ask questions, and received from the doctor a full account of what had occurred.

He had been washed ashore, he was told—he and *madame* his wife—lashed fast together. The ship had been wrecked within half a mile of the land. But the seas had been terrific. There had not been many survivors.

Carey digested the news in silence. He had had no friends on board, having embarked only at Gibraltar.

At length he looked up with a faint smile at his faithful attendant. "And where is—*madame*?" he asked.

The little doctor hesitated, and spread out his hands deprecatingly.

"Oh, *monsieur*, I regret—I much regret—to have to inform you that she is already departed for Paris. Her solicitude for you was great, was pathetic. The first words she speak were: 'My husband, do not let him know!' as though she feared that you would be distressed for her. And then she recover quick, quick, and say that she must go—that *monsieur* when he know, will understand. And so she depart early in the morning of yesterday while *monsieur* is still asleep."

He was watching Carey with obvious anxiety as he ended, but the Englishman's face expressed nothing but a somewhat elaborate indifference.

"I see," he said, and relapsed into silence.

He made no further reference to the matter, and the doctor discreetly abstained from asking questions. He presently showed him an English paper which contained the information that Mr. and Mrs. Carey were among the rescued.

"That," he remarked, "will alleviate the anxiety of your friends."

To which Carey responded, with a curt laugh: "No one knew that we were on board."

He left for Paris on the following day, allowing the doctor to infer that he was on his way to join his wife.

I

It was growing dark in the empty class-room, but there was nothing left to do, and the French mistress, sitting alone at her high desk, made no move to turn on the light. All the lesson books were packed away out of sight. There was not so much as a stray pencil trespassing upon that desert of orderliness. Only the waste-paper basket, standing behind *Mademoiselle* Trèves's chair, gave evidence of the tempest of energy that had preceded this empty calm in the midst of which she sat alone. It was crammed to overflowing with torn exercise books, and all manner of schoolgirls' rubbish, and now and then it creaked eerily in the desolate silence as though at the touch of an invisible hand.

It was very cold in the great room, for the fire had gone out long ago. There was no one left to enjoy it except *mademoiselle*, who apparently did not count. For most of the pupils had departed in the morning, and those who were left were collected in the great hall speeding one after another upon their homeward way. All day the wheels of cabs had crunched the gravel below the class-room window, but they were not so audible now, for the ground was thickly covered with snow, which had been drearily falling throughout the afternoon.

It lay piled upon the window-sill, casting a ghostly light into the darkening room, vaguely outlining the slender figure that sat so still before the high desk.

Another cab-load of laughing girls was just passing out at the gate. There could not be many left. The darkness increased, and *mademoiselle* drew a quick breath and shivered. She wished the departures were all over.

There came a light step in the passage, and a daring whistle, which broke off short as a hand impetuously opened the class-room door.

"Why, *mademoiselle!*" cried a fresh young voice. "Why, *chérie!*" Warm arms encircled the lonely figure, and eager lips pressed the cold face. "Oh, *chérie*, don't grizzle!" besought the newcomer. "Why, I've never known you do such a thing before. Have you been here all this time? I've been looking for you all over the place. I couldn't leave without one more good-bye. And see here, *chérie*, you must—you must—come to my birthday-party on New Year's Eve. If you won't come and stay with me, which I do think you might, you must come down for that one night. It's no distance, you know. And it's only a children's show. There won't be any grown-ups except my cousin Reggie, who is the sweetest man in the world, and Mummy's Admiral who comes next. Say you will, *chérie*, for I shall be sixteen—just think of it!—and I do want you to be there. You will, won't you? Come, promise!"

It was hard to refuse this petitioner, so warmly fascinating was she. *Mademoiselle*, who, it was well known, never accepted any invitations, hesitated for the first time—and was lost.

"If I came just for that one evening then, Gwen, you would not press me to stay longer?"

"Bless you, no!" declared Gwen. "I'll drive you to the station myself in Mummy's car to catch the first train next morning, if you'll come. And I'll make Reggie come too. You'll just love Reggie, *chérie*. He's my exact ideal of what a man ought to be—the best friend I have, next to you. Well, it's a bargain then, isn't it? You'll come and help dance with the kids—you promise? That's my own sweet *chérie*! And now you mustn't grizzle here in the dark any longer. I believe my cab is at the door. Come down and see me off, won't you?"

Yet again she was irresistible. They went out together, hand in hand, happy child and lonely woman, and the door of the deserted class-room banged with a desolate echoing behind them.

II

It was ten days later, on a foggy evening, in the end of the year, that Reginald Carey alighted at a small wayside station, and grimly prepared himself for a five-mile trudge through dark and muddy lanes to his destination.

The only conveyance in the station yard was a private motor car, and his first glance at this convinced him that it was not there to await him. He paused under the lamp outside to turn up his collar, and, as he did so, a man of gigantic breadth and stature, wearing goggles, came out of the station behind him and strode past. He glanced at Carey casually as he went by, looked again, then suddenly stopped and peered at him.

"Great Scotland!" he exclaimed abruptly. "I know you—or ought to. You're the little newspaper chap who saved my life at Magersfontein. Thought there was something familiar about you the moment I saw you. You remember me, eh?"

He turned back his goggles impetuously, and showed Carey his face.

Yes; Carey remembered him very well indeed, though he was not sure that the acquaintance was one he desired to improve. He took the proffered hand with a certain reserve.

"Yes; I remember you. I don't think I ever heard your name, but that's a detail. You came out of it all right, then?"

"Oh, yes; more or less. Nothing ever hurts me." The big man's laugh had in it a touch of bitterness. "Where are you bound for? Come along with me in the car; I'll take you where you want to go." He seized Carey by the shoulder, impelling him with boisterous cordiality towards the vehicle. "Jump in, my friend. My name is Coningsby—Major Coningsby, of Crooklands Manor—mad Coningsby I'm called about here, because I happen to ride straighter to hounds than most of 'em. A bit of a compliment, eh? But they're a shocking set of muffs in these parts. You don't live here?"

"No; I am down on a visit to my cousin, Lady Emberdale. She lives at Crooklands Mead. I've come down a day sooner than I was expected, and the train was two hours late. I'm Reginald Carey." He stopped before the step of the car. "It's very good of you, but I won't take you out of your way on such a beastly night. I can quite well walk."

"Nonsense, man! It's no distance, and it isn't out of the way. I've only just motored down to get an evening paper. You're just in time to dine with me. I'm all alone, and confoundedly glad to see you. I know Lady Emberdale well. Come, jump in!"

Thus urged, Carey yielded, not over-willingly, and took his seat in the car.

Directly they started, he knew the reason for his companion's pseudonym, for they whizzed out of the yard at a speed which must have disquieted the stoutest nerves.

It was the maddest ride he had ever experienced, and he wondered by what instinct Major Coningsby kept a straight course through the darkness. Their own lamps provided the only light there was, and when they presently turned sharply at right angles he gathered himself together instinctively in preparation for a smash.

But nothing happened. They tore on a little farther in darkness, travelling along a private road; and then the lights of a house pierced the gloom.

Coningsby brought his car to a standstill.

"Tumble out! The front door is straight ahead. My man will let you in and look after you. Excuse me a moment while I take the car round!"

He was gone with the words, leaving Carey to ascend a flight of steps to the hall door. It opened at once to admit him, and he found himself in a great hall dimly illumined by firelight. A servant helped him to divest himself of his overcoat, and silently led the way.

The room he entered was furnished as a library. He glanced round it as he stood on the hearth-rug, awaiting his host, and was chiefly struck by the general atmosphere of dreariness that pervaded it. Its sombre oak furniture seemed to absorb instead of reflecting the light. There was a large oil-painting above the fireplace, and after a few seconds he turned his head and saw it. It was the portrait of a woman.

Young, beautiful, queenly, the painted face looked down into his own, and the man's heart gave a sudden, curious throb that was half rapture and half pain. In a moment the room he had just entered, with all the circumstances that had taken him there, was blotted from his brain. He was standing once more on the rocking deck of a steamer, in a tempest of wind and rain and furious sea, facing the storm, exultant, with a woman's hand fast gripped in his.

"Are you looking at that picture?" said a voice. "It's my wife—dead now—lost—five years ago—at sea!"

Carey wheeled sharply at the jerky utterance. Coningsby was standing by his side. He was staring upwards at the portrait, a strange gleam darting in his eyes—a gleam not wholly sane.

"It doesn't do her justice," he went on in the same abrupt, headlong fashion. "But it's better than nothing. She was the only woman who ever satisfied me. Her loss damaged me badly. I've never been the same since. There've been others, of course, but she was always first—an easy first. I shall want her—I shall go on wanting her—till I'm in my grave." His voice was suddenly husky, as the voice of a man in pain. "It's like a fiery thirst," he said. "I try to quench it—Heaven knows I try! But it comes back—it comes back."

He swung round on his heel and went to the table. There followed the clink of glasses, but Carey did not turn. His eyes had left the picture, and were fixed, stern and unwinking, upon the fire that glowed at his feet.

Again he seemed to feel the clasp of a woman's hand, free and confiding, within his own. Again his heart stirred responsively in the quick warmth of a woman's perfect sympathy.

And he knew that into his keeping had been given the secret of that woman's existence. The five years' mystery was solved at last. He understood, and, understanding, he kept silent faith with her.

III

It was two hours later that Carey presented himself at his cousin's house. He entered unobtrusively, as his manner was, knowing himself to be a welcome guest.

The first person to greet him was Gwen, who, accompanied by a college youth of twenty, was roasting chestnuts in front of the hall fire. She sprang up at the sound of his voice, and, flushed and eager, rushed to meet him.

"Why, Reggie, my dear old boy, who would have thought of seeing you to-night? Come right in! Aren't you very cold? How did you get here? Have you dined? This is Charlie Rivers, the Admiral's son. Charlie, you have heard me speak of my cousin, Mr. Carey."

Charlie had, several times over, and said so, with a grin, as he made room for Carey in front of the blaze, taking care to keep himself next to Gwen.

Carey considerately fell in with the manoeuvre and, greetings over, they huddled sociably together over the fire, and fell to discussing the birthday party which was to be held on the morrow.

Gwen was a curious blend of excitement and common sense. She had been busily preparing all day for the coming festivity.

"There's one visitor I want you both to be very good to," she said, "and see that she takes plenty of refreshments, whether she wants them or not."

Young Rivers grimaced at Carey.

"You can have my share of this unattractive female," he said generously. "It's Gwen's schoolmistress, and I'll bet she's as heavy as a sack of coals."

"I can't dance. I'm lame," said Carey. "But I don't mind sitting out in the refreshment room to please Gwen. How old is she, Gwen? About twice my age?"

Gwen did not stop to calculate.

"Older than that, I should think. Her hair is quite grey, and she's very sad and quiet. I am sure she has had a lot of trouble. Very likely she won't want to dance either, so there will be a pair of you. Her name is *Mademoiselle* Trèves, but she is only half French, and speaks English better than I do. She never goes anywhere, so I do want her to have a good time. You will be kind to her, won't you? I'll introduce you to her as early as possible. We are all going to wear masks till midnight."

"Stupid things—masks," said Charlie very decidedly. "Don't like 'em."

Gwen turned upon him.

"It's much the fairest way. If we didn't wear them, the pretty girls would get all the best dances."

"Oh, well, you wouldn't be left out, anyway," he assured her.

At which compliment Gwen sniffed contemptuously, and pointedly requested Carey to give her a few minutes in strict privacy before they parted for the night.

He saw that she meant it; and when Charlie had reluctantly taken himself off he went with his young cousin to her own little sitting-room upstairs before seeking Lady Emberdale in the drawing-room.

Gwen could scarcely wait till the door was closed before she began to lay her troubles before him.

"It's Mummy!" she told him very seriously. "You can't think how sick and disgusted I am. Sit down, Reggie, and I'll tell you all about it! Being Mummy's trustee, perhaps you will have some influence over her. I have none. She thinks I'm prejudiced. And I'm not, Reggie. There's nothing to make me so except that Charlie is a nice boy, and the Admiral a perfect darling."

She paused for breath, and Carey patiently waited for further enlightenment. It came.

"Of course," she said, seating herself on the arm of his chair, "I've always known that Mummy would marry again some day or other. She's so young and pretty; and I haven't minded the idea a bit. Poor, dear Dad was always such a very, very old man! But I do want her to marry someone nice now the time has come. All through the summer holidays I felt sure it was going to be the Admiral, and I was so pleased about it. Charlie and I used to make bets about its coming off before Christmas. He was ever so pleased, too, and we'd settled to join together for the wedding present so as to get something decent. It was all going to be so jolly. And now," with a great sigh, "everything's spoilt. There's—there's someone else."

"Good heavens!" said Carey. "Who?"

He had been suppressing a laugh during the greater part of Gwen's confidence, but this last announcement startled him into sobriety. A very faint misgiving stirred in his soul. What if—but no; it was preposterous. He thrust it from him.

Gwen slid a loving arm about his neck.

"I like telling you things, Reggie. You always understand, and they never worry me so much afterwards. For I am—horribly worried. Mummy met him in the hunting field. He has come to live quite near us—oh, such a brute he is, loud and coarse and bullying! He rode a horse to death only a few weeks ago. They say he's mad, and I'm nearly sure he drinks as well. And he and Mummy have chummed up. They are as thick as thieves, and he's always coming to the house, dropping in at odd hours. The poor, dear Admiral hasn't a chance. He's much too gentlemanly to elbow his way in like—like this horrid Major Coningsby. Oh, Reggie, do you think you can do anything to stop it? I don't want her to marry him, neither does Charlie. My, Reggie, what's the matter? You don't know him, do you? You don't know anything bad about him?"

Carey was on his feet, pacing slowly to and fro. One hand—the maimed left hand—was thrust away out of sight, as his habit was in a woman's presence. The other was clenched hard at his side.

He did not at once answer Gwen's agitated questioning. She sat and watched him in some anxiety, wondering at the stern perplexity with which he reviewed the problem.

Suddenly he stopped in front of her.

"Yes; I know the man," he said. "I knew him years ago in South Africa, and I met him again to-night. I must think this matter over, and consider it carefully. You are quite sure of what you say—quite sure he is attracted by your mother?"

Gwen nodded.

"Oh, there's no doubt of that. He treats her already as if she were his property. You won't tell her I told you, Reggie? It will simply precipitate matters if you do."

"No; I shan't tell her. I never argue with women." Carey spoke almost savagely. He was staring at something that Gwen could not see.

"Do you think you will be able to stop it?" she asked him, with a slightly nervous hesitation.

His eyes came back to her. He seemed to consider her for a moment. Then, seeing that she was really troubled, he spoke with sudden kindliness:

"I think so, yes. But never mind how! Leave it to me and put it out of your head as much as possible! I quite agree with you that it is an arrangement that wouldn't do at all. Why on earth couldn't your friend the Admiral speak before?"

"I wish he had," said Gwen, from her heart. "And I believe he does, too, now. But men are so idiotic, Reggie. They always miss their opportunities."

"Think so?" said Carey. "Some men never have any, it seems to me."

And he left her wondering at the bitterness of his speech.

IV

The winter sunlight was streaming into Major Coningsby's gloomy library when Carey again stood within it. The Major was out riding, he had been told, but he was expected back ere long; and he had decided to wait for him.

And so he stood waiting before the portrait; and closely, critically, he studied it by the morning light.

It was the face which for five years now he had carried graven on his heart. She was the one woman to him—the woman of his dream. Throughout his wanderings he had cherished the memory of her—a secret and priceless possession to which he clung day and night, waking and sleeping. He had made no effort to find her during those years, but silently, almost in spite of himself, he had kept her in his heart, had called her to him in his dreams, yearning to her across the ever-widening gulf, hungering dumbly for the voice he had never heard.

He knew that he was no favourite with women. All his life his reserve had been a barrier that none had ever sought to pass till this woman—the woman who should have been his fate—had been drifted to him through life's stress and tumult and had laid her hand with perfect confidence in his. And now it was laid upon him to betray that confidence. He no longer had the right to keep her secret. He had protected her once, and it had been as a hidden, sacred bond invisibly linking them together. But it could do so no longer. The time had come to wrest that precious link apart.

Sharply he turned from the picture. The dark eyes tortured him. They seemed to be pleading with him, entreating him. There came a sudden clatter without, the tramp of heavy feet, the jingle of spurs. The door was flung noisily back, and Major Coningsby strode in.

"Hullo! Very good of you to look me up so soon. Sorry I wasn't in to receive you. Haven't you had a drink yet?"

He tossed his riding-whip down upon the table, and busied himself with the glasses.

Carey drew near; his face was stern.

"I have something to say to you," he said, "before we drink, if you have no objection."

His voice was quiet and very even, but Coningsby looked up with a quick frown.

"Confound you, Carey! What are you pulling a long face about this time of the morning? Better have a drink; it'll make you feel more sociable."

He spoke with sharp irritation. The hand that held the spirit-decanter was not over-steady. Carey watched him—coldly critical.

"That portrait over the mantelpiece," he said; "your wife, I think you told me?"

Coningsby swore a deep oath.

"I may have told you so. I don't often mention the subject. She is dead."

"I beg your pardon; I am forced to mention it." Carey's tone was deliberate, emotionless, hard. "That lady—the original of that portrait—is still alive, to the best of my belief. At least, she was not lost at sea on the occasion of the wreck of the *Denver Castle* five years ago."

"What?" said Coningsby. He turned suddenly white—white to the lips, and set down the decanter he was still holding as if he had been struck powerless. "What?" he said again, with starting eyes upon Carey's face.

"I think you understood me," Carey returned coldly. "I have told you because, upon consideration, it seemed to me you ought to know."

The thing was done and past recall, but deep in his heart there lurked a savage resentment against this man who had forced him to break his silence. He felt no sympathy with him; he only knew disgust.

Coningsby moved suddenly with a frantic oath, and gripped him by the shoulder. The blood was coming back to his face in livid patches; his eyes were terrible.

"Go on!" he said thickly. "Out with it! Tell me all you know!"

He towered over Carey. There was violence in his grip, but Carey did not seem to notice. He faced the giant with absolute composure.

"I can tell you no more," he said. "I knew she was saved, because I was saved with her. But she left Brittany while I was still too ill to move."

"You must know more than that!" shouted Coningsby, losing all control of himself, and shaking his informant furiously by the shoulder. "If she was saved, how did she come to be reported missing?"

For a single instant Carey hesitated; then, with steady eyes upon the bloated face above him, he made quiet reply:

"Her name was among the missing by her own contrivance. Doubtless she had her reasons."

Coningsby's face suddenly changed: his eyes shone red.

"You helped her!" he snarled, and lifted a clenched fist.

Carey's maimed hand came quietly into view, and closed upon the man's wrist.

"It is not my custom," he coldly said, "to refuse help to a woman."

"Confound you!" stormed Coningsby. "Where is she now? Where? Where?"

There fell a sudden pause. Carey's eyes were like steel; his grasp never slackened.

"If I knew," he said deliberately, at length, "I should not tell you! You are not fit for the society of any good woman."

The words fell keen as a whip-lash, and as pitiless. Coningsby glared into his face like a goaded bull; his look was murderous. And then by some chance his eyes fell upon the hand that gripped his wrist. He looked at it closely, attentively, for a few seconds, and finally set Carey free.

"You may thank that," he said more quietly, "for getting you out·of the hottest corner you were ever in. I didn't notice it yesterday, though I remember now that you were wounded. So you parted with half your hand to drag me out of that hell, did you? It was a rank, bad investment on your part."

He flung away abruptly, and helped himself to some brandy. A considerable pause ensued before he spoke again.

"Egad!" he said then, with a harsh laugh, "it's a deuced ingenious lie, this of yours. I suppose you and that imp of mischief, Gwen, hatched it up between you? I saw she had got her thinking-cap on yesterday. I am not considered good enough for her lady mother. But, mark you, I'm going to have her for all that! It isn't good for man to live alone, and I have taken a fancy to Evelyn Emberdale."

"You don't believe me?" Carey asked.

Somehow, though he had been prepared for bluster and even violence, he had not expected incredulity.

Coningsby filled and emptied his glass a second time before he answered.

"No," he said then, with sudden savagery: "I don't believe you! You had better get out of my house at once, or—I warn you—I may break every bone in your blackguardly body yet!" He turned on Carey, leaping madness in his eyes.

But Carey stood like a rock. "You know the truth," he said quietly.

Coningsby broke into another wild laugh, and pointed up at the picture above his head.

"I shall know it," he declared, "when the sea gives up its dead. Till that day I am free to console myself in my own way, and no one shall stop me."

"You are not free," Carey said. Very steadily he faced the man, very distinctly he spoke. "And, however you console yourself, it will not be with my cousin Lady Emberdale."

Coningsby turned back to the table to fill his glass again. He spilt the spirit over the cloth as he did it.

"Man alive," he gibed, "do you think she will believe you if I don't?"

It was the weak point of his position, and Carey realised it. It was more than probable that Lady Emberdale would take Coningsby's view of the matter. If the man really attracted her it was almost a foregone conclusion. He knew Gwen's mother well—her inconsequent whims, her obstinacy.

Yet, even in face of this check, he stood his ground.

"I may find some means of proving what I have told you," he said, with unswerving resolution.

Coningsby drained his glass for the third time, and, with a menacing sweep of the hand, seized his riding-whip.

"I don't advise you to come here with your proofs," he snarled. "The only proof I would look at is the woman herself. Now, sir, I have warned you fairly. Are you going?"

His attitude was openly threatening, but Carey's eyes were piercingly upon him, and, in spite of himself, he paused. So for the passage of seconds they stood; then slowly Carey turned away.

"I am going," he said, "to find your wife."

He did not glance again at the picture as he passed from the room. He could not bring himself to meet the dark eyes that followed him.

V

Yes; he would find her. But how? There was only one course open to him, and he shrank from that with disgust unutterable. It was useless to think of advertising. He was convinced that she would never answer an advertisement.

The only way to find her was to employ a detective to track her down. He clenched his hands in impotent revolt. Not only had it been laid upon him to betray her confidence, but he must follow this up by dragging her from her hiding-place, and returning her to the bitter bondage from which he had once helped her to escape.

That she still lived he was inwardly convinced. He would have given all he had to have known her dead.

But, for that day, at least, there was no more to be done, and Gwen must not have her birthday spoilt by the knowledge of his failure. He decided to keep out of her way till the evening.

When he entered the ball-room at the appointed time she pounced upon him eagerly, but her young guests were nearly all assembled, and it was no moment for private conversation.

"Oh, Reggie! There you are! How dreadful you look in a mask! This is my cousin, *mademoiselle*," turning to a lady in black who accompanied her. "I've been wanting to introduce him to you. Don't forget that the masks are not to come off till midnight. We're going to boom the big gong when the clock strikes twelve."

She flitted away in her shimmering fairy's dress, closely attended by Charlie Rivers, to persuade his father to give her a dance. The room was crowded with masked guests, Lady Emberdale, handsome and brilliant, and Admiral Rivers, her bluff but faithful admirer, being the only exceptions to the rule of the evening.

Carey found himself standing apart with Gwen's particular *protégée*, and he realised at once that he could expect no help from Charlie in this quarter. For, though slim and graceful, *Mademoiselle* Trèves's general appearance was undeniably sombre and elderly. The hair that she wore coiled regally upon her head was silver-grey, and there was a certain weariness about the mouth that, though it did not rob it of its sweetness, deprived it of all suggestion of youth.

"I don't know if I am justified in asking for a dance," Carey said. "My own dancing days are over."

She smiled at him, and instantly the weariness vanished. There was magic in her smile.

"I am no dancer either, except with the little ones. If you care to sit out with me, I shall be very pleased."

Her voice was low and musical. It caught his fancy so that he was aware of a sudden curiosity to see the face that the black mask concealed.

"Give me the twelve-o'clock dance," he said, "if you can spare it!"

She consulted the programme that hung from her wrist. He bent over it as she held it, and scrawled his initials against the dance in question.

"Perhaps I shall not stay for that one," she said, with slight hesitation.

He glanced up at her.

"I thought you were here for the night."

She bent her head.

"But I may slip away before twelve for all that."

Carey smiled.

"I don't think you will, not anyhow if I have a voice in the matter. I am Gwen's lieutenant, you know, specially enrolled to prevent any deserting. There is a heavy penalty for desertion."

"What is it?"

Carey bent again over the programme.

"Deserters will be brought back ignominiously and made to dance with everyone in the room in turn."

He glanced up again at the sound of her low laugh. There was something elusively suggestive about her personality.

"May I have another?" he said. "I hope you don't mind holding the card for me."

"You have hurt your hand?" she asked.

It was thrust away, as usual, in his pocket.

"Some years ago," he told her. "I don't use it more than I can help."

"How disagreeable for you!" she murmured.

He shrugged his shoulders.

"I am used to it. It is worse for others than it is for me. May I have No. 9? It includes the supper interval. Thanks! And any more you can spare. I'm only lounging about and seeing that the kids enjoy themselves. I shall be delighted to sit out with you when you are tired of dancing."

"You are very kind," she said.

He made her an abrupt bow.

"Then I hope you won't snub my efforts by deserting?"

She laughed again.

"No, lieutenant, I will not desert. I am going to help you."

She spoke with a winning and impulsive graciousness that stirred again within him that curious sense of groping in the dark among objects familiar but unrecognisable. Surely he had met this stranger somewhere before—in a crowded thoroughfare, in a train, possibly in a theatre, or even in a church!

She looked at him questioningly as he lingered, and with another bow he turned and left her. Doubtless, when he saw her face he would remember, or realise that he had been mistaken.

VI

Mademoiselle Trèves kept her word, and wherever the fun was at its height she was invariably the centre of it. The shy children crowded about her. She seemed to possess a special charm for them.

Gwen was delighted, and was obviously enjoying herself to the utmost. In the absence of her *bête noire* whom she had courageously omitted to invite, she rejoiced to see that her mother was being unusually gracious to her beloved Admiral, who was as merry as a schoolboy in consequence.

She was shrewdly aware, however, that the welcome change was but temporary. Incomprehensible though it was to Gwen, she knew that Major Coningsby's power over her gay and frivolous young mother was absolute. He ruled her with a rod of iron, and Lady Emberdale actually enjoyed his tyranny. The rough court he paid her served to turn her head completely, and she never attempted to resist his influence.

It was all very distasteful to Gwen, who hated the man with the whole force of her nature. She was thankful to feel that Carey was enlisted on her side. She looked upon him as a tower of strength, and, forebodings notwithstanding, she was able to throw herself heart and soul into the evening's festivities, and to beam delightedly upon her cousin as she walked behind him with Charlie to the supper room.

Carey was escorting the French governess. He found a comfortable corner for her in the thronged room at a table laid for two.

"I am bearing in mind your promise to stand by till twelve o'clock," he said. "It's the only thing that keeps me going, for I have a powerful longing to remove my mask in defiance of orders. It feels like a porous plaster. I shall only hold out till midnight with your gallant assistance."

He stooped with the words to pick up her fan which she had dropped. He was obliged to use his left hand, and he knew that she gave a quick start at sight of it. But she spoke instantly and he admired her ready self-control.

"It was rather a rash promise, I am afraid."

Her voice sounded half shy and wholly sweet, and again he was caught by that elusive quality about her that had puzzled him before. It was stronger than ever, so strong that he felt for a moment on the verge of discovery. But yet again it baffled him, making him all the more determined to pursue it to its source.

"You're not going to cry off?" he said, with a smile.

He saw her flush behind her mask.

"Only with your permission," she answered.

He heard the note of pleading in her voice, but he would not notice it.

"Oh, I can't let you off!" he said lightly. "Gwen would never forgive me. Besides, I don't want to."

She said no more, probably realising that he meant to have his way. They talked upon indifferent topics in the midst of the general buzz of merriment till, supper over, they separated.

"I shall come for that midnight dance," were Carey's last words, as he bowed and left her.

And during the hour that intervened he kept a sharp eye upon her, lest her evident reluctance to remain should prove too much for her integrity. He was half amused at his own tenacity in the matter. Not for years had a chance acquaintance so excited his curiosity.

A few minutes before midnight he was standing before her. The last dance of the evening had just begun. Gwen had decreed that everyone should stop upon the stroke of twelve, while every mask was removed, after which the dance was to be continued to the finish.

"Shall we go upstairs?" suggested Carey.

To his surprise he felt that the hand she laid upon his arm was trembling.

"By all means," she answered. "Let us get away from the crowd!"

It was an unexpected request, but he showed no surprise. He piloted her to a secluded spot in the upper regions, and they sat down on a lounge at the end of a corridor.

A queer sense of uneasiness had begun to oppress Carey, as strong as it was inexplicable. He made a resolute effort to ignore it. The music downstairs was sinking away. He took out his watch.

"The dramatic moment approaches," he remarked, after a pause. "Are you ready?"

She did not speak.

"I'll tell you why I want to see you unmask," he said, speaking very quietly. "It is because there is something about you that reminds me of someone I know, but the resemblance is so subtle that it has eluded me all the evening."

"You do not know me," she said. And he felt that she spoke with an effort.

"I am not so sure," he answered. "But in any case—"

He paused. The music had ceased altogether, and an expectant silence prevailed. He looked at her intently as he waited, till aware that she shrank from his scrutiny.

A long deep note boomed through the house, echoing weirdly through the intense silence. Carey put up his hand without speaking, and stripped off his mask. He crumpled it into a ball as the second note struck, and looked at her. She had not moved. He waited silently.

At the sixth note she made a sudden, almost passionate gesture and rose. Carey remained motionless, watching her. Swiftly she turned, and began to walk away from him. He leaned forward. His eyes were fixed upon her.

Three more strokes! She stopped abruptly, turning back as if he had spoken. Moving slowly, and still masked, she came back to him. He met her under a lamp. His face was very pale, but his eyes were steady and piercingly keen. He took her hand, bending over it till his lips touched her glove.

"I know you now," he said, his voice very low.

Three more strokes, and silence.

A ripple of laughter suddenly ran through the house, a gay voice called for three cheers, and as though a spell had been lifted the merriment burst out afresh in tune to the lilting dance-music.

Carey straightened himself slowly, still holding the slender hand in his. Her mask had gone at last, and he stood face to face with the woman of his dream—the woman whose hard-won security he had only that morning pledged himself to shatter.

VII

"You know me," she said.

"Yes; I know you. And I know your secret, too."

The words sounded stern. He was putting strong restraint upon himself.

She faced him without flinching, her look as steady as his own. And yet again it was to Carey as though he stood in the presence of a queen. She did not say a word.

"Will you believe me," he said slowly, "when I tell you that I would give all I have not to know it?"

She raised her beautiful brows for a moment, but still she said nothing.

He let her hand go. "I was on the point of searching to the world's end for you," he said. "But since I have found you here of all places, I am bound to take advantage of it. Forgive me, if you can!"

He saw a gleam of apprehension in her eyes.

"What is it you want to say to me?" she asked.

He passed the question by.

"You know me, I suppose?"

She bent her head.

"I fancied it was you from the first. When I saw your hand at supper, I knew."

"And you tried to avoid me?"

"When you have something to conceal, it is wise to avoid anyone connected with it."

She answered him very quietly, but he knew instinctively that she was fighting him with her whole strength. It was almost more than he could bear.

"Believe me," he said, "I am not a man to wantonly betray a woman's secret. I have kept yours faithfully for years. But when within the last few days I came to know who you were, and that your husband, Major Coningsby, was contemplating making a second marriage, I was in honour bound to speak."

"You told him?" She raised her eyes for a single instant, and he read in them a reproach unutterable.

His heart smote him. What had she endured, this woman, before taking that final step to cut herself off from the man whose name she had borne? But he would not yield an inch. He was goaded by pitiless necessity.

"I told him," he answered. "But I had no means of proving what I said. And he refused to believe me."

"And now?" she almost whispered.

He heard the note of tragedy in the words, and he braced himself to meet her most desperate resistance.

"Before I go further," he said, "let me tell you this! Slight though you may consider our acquaintance to be, I have always felt—I have always known—that you are a good woman."

She made a quick gesture of protest.

"Would a good woman have left the man who saved her life lying ill in a strange land while she escaped with her miserable freedom?"

He answered her without hesitation, as he had long ago answered himself.

"No doubt the need was great."

She turned away from him and sat down, bowing her head upon her hand.

"It was," she said, her voice very low. "I was nearly mad with trouble. You had pity then—without knowing. Have you—no pity—now?"

The appeal went out into silence. Carey neither spoke nor moved. His face was like a stone mask—the face of a strong man in torture.

After a pause of seconds she spoke again, her face hidden from him.

"The first Mrs. Coningsby is dead," she said. "Let it be so! Nothing will ever bring her back. Geoffrey Coningsby is free to marry—whom he will."

The words were scarcely more than a whisper, but they reached and pierced him to the heart. He drew a step nearer to her, and spoke with sudden vehemence.

"I would help you, Heaven knows, if I could! But you will see—you must see presently—that I have no choice. There is only one thing to be done, and it has fallen to me to see it through, though it would be easier for me to die!"

He broke off. There was strangled passion in his voice. Abruptly he turned his back upon her, and began to pace up and down. Again there fell a long pause. The music and the tramp of dancing feet below rose up in his ears like a shout of mockery. He was fighting the hardest battle of his life, fighting single-handed and grievously wounded for a victory that would cripple him for the rest of his days.

Suddenly he stood still and looked at her, though she had not moved, unless her head with its silvery hair were bowed a little lower than before. For a single instant he hesitated, then strode impulsively to her, and knelt down by her side.

"God help us both!" he said hoarsely.

His hands were on her shoulders. He drew her to him, taking the bowed head upon his breast. And so, silently, he held her. When she looked up at last, he knew that the bitter triumph was his. Her face was deathly, but her eyes were steadfast. She drew herself very gently out of his hold.

"I do not think," she said, "that there is anyone else in the world who could have done for me what you have done tonight." She paused a moment looking straight into his eyes, then laid her hands in his without a quiver. "Years ago," she said, "you saved my life. Tonight—you have saved something infinitely more precious than that. And I—I am grateful to you. I will do—whatever you think right."

It was a free surrender, but it wrung his heart to accept it. Even in that moment of tragedy there was to him something of that sublime courage with which she had faced the tumult of a stormy sea with him five years before. And very poignantly it came home to him that he was there to destroy and not to deliver. Like a wave of evil, it rushed upon him, overwhelming him.

He could not trust himself to speak. The wild words that ran in his brain were such as he could not utter. And so he only bent his head once more over the hands that lay so trustingly in his, and with great reverence he kissed them.

VIII

It was on a cold, dark evening two days later that Major Coningsby returned from the first run of the year, and tramped, mud-splashed and stiff from hard riding, into his gloomy house. A gust of rain blew swirling after him, and he turned, swearing, and shut the great door with a bang. It had not been a good day for sport. The ground had been sodden, and the scent had washed away. He had followed the hounds for miles to no purpose and had galloped home at last in sheer disgust. To add to his grievances he had called upon Lady Emberdale on his way back, and had not found her in. "Gone to tea with her precious Admiral, I suppose!" he had growled, as he rode away, which, as it chanced, was the case. The suspicion had not improved his mood, and he was very much out of humour when he finally reached his own domain. Striding into the library, he turned on the threshold to curse his servant for not having lighted the lamp, and the man hastened forward nervously to repair the omission. This accomplished, he as hastily retired, glancing furtively over his shoulder as he made his escape.

Coningsby tramped to the hearth, and stood there, beating his leg irritably with his riding-whip. There was a heavy frown on his face. He did not once raise his eyes to the picture above him. He was still thinking of

Lady Emberdale and the Admiral. Finally, with a sudden idea of refreshing himself, he wheeled towards the table. The next instant, he stood and stared as if transfixed.

A woman dressed in black, and thickly veiled, was standing facing him under the lamp.

He gazed at her speechlessly for a second or two, then passed his hand across his eyes.

"Great heavens!" he said slowly, at last.

She made a quick movement of the hands that was like a gesture of shrinking.

"You don't know me?" she asked, in a voice so low as to be barely audible.

For a moment there flashed into his face the curious, listening look that is seen on the faces of the blind. Then violently he strode forward.

"I should know that voice in ten thousand!" he cried, his words sharp and quivering. "Take off your veil, woman! Show me your face!"

The hunger in his eyes was terrible to see. He looked like a dying man reaching out impotent hands for some priceless elixir of life.

"Your face!" he gasped again hoarsely, brokenly. "Show me your face!"

Mutely she obeyed him, removed hat and veil with fingers that never faltered, and turned her sad, calm face towards him. For seconds longer he stared at her, stared devouringly, fiercely, with the eyes of a madman. Then, suddenly, with a great cry, he stumbled forward, flinging himself upon his knees at the table, with his face hidden on his arms.

"Oh, I know you! I know you!" he sobbed. "You've tortured me like this before. You've made me think I had only to open my arms to you, and I should have you close against my heart. It's happened night after night, night after night! Naomi! Naomi! Naomi!"

His voice choked, and he became intensely still crouching there before her in an anguish too great for words.

For a long time she was motionless too, but at last, as he did not move, she came a step toward him, pity and repugnance struggling visibly for the mastery over her. Reluctantly she stooped and touched his shoulder.

"Geoffrey!" she said, "it is I, myself, this time."

He started at her touch but did not lift his head.

She waited, and presently he began to recover himself. At last he blundered heavily to his feet.

"It's true, is it?" he said, peering at her uncertainly. "You're here—in the flesh? You've been having just a ghastly sort of game with me all these years, have you? Hang it, I didn't deserve quite that! And so the little newspaper chap spoke the truth, after all."

He paused; then suddenly flung out his arms to her as he stood.

"Naomi!" he cried, "come to me, my girl! Don't be afraid. I swear I'll be good to you, and I'm a man that keeps his oath! Come to me, I say!"

But she held back from him, her face still white and calm.

"No, Geoffrey," she said very firmly, "I haven't come back to you for that. When I left you, I left you for good. And you know why. I never meant to see your face again. You had made my life with you impossible. I have only come to-day as—as a matter of principle, because I heard you were going to marry again."

The man's arms fell slowly.

"You were always rather great on principle," he said, in an odd tone.

He was not angry—that she saw. But the sudden dying away of the eagerness on his face made him look old and different. This was not the man whose hurricanes of violence had once overwhelmed her, whose unrestrained passions had finally driven her from him to take refuge in a lie.

"I should not have come," she said, speaking with less assurance, "if it had not been to prevent a wrong being done to another woman."

His expression did not change.

"I see," he said quietly. "Who sent you? Carey?"

She flushed uncontrollably at the question, though there was no offence in the tone in which it was uttered.

"Yes," she answered, after a moment.

Coningsby turned slowly and looked into the fire.

"And how did he persuade you?" he asked. "Did he tell you I was going blind?"

"No!" There was apprehension as well as surprise in her voice; and he jerked his head up as though listening to it.

"Ah, well!" he said. "It doesn't much matter. There is a remedy for all this world's evils. No doubt I shall take it sooner or later. So you're going again are you? I'm not to touch you; not to kiss your hand? You won't have me as husband, slave, or dog! Egad!" He laughed out harshly. "I used not to be so humble. If you were queen, I was king, and I made you know it.

There! Go! You have done what you came to do, and more also. Go quickly, before I see your face again! I'm only mortal still, and there are some things that mortals can't endure—even strong men—even giants. So—good-bye!"

He stopped abruptly. He was gripping the high mantelpiece with both hands. Every bone of them stood out distinctly, and the veins shone purple in the lamplight. His head was bowed forward upon his chest. He was fighting fiercely with that demon of unfettered violence to which he had yielded such complete allegiance all his life.

Minutes passed. He dared not turn his head to look but he knew that she had not gone. He waited dumbly, still forcing back the evil impulse that tore at his heart. But the tension became at last intolerable, and slowly, still gripping himself with all his waning strength, he stood up and turned.

She was standing close to him. The repugnance had all gone out of her face. It held only the tenderness of a great compassion.

As he stared at her dumbfounded, she held out her hands to him.

"Geoffrey," she said, "if you wish it, I will come back to you."

He stared at her, still wide-eyed and mute, as though a spell were upon him.

"Won't you have me, Geoffrey?" she said, a faint quiver in her voice.

He seized her hands then, seized them, and drew her to him, bowing his head down upon her shoulder with a great sob.

"Naomi, Naomi," he whispered huskily, "I will be good to you, my darling—so help me, God!"

Her own eyes were full of tears. She yielded herself to him without a word.

IX

"Can I come in a moment, Reggie?"

Gwen's bright face peered round the door at him as he sat at the writing-table in his room, with his head upon his hand. He looked up at her.

"Yes, come in, child! What is it?"

She entered eagerly and went to him.

"Are you busy, dear old boy? It is horrid that you should be going away so soon. I only wanted just to tell you something that the dear old Admiral has just told me."

She sat down in her favourite position on the arm of his chair, her arm about his neck. Her eyes were shining. Carey looked up at her.

"Well?" he said. "Has he plucked up courage at last to ask for what he wants?"

"Yes; he actually has." There was a purr of content in Gwen's voice. "And it's quite all right, Reggie. Mummy has said 'yes,' as I knew she would, directly I told her about Major Coningsby finding his wife again. All she said to that was: 'Dear me! How annoying for poor Major Coningsby!' I thought it was horrid of her to say that, but I didn't say so, for I wanted it all to come quite casually. And after that I wrote to Charlie, and he told the Admiral. And he came straight over only this morning and asked her. He's been telling me all about it, and he's so awfully happy! He says he was a big fool not to ask her long ago in the summer. For what do you think she said, Reggie, when he told her that he'd been wanting to marry her for ever so long, but couldn't be quite sure how she felt about it? Why, she said, with that funny little laugh of hers—you know her way—'My dear Admiral, I was only waiting to be asked.' The dear old man nearly cried when he told me. And I kissed him. And he and Charlie are coming over to dine this evening. So we can all be happy together."

Gwen paused to breathe, and to give her cousin an ardent hug.

"You've been a perfect dear about it," she ended with enthusiasm. "It would never have happened but for you, and—and Mademoiselle Trèves. Do you think she hated going back to that man very badly?"

"I think she did," said Carey.

He was looking, not at Gwen, but straight at the window in front of him. There were deep lines about his eyes, as if he had not slept of late.

"But she needn't have stayed," urged Gwen.

He did not answer. In his pocket there lay a slip of paper containing a few brief lines in a woman's hand.

"I have taken up my burden again, and, God helping me, I will carry it now to the end. You know what it means to me, but I shall always thank you in my heart, because in the hour of my utter weakness you were strong.— NAOMI CONINGSBY."

The splendid courage that underlay those few words had not hidden from the man the cost of her sacrifice. She had gone voluntarily back into the bondage that once had crushed her to the earth. And he—and he only— knew what it meant to her.

He was brought back to his surroundings by the pressure of Gwen's arm. He turned and found her looking closely into his face.

"Reggie," she said, with a touch of shyness, "are you—unhappy—about something?" He did not answer her at once, and she slipped suddenly down upon her knees by his side. "Forgive me, dear old boy! Do you know, I couldn't help guessing a little? You're not vexed?"

He laid a silencing hand upon her shoulder.

"I don't mind your knowing, dear," he said gently.

And he stooped, and kissed her forehead. She clung to him closely for a second. When she rose, her eyes were wet. But, obedient to his unspoken desire, she did not say another word.

When she was gone Carey roused himself from his preoccupation, and concentrated his thoughts upon his correspondence. He was leaving England in two days, and travelling to the East on a solitary shooting expedition. He did not review the prospect with much relish, but inaction had become intolerable to him, and he had an intense longing to get away. He had arranged to return to town that afternoon.

It was towards luncheon-time that he left his room, and, descending, came upon Lady Emberdale in the hall. She turned to meet him, a slight flush upon her face.

"No doubt Gwen has told you our piece of news?" she said.

He held out his hand.

"It is official, is it? I am very glad. I wish you joy with all my heart."

She accepted his congratulations with a gracious smile.

"I think everyone is pleased, including those absurd children. By the way, here is a note just come for you, brought by a groom from Crooklands Manor. I was going to bring it up to you, as he is waiting for an answer."

He took it up and opened it hastily, with a murmured excuse. When he looked up, Lady Emberdale saw at once that there was something wrong. She began to question him, but he held the note out to her with a quick gesture, and she took it from him.

> "My husband met with an accident while motoring this morning," she read. "He has been brought home, terribly injured, and keeps asking for you. Can you come?
> "N. CONINGSBY."

Glancing up, she saw Carey, pale and stern, waiting to speak.

"Send back word, 'Yes, at once,'" he said. "And perhaps you can spare me the car?"

He turned away without waiting for her reply, and went back to his room, crushing the note unconsciously in his hand.

X

"And the sea—gave up—the dead—that were in it." Haltingly the words fell through the silence. There was a certain monotony about them, as if they had been often repeated. The speaker turned his head from side to side upon the pillow uneasily, as if conscious of restraint, then spoke again in the tone of one newly awakened. "Why doesn't that fellow come?" he demanded restlessly. "Did you tell him I couldn't wait?"

"He is coming," a quiet voice answered at his side. "He will soon be here."

He moved his head again at the words, seeming to listen intently.

"Ah, Naomi, my girl," he said, "you've turned up trumps at last. It won't have been such a desperate sacrifice after all, eh, dear? It's wonderful how things get squared. Is that the doctor there? I can't see very well."

The doctor bent over him.

"Are you wanting anything?"

"Nothing—nothing, except that fellow Carey. Why in thunder doesn't he come? No; there's nothing you can do. I'm pegging out. My time is up. You can't put back the clock. I wouldn't let you if you could—not as things are. I have been a blackguard in my time, but I'll take my last hedge straight. I'll die like a man."

Again he turned his head, seeming to listen.

"I thought I heard something. Did someone open the door? It's getting very dark."

Yes; the door had opened, but only the dying brain had caught the sound. As Carey came noiselessly forward only the dying man greeted him.

"Ah, here you are! Come quite close to me! I want to see you, if I can. You're the little newspaper chap who saved my life at Magersfontein?"

"Yes," Carey said.

He sat down by Coningsby's side, facing the light.

"I was told you wanted me," he said.

"Yes; I want you to give me a promise." Coningsby spoke rapidly, with brows drawn together. "I suppose you know I'm a dead man?"

"I don't believe in death," Carey answered very quietly.

Coningsby's eyes burned with a strange light.

"Nor I," he said. "Nor I. I've been too near it before now to be afraid. Also, I've lived too long and too hard to care overmuch for what is left. But there's one thing I mean to do before I go. And you'll give me your promise to see it through?"

He paused, breathing quick and short; then went on hurriedly, as a man whose time is limited.

"You'll stick to it, I know, for you're a fellow that speaks the truth. I nearly thrashed you for it, once. Remember? You said I wasn't fit for the society of any good woman. And you were right—quite right. I never have been. Yet you ended by sending me the best woman in the world. What made you do that, I wonder?"

Carey did not answer. His face was sternly composed. He had not once glanced at the woman who sat on the other side of Coningsby's bed.

Coningsby went on unheeding.

"I drove her away from me, and you—you sent her back. I don't think I could have done that for the woman I loved. For you do love her, eh, Carey? I remember seeing it in your face that first night I brought you here. It comes back to me. You were standing before her portrait in the library. You didn't know I saw you. I was drunk at the time. But I've remembered it since."

Again he paused. His breath was slowing down. It came spasmodically, with long silences between.

Carey had listened with his eyes fixed and hard, staring straight before him, but now slowly at length he turned his head, and looked down at the man who was dying.

"Hadn't you better tell me what it is you want me to do?" he said.

"Ah!" Coningsby seemed to rouse himself. "It isn't much, after all," he said. "I made my will only this morning. It was on my way back that I had the smash. I was quite sober, only I couldn't see very well, and I lost control. All my property goes to my wife. That's all settled. But there's one thing left—one thing left—which I am going to leave you. It's the only thing I value, but there's no nobility about it, for I can't take it with me where I'm going. I want you, Carey—when I'm dead—to marry the woman you love, and give her happiness. Don't wait for the sake of decency! That consideration never appealed to me. I say it in her presence, that she may know it is my wish. Marry her, man—you love each other—did you think I didn't know? And take her away to some Utopia of your own, and—and—teach her—to forget me."

His voice shook and ceased. His wife had slipped to her knees by the bed, hiding her face. Carey sat mute and motionless, but the grim look had passed from his face. It was almost tender.

Gaspingly at length Coningsby spoke again: "Are you going to do it, Carey? Are you going to give me your promise? I shall sleep the easier for it."

Carey turned to him and gripped one of the man's powerless hands in his own. For a moment he did not speak—it almost seemed he could not. Then at last, very low, but resolute his answer came:

"I promise to do my part," he said.

In the silence that followed he rose noiselessly and moved away.

He left Naomi still kneeling beside the bed, and as he passed out he heard the dying man speak her name. But what passed between them he never knew.

When he saw her again, nearly an hour later, Geoffrey Coningsby was dead.

XI

It was on a day of frosty sunshine, nearly a fortnight later, that Carey dismounted before the door of Crooklands Manor, and asked for its mistress.

He was shown at once into the library, where he found her seated before a great oak bureau with a litter of papers all around her.

She flushed deeply as she rose to greet him. They had not met since the day of her husband's funeral.

"I see you're busy," he said, as he came forward.

"Yes," she assented. "Such stacks of papers that must be examined before they can be destroyed. It's dreary work, and I have been very thankful to have Gwen with me. She has just gone out riding."

"I met her," Carey said. "She was with young Rivers."

"It is a farewell ride," Naomi told him. "She goes back to school to-morrow. Dear child! I shall miss her. Please sit down!"

The colour had ebbed from her face, leaving it very pale. She did not look at Carey, but began slowly to sort afresh a pile of correspondence.

He ignored her request, and stood watching her till at last she laid the packet down.

Then somewhat abruptly he spoke: "I've just come in to tell you my plans."

"Yes?" She took up an old cheque-book, as if she could not bear to be idle, and began to look through it, seeming to search for something.

Again he fell silent, watching her.

"Yes?" she repeated after a moment, bending a little over the book she held.

"They are very simple," he said quietly. "I'm going to a place I know of in the Himalayas where there is a wonderful river that one can punt along all day and all night, and never come to an end."

Again he paused. The fingers that held the memorandum were not quite steady.

"And you have come to say good-bye?" she suggested in her deep, sad voice.

His eyes were turned gravely upon her, but there was a faint smile at the corners of his mouth.

"No," he said in his abrupt fashion. "That isn't in the plan. Good-bye to the rest of the world if you will, but never again to you!"

He drew close to her and gently took the cheque-book out of her grasp.

"I want you to come with me, Naomi," he said very tenderly. "My darling, will you come? I have wanted you—for years."

A great quiver went through her, as though every pulse leapt to the words he uttered. For a second she stood quite still, with her face lifted to the sunlight. Then she turned, without question or words of any sort, as she had turned long ago—yet with a difference—and laid her hand with perfect confidence in his.

THE RETURN GAME

I

"Well played, Hone! Oh, well played indeed!"

A great roar of applause went up from the polo-ground like the surge and wash of an Atlantic roller. The regimental hero was distinguishing himself—a state of affairs by no means unusual, for success always followed Hone. His luck was proverbial in the regiment, as sure and as deeply-rooted as his popularity.

"It's the devil's own concoction," declared Teddy Duncombe, Major Hone's warmest friend and admirer, who was watching from the great stand near the refreshment-tent. "It never fails. We call him Achilles because he always carries all before him."

"Even Achilles had his vulnerable point," remarked Mrs. Perceval, to whom the words were addressed.

She spoke with her dark eyes fixed upon the distant figure. Seen from a distance, he seemed to be indeed invincible—a magnificent horseman who rode like a fury, yet checked and wheeled his pony with the skill of a circus rider. But there was no admiration in Mrs. Perceval's intent gaze. She looked merely critical.

"Pat hasn't," replied Duncombe, whose love for Hone was no mean thing, and who gloried in his Irish major's greatness. "He's a man in ten thousand—the finest specimen of an imperfect article ever produced."

His enthusiasm fell on barren ground. Mrs. Perceval was not apparently bestowing much attention upon him. She was watching the play with brows slightly drawn.

Duncombe looked at her with faint surprise. She was not often unappreciative, and he could not imagine any woman failing to admire Hone. Besides, Mrs. Perceval and Hone were old friends, as everyone knew. Was it not Hone who had escorted her to the East seven years ago when she had left Home to join her elderly husband? By Jove, was it really seven years since Perceval's beautiful young wife had taken them all by storm?

She looked a mere girl yet, though she had been three years a widow. Small and dark and very regal was Nina Perceval, with the hands and feet of a fairy and the carriage of a princess. He had seen nothing of her during those last three years. She had been living a life of retirement in the hills. But now she was going back to England and was visiting her old haunts to bid her friends farewell. And Teddy Duncombe found her as captivating as ever. She was more than beautiful. She was positively dazzling.

What a splendid pair she and Pat would make, Duncombe thought to himself as he watched her. A man like Major Hone, V.C., ought to find a mate. Every king should have a queen.

The thought was still in his mind, possibly in his eyes also, when abruptly Mrs. Perceval turned her head and caught him.

"Taking notes, Captain Duncombe?" she asked, with a smile too careless to be malicious.

"Playing providence, Mrs. Perceval," he answered without embarrassment.

He had never been embarrassed in her presence yet. She had a happy knack of setting her friends at ease.

"I hope you are preparing a kind fate for me," she said.

He laughed a little. "What would you call a kind fate?"

Her dark eyes flashed. She looked for a moment scornful. "Not the usual woman's Utopia," she said. "I have been through that and come out on the other side."

"I can hardly believe it," protested Teddy.

"Don't you know I am a cynic?" she said, with a little reckless laugh.

A second wild shout from the spectators on all sides of them swept their conversation away. On the further side of the ground Hone, with steady wrist and faultless aim, had just sent the ball whizzing between the posts.

It was the end of the match, and Hone was once more the hero of the hour.

"Really, I sometimes think the gods are too kind to Major Hone," smiled Mrs. Chester, the colonel's wife, and Mrs. Perceval's hostess. "It can't be good for him to be always on the winning side."

Hone was trotting quietly down the field, laughing all over his handsome, sunburnt face at the cheers that greeted him. He dismounted close to Mrs. Perceval, and was instantly seized by Duncombe and thumped upon the back with all the force of his friend's goodwill.

"Pat, old fellow, you're the finest sportsman in the Indian Empire. Those chaps haven't been beaten for years."

Hone laughed easily and swung himself free. "They've got some knowing little brutes of ponies, by the powers," he said. "They slip about like minnows. The Ace of Trumps was furious. Did you hear him squeal?"

He turned with the words to his own pony and kissed the velvet nose that was rubbing against his arm.

"And a shame it is to make him carry a lively five tons," he murmured in his caressing Irish brogue.

For Hone was a giant as well as a hero and he carried his inches, as he bore his honours, like a man.

Raising his head, he encountered Mrs. Perceval's direct look. She bowed to him with that regal air of hers that for all its graciousness yet managed to impart a sense of remoteness to the man she thus honoured.

"I have been admiring your luck, Major Hone," she said. "I am told you are always lucky."

He smiled courteously.

"Sure, Mrs. Perceval, you can hardly expect me to plead guilty to that."

"Anyway, you deserved your luck, Pat," declared Duncombe. "You played superbly."

"Major Hone excels in all games, I believe," said Mrs. Perceval. "He seems to possess the secret of success."

She spoke with obvious indifference; yet an odd look flashed across Hone's brown face at the words. He almost winced.

But he was quick to reply. "The secret of success," he said, "is to know how to make the best of a beating."

He was still smiling as he spoke. He met Mrs. Perceval's eyes with baffling good-humour.

"You speak from experience, of course?" she said. "You have proved it?"

"Faith, that is another story," laughed Hone, hitching his pony's bridle on his arm. "We live and learn, Mrs. Perceval. I have learnt it."

And with that he bowed and passed on, every inch a soldier and to his finger-tips a gentleman.

II

"Hullo, Pat!"

Teddy Duncombe, airily clad in pyjamas, stood a moment on the verandah to peer in upon his major, then stepped into the room with the assurance of one who had never yet found himself unwelcome.

"Hullo, my son!" responded Hone, who, clad still more airily, was exercising his great muscles with dumb-bells before plunging into his morning tub.

Duncombe seated himself to watch the operations with eyes of keen appreciation.

"By Jove," he said admiringly at length, "you are a mighty specimen! I believe you'll live for ever."

"Not on this plaguey little planet, let us trust!" said Hone, speaking through his teeth by reason of his exertions.

"You ought to marry," said Duncombe, still intently observant. "Giants like you have no right to remain single in these degenerate days."

"Faith!" scoffed Hone. "It's an age of feather-weights, and I'm out of date entirely."

He thumped down his dumb-bells, and stood up with arms outstretched. He saw the open admiration in his friend's eyes, and laughed at it.

But Duncombe remained serious.

"Why don't you get married, Pat?" he said.

Hone's arms slowly dropped. His brown face sobered. But the next instant he smiled again.

"Find the woman, Teddy!" he said lightly.

"I've found her," said Teddy unexpectedly.

"The deuce you have!" said Hone. "Sure, and it's truly grateful I am! Is she young, my son, and lovely?"

"She is the loveliest woman I know," said Teddy Duncombe, with all sincerity.

"Faith!" laughed the Irishman. "But that's heartfelt! Why don't you enter for the prize yourself?"

"I'm going to marry little Lucy Fabian as soon as she will have me," explained Duncombe. "We settled that ages ago, almost as soon as she came out. It's not a formal engagement even yet, but she has promised to bear it in mind. We had a talk last night, and—I believe I haven't much longer to wait."

"Good luck to you, dear fellow!" said Hone. "You deserve the best." He laid his hand for a moment on Duncombe's shoulder. "It's been a good partnership, Teddy boy," he said. "I shall miss you."

Teddy gripped the hand hard.

"You'll have to get married yourself, Pat," he declared urgently. "It isn't good for man to live alone."

"And so you are going to provide for my future also," laughed Hone. "And the lady's name?"

"Oh, she's an old friend!" said Duncombe. "Can't you guess?"

Hone shook his head.

"I can't imagine any old friend taking pity on me. Have you sounded her feelings on the subject? Or perhaps she hasn't got any where I am concerned."

"Oh, yes, she has her feelings about you!" said Duncombe, with confidence. "But I don't know what they are. She wasn't particularly communicative on that point."

"Or you, my son, were not particularly penetrating," suggested Hone.

"I certainly didn't penetrate far," Duncombe confessed. "It was a case of 'No admission to outsiders.' Still, I kept my eyes open on your behalf; and the conclusion I arrived at was that, though reticent where you were concerned, she was by no means indifferent."

Hone stooped and picked up his dumb-bells once more.

"Your conclusions are not always very convincing, Teddy," he remarked.

Duncombe got to his feet in leisurely preparation for departure.

"There was no mistake as to her reticence anyhow," he observed. "It was the more conspicuous, as all the rest of us were yelling ourselves hoarse in your honour. I was watching her, and she never moved her lips, never even smiled. But her eyes saw no one else but you."

Hone grunted a little. He was poising the dumb-bells at the full stretch of his arms.

Duncombe still loitered at the open window.

"And her name is Nina Perceval," he said abruptly, shooting out the words as though not quite certain of their reception.

The dumb-bells crashed to the ground. Hone wheeled round. For a single instant the Irish eyes flamed fiercely; but the next he had himself in hand.

"A pretty little plan, by the powers!" he said, forcing himself to speak lightly. "But it won't work, my lad. I'm deeply grateful all the same."

"Rats, man! She is sure to marry again." Duncombe spoke with deliberate carelessness. He would not seem to be aware of that which his friend had suppressed.

"That may be," Hone said very quietly. "But she will never marry me. And—faith, I'll be honest with you, Teddy, for the whole truth told is better than a half-truth guessed—for her sake I shall never marry another woman."

He spoke with absolute steadiness, and he looked Duncombe full in the eyes as he said it.

A brief silence followed his statement; then impulsively Duncombe thrust out his hand.

"Hone, old chap, forgive me! I'm a headlong, blundering jackass!"

"And the best friend a man ever had," said Hone gently. "It's an old story, and I can't tell you all. It was just a game, you know; it began in jest, but it ended in grim earnest, as some games do. It happened that time we travelled out together, eight years ago. I was supposed to be looking after her; but, faith, the monkey tricked me! I was a fool, you see, Teddy." A faint smile crossed his face. "And she gave me an elderly spinster to dance attendance upon while she amused herself. She was only a child in those days. She couldn't have been twenty. I used to call her the Princess, and I was St. Patrick to her. But the mischief was that I thought her free, and—I made love to her." He paused a moment. "Perhaps it's hardly fair to tell you this. But you're in love yourself; you'll understand."

"I understand," Duncombe said.

"And she was such an innocent," Hone went on softly. "Faith, what an innocent she was! Till one day she saw what had happened to me, and it nearly broke her heart. For she hadn't meant any harm, bless her. It was all a game with her, and she thought I was playing, too, till—till she saw otherwise. Well, it all came to an end at last, and to save her from grieving I pretended that I had known all along. I pretended that I had trifled with her from start to finish. She didn't believe me at first, but I made her—Heaven pity me!—I made her. And then she swore that she would never forgive me. And she never has."

Hone turned quietly away, and put the dumb-bells into a corner. Duncombe remained motionless, watching him.

"But she will, old chap," he said at last. "She will. Women do, you know—when they understand."

"Yes, I know," said Hone. "But she never can understand. I tricked her too thoroughly for that." He faced round again, his grey eyes level and very steady.

"It's just my fate, Teddy," he said; "and I've got to put up with it. However it may appear, the gods are not all-bountiful where I am concerned. I may win everything in the world I turn my hand to, but I have lost for ever the only thing I really want!"

III

It was two days later that Mrs. Chester decided to give what she termed a farewell *fête* to all Nina Perceval's old friends. Nina had always been a great favourite with her, and she was determined that the function should be worthy of the occasion.

To ensure success, she summoned Hone to her assistance. Hone always assisted everybody, and it was well known that he invariably succeeded in that to which he set his hand. And Hone, with native ingenuity, at once suggested a water expedition by moonlight as far as the ruined Hindu temple on the edge of the jungle that came down to the river at that point. There was a spice of adventure about this that at once caught Mrs. Chester's fancy. It was the very thing, she declared; a water-picnic was so delightfully informal. They would cut for partners, and row up the river in couples.

To Nina Perceval the plan seemed slightly childish, but she veiled her feelings from her friend as she veiled them from all the world; for very soon it would be all over, sunk away in that grey, grey past into which she would never look again. She even joined in conference with Mrs. Chester and Hone over the details of the expedition, and if now and then the Irishman's eyes rested upon her as though they read that which she would fain have hidden, she never suffered herself to be disconcerted thereby.

When the party assembled on the eventful evening to settle the question of partners, Hone was, as usual, in the forefront. The lots were drawn under his management, not by his own choice, but because Mrs. Chester insisted upon it. He presided over two packs of cards that had been reduced to the number of guests. The men drew from one pack, the women from the other; and thus everyone in the room was bound at length to pair.

Hone would have foregone this part of the entertainment, but the colonel's wife was firm.

"People never know how to arrange themselves," she declared. "And I decline any responsibility of that sort. The Fates shall decide for us. It will be infinitely more satisfactory in the end."

And Hone could only bow to her ruling.

Nina Perceval was the first to draw. Her card was the ace of hearts. She slung it round her neck in accordance with Mrs. Chester's decree, and sat down to await her destiny.

It was some time in coming. One after another drew and paired in the midst of much chaff and merriment; but she sat solitary in her corner watching the pile of cards diminish while she remained unclaimed.

"Most unusual!" declared Mrs. Chester. "Whom can the Fates be reserving for you, I wonder?"

Nina had no answer to make. She sat with her dark eyes fixed upon the few cards that were left in front of Hone, not uttering a single word. He sat motionless, too, Teddy Duncombe, who had paired with his hostess, standing by his side. He was not looking in her direction, but by some mysterious means she knew that his attention was focussed upon herself. She was convinced in her secret soul that, though he hid his anxiety, he was closely watching every card in the hope that he might ultimately pair with her.

The last man drew and found his partner. One card only was left in front of Hone. He laid his hand upon it, paused for an instant, then turned it up. The ace of hearts!

She felt herself stiffen involuntarily, and something within her began to pound and race like the hoofs of a galloping horse. A brief agitation was hers, which she almost instantly subdued, but which left her strangely cold.

Hone had risen from the table. He came quietly to her side. There was no visible elation about him. His grey eyes were essentially honest, but they were deliberately emotionless at that moment.

In the hubbub of voices all about them he bent and spoke.

"It may not be the fate you would have chosen; but since submit we must, shall we not make the best of it?"

She met his look with the aloofness of utter disdain.

"Your strategy was somewhat too apparent to be ascribed to Fate," she said. "I cannot imagine why you took the trouble."

A dark flush mounted under Hone's tan. He straightened himself abruptly, and she was conscious of a moment's sharp misgiving that was strangely akin to fear. Then, as he spoke no word, she rose and stood beside him, erect and regal.

"I submit," she said quietly; "not because I must, but because I do not consider it worth while to do otherwise. The matter is too unimportant for discussion."

Hone made no rejoinder. He was staring straight before him, stern-eyed and still.

But a few moments later, he gravely proffered his arm, and in the midst of a general move they went out together into the moonlit splendour of the Indian night.

IV

Slowly the boats slipped through the shallows by the bank.

Hone sat facing his companion in unbroken silence while he rowed steadily up the stream. But there was no longer anger in his steady eyes. The habit of kindness, which was the growth of a lifetime, had reasserted itself. He had not been created to fulfil a harsh destiny. The chivalry at his heart condemned sternness towards a woman.

And Nina Perceval sat in the stern with the moonlight shining in her eyes and the darkness of a great bitterness in her soul, and waited. Despite her proud bearing she would have given much to have looked into his heart at that moment. Notwithstanding all her scorn of him very deep down in her innermost being she was afraid.

For this was the man who long ago, when she was scarcely more than a child, had blinded her, baffled her, beaten her. He had won her trust, and had used it contemptibly for his own despicable ends. He had turned an innocent game into tragedy, and had gone his way, leaving her life bruised and marred and bitter before it had ripened to maturity. He had put out the sunshine for ever, and now he expected to be forgiven.

But she would never forgive him. He had wounded her too cruelly, too wantonly, for forgiveness. He had laid her pride too low. For even yet, in all her furious hatred of him, she knew herself bound by a chain that no effort of hers might break. Even yet she thrilled to the sound of that soft, Irish voice, and was keenly, painfully aware of him when he drew near.

He did not know it, so she told herself over and over again. No one knew, or ever would know. That advantage, at least, was hers, and she would carry it to her grave. But yet she longed passionately, vindictively, to punish him for the ruin he had wrought, to humble him—this faultless knight, this regimental hero, at whose shrine everybody worshipped—as he had once dared to humble her; to make him care, if it were ever so little—only to make him care—and then to trample him ruthlessly underfoot, as he had trampled her.

She began to wonder how long he meant to maintain that uncompromising silence. From across the water came the gay voices of their fellow-guests, but no other boat was very near them. His face was in the shadow, and she had no clue to his mood.

For a while longer she endured his silence. Then at length she spoke:

"Major Hone!"

He started slightly, as one coming out of deep thought.

"Why don't you make conversation?" she asked, with a little cynical twist of the lips. "I thought you had a reputation for being entertaining."

"Will it entertain you if I ask for an apology?" said Hone.

"An apology!" She repeated the words sharply, and then softly laughed. "Yes, it will, very much."

"And yet you owe me one," said Hone.

"I fear I do not always pay my debts," she answered. "But you will find it difficult to convince me on this occasion that the debt exists."

"Faith, I shall not try!" he returned, with a doggedness that met and overrode her scorn. "The game isn't worth the candle. I know you will think ill of me in either case."

"Why, Major Hone?"

He met her eyes in the moonlight, and she felt as if by sheer force he held them.

"Because," he said slowly, "I have made it impossible for you to do otherwise."

"Surely that is no one's fault but your own?" she said.

"I blame no one else," said Hone.

And with that he bent again to his work as though he had been betrayed into plainer speaking than he deemed advisable, and became silent again.

Nina Perceval trailed her hand in the water and watched the ripples. Those few words of his had influenced her strangely. She had almost for the moment forgotten her enmity. But it returned upon her in the silence. She began to remember those bitter years that stretched behind her, the blind regrets with which he had filled her life—this man who had tricked her, lied to her—ay, and almost broken her heart in those far-off days of her girlhood, before she had learned to be cynical.

"And even if I did believe you," she said, "what difference would it make?"

Hone was silent for a moment. Then—"Just all the difference in the world," he said, his voice very low.

"You value my good opinion so highly?" she laughed. "And yet you will make no effort to secure it?"

He turned his eyes upon her again.

"I would move heaven and earth to win it," he said, and she knew by his tone that he was putting strong restraint upon himself, "if there were the smallest chance of my ever doing so. But I know my limitations; I know it's all no good. Once a blackguard, always a blackguard, eh, Mrs. Perceval? And I'd be a special sort of fool if I tried to persuade you otherwise."

But still she only laughed, in spite of the agitation but half-subdued in his voice.

"I would offer to steer," she remarked irrelevantly, "only I don't feel equal to the responsibility. And since you always get there sooner or later, my help would be superfluous."

"You share the popular belief about my luck?" asked Hone.

"To be sure," she answered gaily. "Even you could scarcely manage to find fault with it."

He drew a deep breath. "Not with you in the boat," he said.

She withdrew her hand from the water, and flicked it in his face.

"Hadn't you better slow down? You are getting overheated. I feel as if I were sitting in front of a huge furnace."

"And you object to it?" said Hone.

"Of course I do. It's unseasonable. You Irish are so tropical."

"It's only by contrast," urged Hone. "You will get acclimatised in time."

She raised her head with a dainty gesture.

"You take a good deal for granted, Major Hone."

"Faith, I know it!" he answered. "It's yourself that has turned my head."

Her laugh held more than a hint of scorn.

"How amusing," she commented, "for both of us!"

"Does it amuse you?" said Hone.

The question did not call for a reply, and she made none. Only once more she gathered up some water out of the magic moonlit ripples, and tossed it in his face.

V

They reached their destination far ahead of any of the others. A thick belt of jungle stretched down to the river where they landed, enveloping both banks a little higher up the stream.

"What an awesome place!" remarked Mrs. Perceval, as she stepped ashore. "I hope the rest will arrive soon, or I shall develop an attack of nerves."

"You've got me to take care of you," suggested Hone.

She uttered her soft, little laugh.

"Faith, Major Hone, and I'm not at all sure that it isn't yourself I want to run away from!"

Hone was securing the boat, and made no immediate response. But as he straightened himself, he laughed also.

"Am I so formidable, then?"

She flashed a swift glance at him.

"I haven't quite decided."

"You have known me long enough," he protested.

She shrugged her shoulders lightly.

"Have I ever met you before to-night? I have no recollection of it."

And mutely, with that chivalry which was to him the very air he breathed, Hone bowed to her ruling. She would have no reference to the past. It was to be a closed book to them both. So be it, then! For this night, at least, she would have her way.

He stepped forward in silence into the chequered shadow of the trees that surrounded the ruin, and she walked lightly by his side with that dainty, regal carriage of hers that made him yet in his secret heart call her his princess.

The place was very dark and eerie. The shrill cries of flying-foxes, disturbed by their appearance, came through the magic silence. But no living thing was to be seen, no other sound to be heard.

"I'm frightened," said Nina suddenly. "Shall we stop?"

"Hold my hand!" said Hone.

"I'm not joking," she protested, with a shudder.

"Nor am I," he said gently.

She looked up at him sharply, as though she did not quite believe him, and then unexpectedly and impulsively she laid her hand in his.

His fingers closed upon it with a friendly, reassuring pressure, and she never knew how the man's heart leapt and the blood turned to liquid fire in his veins at her touch.

She gave a shaky little laugh as though ashamed of her weakness. "We are coming to an open space," she said. "We shall see the satyrs dancing directly."

"Faith, if we do, we'll join them," declared Hone cheerily.

"They would never admit us," she answered. "They hate mortals. Can't you feel them glaring at us from every tree? Why, I can breathe hostility in the very air."

She missed her footing as she spoke, and stumbled with a sharp cry. Hone held her up with that steady strength of his that was ever equal to emergencies, but to his surprise she sprang forward, pulling him with her, almost before she had fully recovered her balance.

"Oh, come, quick, quick!" she gasped. "I trod on something—something that moved!"

He went with her, for she would not be denied, and in a few seconds they emerged into a narrow clearing in the jungle in which stood the ruin of a small domed temple.

Nina Perceval was shaking all over in a positive frenzy of fear, and clinging fast to Hone's arm.

"What was it?" he asked her, trying gently to disengage himself. "Was it a snake that scared you?"

She shuddered violently. "Yes, it must have been. A cobra, I should think. Oh, what are you going to do?"

"It's all right," Hone said soothingly. "You stay here a minute! I've got some matches. I'll just go back a few yards and investigate."

But at that she cried out so sharply that he thought for a moment that something had hurt her. But the next instant he understood, and again his heart leapt and strained within him like a chained thing.

"No, Pat! No, no, no! You shall do no such thing!" Incoherently the words rushed out, and with them the old familiar name, uttered all unawares. "Do you think I'd let you go? Why, the place may be thronged with snakes. And you—you have nothing to defend yourself with. How can you dream of such a thing?"

He heard her out with absolute patience. His face betrayed no sign of the tumult within. It remained perfectly courteous and calm. Yet when he spoke he, too, it seemed, had gone back to the old intimate days that lay so far behind them.

"Yes, but, Princess," he said, "what about our pals? If there is any real danger we can't let them come stumbling into it. We'll have to warn them."

She was still clinging to his arm, and her hands tightened. For an instant she seemed about to renew her wild protest, but something—was it the expression in the man's steady eyes?—checked her.

She stood a moment silent. Then, "You're quite right, Pat," she said, her voice very low. "We'll go straight back to the boat and stop them."

Her hands relaxed and fell from his arm, but Hone stood hesitating.

"You'll let me go first?" he said. "You stay here in the open! I'll come back for you."

But at that her new-found docility at once evaporated. "I won't!" she declared vehemently. "I won't! Don't be so ridiculous! Of course I am coming with you. Do you suppose I would let you go alone?"

"Why not?" said Hone.

He remembered later that she passed the question by. "We are wasting time," she said, "Let us go!"

And so together they went back into the danger that lurked in the darkness.

VI

They went side by side, for she would not let him take the lead. Her hand was in his, and he knew by its convulsive pressure something of the sheer panic that possessed her. And he marvelled at the power that nerved her, though he held his peace.

They entered the dense shadow of the strip of jungle that separated them from the stream, and very soon he paused to strike a match. She stood very close to him. He was aware that she was trembling in every limb.

He peered about him, but could see very little beyond the fact that the path ahead of them lay clear. On both sides of this the undergrowth baffled all scrutiny. He seemed to hear a small mysterious rustling sound, but his most minute attention failed to locate it. The match burned down to his fingers, and he tossed it away.

"There's nothing between us and the water," he said cheerily. "We'll make a dash for it."

"Stay!" she whispered, under her breath. "I heard something!"

"It's only a bit of a breeze overhead," said Hone. "We won't stop to listen anyway."

He caught her hand in his once more, grasping it firmly, and they moved forward again. They could see the moonlight glimmering on the water ahead, and in another yard or two the low-growing bush to which Hone had moored the boat became visible.

In that instant, with a jerk of terror, Nina stopped short. "Pat! What is that?"

Hone stood still. "There! Don't be scared!" he said soothingly. "What would it be at all? There's nothing but shadow."

"But there is!" she gasped. "There is! There! On the bank above the boat! What is it, Pat? What is it?"

Hone's eyes followed her quivering finger, discerning what appeared to be a blot of shadow close to the bush above the water.

"Sure, it's only shadow—" he began.

But she broke in feverishly. "It's not, Pat! It's not! There's nothing to cast it. It's in the full moonlight."

"You stay here!" said Hone. "I'll go and have a look."

"I won't!" she rejoined in a fierce whisper, holding him fast. "You—you shan't go a step nearer. We must get away somehow—somehow!" with a hunted glance around. "Not through the undergrowth, that's certain. We—we shall have to go back."

Hone was still staring at the motionless blot in the moonlight. He resisted her frantic efforts to drag him away.

"I must go and see," he said at last. "I'm sure there's nothing to alarm us. We can't run away from shadows, Princess. We should never hold up our heads again."

"Oh, Pat, you fool!" she exclaimed, almost beside herself. "I tell you that is no shadow! It's a snake! Do you hear? It's a huge python! And it was a snake I trod on just now. And they are everywhere—everywhere! The whole place is rustling with them. They are closing in on us. I can hear them! I can feel them! I can smell them! Pat, what shall we do? Quick, quick! Think of something! See now! It's moving—uncoiling! Look, look! Did you ever see anything so horrible? Pat!"

Her voice ended in a breathless shriek. She suddenly collapsed against him, her face hidden on his breast. And Hone, stooping impulsively, caught her up in his arms.

"We'll get out of it somehow," he said. "Never fear!"

But even his eyes had widened with a certain horror, for the blot in the moonlight was beyond question moving, elongating, quivering, subtly changing under his gaze.

He held his companion pressed tightly to his heart. She made no further attempt to urge him. Only by the tense clinging of her arms about his neck did he know that she was conscious.

Again he heard that vague rustling which he had set down to a sudden draught overhead. It seemed to come from all directions.

"Ye gods!" he muttered softly to himself. And again, more softly, "Ye gods!"

To the woman in his arms he uttered no word whatever. He only pressed the slender figure ever closer, while the blood surged and sang tumultuously in his veins. Though he stood in the midst of mortal danger, he was conscious of an exultation so mad as to be almost delirious. She was his—his—his!

Something stirred in the undergrowth close to him, and in a moment his attention was diverted from the slow-moving monster ahead of him. He became aware of a dark object, but vaguely discernible, that swayed to and fro about three feet from the ground seeming to menace him.

The moment he saw this thing, his brain flashed into sudden illumination. The shrewdness of the hunted creature entered into him. Without panic, he became most vividly, most intensely alive to the ghastly danger that threatened him. He stopped to ascertain nothing further. Swift as a lightning flash he acted—leapt backwards, leapt sideways, landed upon something that squirmed and thrashed hideously, nearly overthrowing him; and the next moment was breaking madly through the undergrowth, regardless of direction, running blindly through the jungle, fighting furiously every obstacle—forcing by sheer giant strength a way for himself and for the woman he carried through the opposing tangle of vegetation.

Branches slapped him in the face as he went, clutched at him, tore him, but could not stay his progress. Many times he stumbled, many times he recovered himself, dashing wildly on and still on like a man possessed. A marvellous strength was his. Titan-like, he accomplished that which to any ordinary man would have been an utter impossibility. Save that he was in perfect condition, even he must have failed. But that fact was his salvation, that and the fierce passion that urged him, endowing him with an endurance more than human.

Headlong as was his flight, the working of his brain was even swifter, and very soon, without slackening his speed, he was swerving round again towards the open. He could see the moonlight gleaming through the trees, and he made a dash for it, utterly reckless, since caution was of no avail, but alert for every danger, cunning for every advantage, keen as the born fighter for every chance that offered.

And so at last, torn, bleeding, but undismayed, he struggled free from the undergrowth, and sprang away from that place of horrors, staggering slightly but running strongly still, till the dark line of jungle fell away behind him and he reached the river bank once more.

Here he stopped and loosened his grip upon the slight form he carried. Her arms dropped from his neck. She had fainted.

For a few seconds he stared down into her white face, seeing nothing else, while the fiery heart of him leapt and quivered like a wild thing in leash. Then, suddenly, from the water a voice hailed him, and he looked up with a start.

"Hullo, Pat! What on earth is the matter? You have landed the wrong side of the stream. Is anything wrong?"

It was Teddy Duncombe in a boat below him. He saw his face of concern in the moonlight.

He pulled himself together.

"I was coming to warn you. This infernal jungle is full of snakes. We've had to run for it, and leave the boat behind."

"Great Scotland! And Mrs. Perceval?"

Again Hone's eyes sought the white face on his arm.

"No, she isn't hurt. It's just a faint. Pull up close, and I'll hand her down to you!"

Between them, they lowered her into the boat. Hone followed, and raised her to lean against his knee.

Duncombe began to row swiftly across the stream, with an uneasy eye upon the two in the stern.

"What in the world made you go wrong, I wonder?" he said. "No one ever goes that side, not even the natives. They say it's haunted. We all landed near the old bathing *ghat*."

Hone was moistening Nina Perceval's face with his handkerchief. He made no reply to Teddy's words. He was anxiously watching for some sign of returning consciousness.

It came very soon. The dark eyes opened and gazed up at him, at first uncomprehendingly, then with a dawning wonder.

"St. Patrick!" she whispered.

"Princess!" he whispered back.

With an effort she raised herself, leaning against him.

"What happened? Were you hurt? Your face is all bleeding!"

"It's nothing!" he said jerkily. "It's nothing!"

She took his handkerchief in her trembling hand and wiped the blood away. She said no more of any sort. Only when she gave it back to him her eyes were full of tears.

And Hone caught the little hand in passionate, dumb devotion, and pressed it to his lips.

VII

"I am so sorry, Major Hone, but she is seeing no one. I would ask you to dine if it would be of any use. But you wouldn't see her if I did."

So spoke the colonel's wife three days later in a sympathetic undertone; while Hone paced beside her *rickshaw* with a gloomy face.

"She isn't ill?" he asked. "You are sure she isn't ill?"

"No, not really ill. Her nerves are upset, of course. That was almost inevitable. But she has determined to start for Bombay on Monday, and nothing I can say will make her change her purpose."

"But she can't mean to go without saying good-bye!" he protested.

Mrs. Chester shook her head.

"She says she doesn't like good-byes. I had the greatest difficulty in persuading her to come here at all. I am afraid that is exactly what she does mean to do."

Hone stood still. His face was suddenly stubborn.

"I must see her," he said, "with her consent or without it. Will you, of your goodness, ask me to dine tonight? I will manage the rest for myself."

Mrs. Chester looked somewhat dubious. Long as she had known Hone, she was not familiar with this mood.

He saw her hesitation, and smiled upon her persuasively.

"You are not going to refuse my petition? It isn't yourself that would have the heart!"

She laughed, in spite of herself.

"Oh, go away, you wheedling Irishman! Yes, you may dine if you like. The Gerrards are coming for bridge, and you'll be odd man out. There will be no one to entertain you."

"Sure, I can entertain myself," grinned Hone. "And it's truly grateful that I am to your worshipful ladyship."

He bowed, with his hand upon his heart, and, turning, went his way.

Mrs. Chester went hers, still vaguely doubtful as to the wisdom of her action. In common with the rest of mankind, she found Hone well-nigh impossible to resist.

When he made his appearance that evening, he presented an absolutely serene aspect to the world at large. He was the gayest of the party, and Mrs. Chester's uneasiness speedily evaporated. Nina Perceval was not present, but this fact apparently did not depress him. He remained in excellent spirits throughout dinner.

When it was over, and the bridge players were established on the veranda, he drifted off to the smoking-room in an aimless, inconsequent fashion, and his hostess and accomplice saw him no more.

She would have given a good deal to have witnessed his subsequent movements, but she would have been considerably disappointed had she done so, for Hone's methods were disconcertingly direct. All he did when he found himself alone was to sit down and scribble a brief note.

"I am waiting to see you" (so ran his message). "Will you come to me now, or must I follow you to the world's end? One or the other it will surely be. — Yours, PAT."

This note he delivered to the *khitmutgar*, with orders to return to him with a reply. Then, with a certain massive patience, he resumed his cigar and settled himself to wait.

The *khitmutgar* did not return, but he showed no sign of exasperation. His eyes stared gravely into space. There was not a shade of anxiety in them.

And it was thus that Nina Perceval found him when at last she came lightly in from the veranda in answer to his message. She entered without the smallest hesitation, but with that regal air of hers before which men did involuntary homage. Her shadowy eyes met his without fear or restraint of any sort, but they held no gladness either. Her remoteness chilled him.

"Why did you send me that extraordinary message?" she said. "Wasn't it a little unnecessary?"

He had risen to meet her. He paused to lay aside his cigar before he answered, and in the pause that dogged expression that had surprised Mrs. Chester descended like a mask and covered the first spontaneous impulse to welcome her that had dominated him.

"It was necessary that I should see you," he said.

"I really don't know why," she returned. "I wrote a note to thank you for the care you took of me the other night. That was days ago. I suppose you received it?"

"Yes, I received it," said Hone. "I have been trying, without success, to see you ever since."

She made a slight impatient movement.

"I haven't seen any one. I was upset after that horrible adventure. I shouldn't be seeing you now, only your ridiculous note made me wonder if there was anything wrong. Is there?"

She faced him with the direct inquiry. There was a faint frown between her brows. Her delicate beauty possessed him like a charm. He felt his blood begin to quicken, but he kept himself in check.

"There is nothing wrong, Princess," he said steadily. "I am, as ever, your humble servant, only I've got to come to the point with you before you go. I've got to make the most of this shred of opportunity which you have given me against your will. You are not disposed to be generous, I see; but I appeal to your sense of justice. Is it fair play at all to fling a man into gaol, and to refuse to let him plead on his own behalf?"

The annoyance passed like a shadow from her face. She began to smile.

"What can you mean?" she said. "Is it a joke—a riddle? Am I supposed to laugh?"

"Heaven help me, no!" he said. "There is only one woman in the world that I can't trifle with, and that's yourself."

"Oh, but what an admission!" She laughed at him, softly mocking. "And I'm so fond of trifling, too. Then what can you possibly want with me? I suppose you have really called to say good-bye."

"No," said Hone. He spoke quickly, and, as he spoke, he leaned towards her. A deep glow had begun to smoulder in his eyes. "It's something else that I've come to say—something quite different. I've come to tell you that you are all the world to me, that I love you with all there is of me, that I have always loved you. Yes, you'll laugh at me. You'll think me mad. But if I don't take this chance of telling you, I'll never have another. And even if it makes no difference at all to you, I'm bound to let you know."

He ceased. The fire that smouldered in his eyes had leaped to lurid flame; but still he held himself in check, he subdued the racing madness in his veins. He was, as ever, her humble servant.

Perhaps she realized it, for she showed no sign of shrinking as she stood before him. Her eyes grew a little wider and a little darker, that was all.

"I don't know what to say to you, Major Hone," she said, after a moment. "I don't know even what you expect me to say, since you expressly tell me that you are not trifling."

"Faith!" he broke in impetuously. "And is it trifling I'd be with the only woman I ever loved or ever wanted? I'm not asking you to flirt. I'm asking a bigger thing of you than that. I'm asking you—Princess, I'm asking you to stay—and be my wife."

He drew nearer to her, but he made no attempt to touch her. Only the flame of his passion seemed to reach her, to scorch her, for she made a slight movement away from him.

She looked at him doubtfully. "I still don't know what to say," she said.

His face altered. With a mighty effort he subdued the fiery impulse that urged him to override her doubts and fears, to take and hold her in his arms, to make her his with or without her will.

He became in a trice the kindly, winning personality that all his world knew and loved. "Sure then, you're not afraid of me?" he said, as though he softly cajoled a child. "It wouldn't be yourself at all if you were, you that could tread me underfoot like a centipede and not be a mite the worse."

She smiled a little, smiled and uttered a sudden quick sigh. "Don't you think you are rather a fool, Pat?" she said. "I gave you credit for more shrewdness. You certainly had more once."

"What do you mean?" There was a sharp note of pain in Hone's voice.

She moved restlessly across the room and paused with her back to him. "None but a fool would conclude that because a woman is pretty she must be good as well," she said, a tremor of bitterness in her voice. "Why do you take it for granted in this headlong fashion that I am all that man could desire?"

"You are all that I want," he said.

She shook her head. "The woman who lived inside me died long ago," she said, "and a malicious spirit took her place."

"None but yourself would ever dare to say that to me," said Hone. "And I won't listen even to you. Princess—"

"You are not to call me that!" She rounded upon him suddenly, a fierce gleam in her eyes. "You must never—never—"

She broke off. He was close to her, with that on his face that stilled her protest. He gathered her to him with a tenderness that yet was irresistible.

"Sure, then," he whispered, with a whimsical humour that cloaked all deeper feeling, "you shall be my queen instead, for by the saints I swear that in some form or other I was created to be your slave."

And though she averted her face and after a moment withdrew herself from his arms, she raised no further protest. She suffered him to plant the flag of his supremacy unhindered.

VIII

Certainly the colonel's wife was in her element. A wedding in the regiment, and that the wedding of its idolized hero, was to her an affair of almost more importance than anything that had happened since her own. The church had been fully decorated under her directions, and she had turned it into as elegant a reception room as circumstances permitted. White favours had been distributed to the dusky warriors under Hone's command who lined the aisle. All was in readiness, from the bridegroom, resplendent in scarlet and gold, waiting in the chancel with Teddy Duncombe, the best man, to the buzzing guests who swarmed in at the west door to be received by the colonel's wife, who in her capacity of hostess seemed to be everywhere at once.

"She was quite ready when I left, and looking sweet," so ran the story to one after another. "Oh, yes, in her travelling dress, of course. That had to be. But quite bridal—the palest silver grey. She looks quite charming, and such a girl. No one would ever think—" and so on, to innumerable acquaintances, ending where she had begun—"yes, she was quite ready when I left, and looking sweet!"

Ready or not, she was undoubtedly late, as is the recognised custom of brides all the world over. The organist, who had been playing an impressive selection, was drawing to the end of his resources and beginning to improvise somewhat spasmodically. The bridegroom betrayed no impatience, but there was undeniable strain in his attitude. He stood stiff and motionless as a soldier on parade. The guests were commencing to peer and wonder. Mrs. Chester made her tenth pilgrimage to the door.

Ah! The carriage at last! She turned back with a beaming face, and rustled up the aisle as though she were the heroine of the occasion. A flutter of expectation went through the church. The organist plunged abruptly into "The Voice that Breathed o'er Eden."

Everyone rose. Everyone craned towards the door. The carriage, with its flying favours, was stopping, had stopped. The colonel was seen descending.

He was looking very pale, whispered someone. Could anything be wrong? He was not wont to suffer from nervousness.

He did not turn to assist the bride. Surely that was strange! Nor did she follow him. Surely—surely the carriage behind him was empty!

Something indeed had happened. She must be ill! A great tremor went through the waiting crowd. No one was singing, but the music pealed on and on till some wild rumour of disaster reached the waiting chaplain, and he stepped across the chancel and touched the organist's shoulder.

Instantly silence fell—a terrible, nerve-racking silence. Colonel Chester had entered. He stood just within the door, pale and stern, whispering to the officer in charge of the men. People stared at him, at each other, at the bridegroom still standing motionless by the chancel steps. And then at last the silence broke into a murmur that spread and spread. Something had happened! Something was wrong! No, the bride was not ill. But there would be no wedding that day.

Someone came hurriedly and spoke to Teddy Duncombe, who turned first crimson, then very white, and finally pulled himself together with a jerk and went to Hone. Everyone craned to see what would happen—how the news would affect him, whether he would be deeply shocked, or whether—whether—ah! A great sigh went through the church. He did not seem startled or even greatly dismayed. He listened to Duncombe gravely, but without any visible discomfiture. There could not be anything very serious the matter, then. A note was put into his hand, which he read with absolute calmness under the eyes of the multitude.

When he looked up from it, the colonel had reached his side. They exchanged a few words, and then Hone, smiling faintly, beckoned to the chaplain. He rested a hand on his shoulder in his careless, friendly way, and spoke into his ear.

The chaplain looked deeply concerned, nodded once or twice, and, straightening himself, faced the crowd of guests.

"I am requested to state," he announced in the midst of dead silence, "that, owing to a most regrettable and unforeseen mischance, the happy event which we are gathered here to celebrate must be unavoidably postponed. The bride has just received an urgent summons to England on a matter of the first importance, which she feels compelled to obey, and she is already on her way to Bombay in the hope of catching the steamer which will sail to-morrow. It only remains for me to express deep sympathy, in which I am sure all present join me, with our friend Major Hone and his bride-elect on their disappointment, and the sincere hope that their happy union may not long be deferred."

He ended with a doubtful glance at Hone, who, standing on the chancel steps, bowed briefly, and, taking Duncombe by the shoulder, marched with him into the vestry. He certainly did not look in the least disconcerted or anxious. It could not be anything really serious. A feeling of relief lightened the atmosphere. People began to talk, to speculate, even to enjoy the sensation. Poor Hone! He was not often unlucky. But, of course, it would be all right. He would probably follow his bride to England, and they would be married there. Doubtless that was his intention, or he could not have looked so undismayed.

So ran the tide of gossip and surmise. And in Hone's pocket lay the twisted note which the woman he loved had left behind—the note which he had read with an unmoved countenance under a host of watching eyes.

"Good-bye, St. Patrick! It has been an amusing game, has it not? Do you remember how you beat me once long ago? I was but a child in those days. I did not know the rules of the game, and so you had the advantage. But you could not hope to have it always. It is my turn now, and I think I may claim the return match for my own. So good-bye, Achilles! Perhaps the gods will send you better luck next time. Who knows?"

No eye but Hone's ever read that heartless note, and his but once. Half an hour after he had received it, it lay in ashes, but every word of it was graven deep upon his brain.

IX

It was in the early hours of the morning that Nina Perceval reached Bombay.

She had sat wide-eyed and motionless all through the night. She had felt no desire to sleep. An intense horror of her surroundings seemed to possess her. She was like a hunted creature seeking to escape from a world of horrors. She would know no rest till she reached the sea, till she was speeding away over the glittering water, and the land—that land which had become more hateful to her than any prison—was left far behind.

She had played her game, she had sped her shaft, and now panic—sheer, unreasoning panic—filled her. She was terrified at what she had done, too terrified yet for coherent thought. She had taken her revenge at last. She had pierced her conqueror to the heart. As he had once laughed at her, as he had once, with a smile and a jest, broken and tossed her aside—so she had done to him. She had gathered up her wounded pride, and she had smitten him therewith. She was convinced that he would never laugh at her again.

He would get over it, of course; men always did. She had known men by the score who played the same merry game, men who broke hearts for sport and went their careless ways, unheeding, uncomprehending. It was the way of the world, this world of countless tragedies. She had learned, in her piteous cynicism, to look for nothing else. Faithfulness had become to her a myth. Surely all men loved—they called it love—and rode away.

No, she did not flatter herself that she had hurt him very seriously. She had dealt his pride a blow, that was all.

She reached Bombay, and secured her berth. The steamer was to sail at noon. There were not a great many passengers, and she managed to engage a cabin to herself. But she could not even attempt to rest in that turmoil of noise and excitement. She went ashore again, and repaired to a hotel for a meal. She took a private room, and lay down; but sleep would not come to her, and presently, urged by that gnawing restlessness, she was pacing up and down, up and down, like a wild creature newly caged.

Sometimes she paused at the window to stare down into the busy thoroughfare below, but she never paused for long. The fever that consumed her gave her no rest, and again she was pacing to and fro, to and fro, eternally, counting the leaden minutes that crept by so slowly.

At last, when flesh and blood could endure no longer, she snatched up her hat and veil, and prepared to go on board. Standing before a mirror, she began to adjust these with trembling fingers, but suddenly stopped dead, gazing speechlessly before her. For her own eyes had inadvertently met the eyes of the haggard woman in the glass, and dumbly, with a new horror clutching at her heart, she stared into their wild depths and read as in a book the tale of torture that they held.

When she turned away at length, she was shivering from head to foot as though she had seen a spectre; and so in truth she had. For those eyes had told her what she had not otherwise begun to realise.

That which she had believed dead for so long had been, only dormant, and had sprung to sudden, burning life. The weapon with which she had thought to pierce her enemy had turned in her grasp and pierced her also, pierced her with an agony unspeakable—ay, pierced her to the heart.

X

As one in a dream she stood on deck and watched India slipping below the horizon. Her restlessness was subsiding at last. She was conscious of an intense weariness, greater than any she had ever known. As soon as that distant line of land had disappeared she told herself that she would go and rest. Her fellow passengers had for the most part settled down. They sat about in groups under the awning. A few, like herself, stood at the rail and gazed astern, but there was no one very near her. She felt as if she stood utterly alone in all the world.

Slowly at last she turned away. Slowly she crossed the deck and began to descend the companion. A knot of people stood talking at the foot. They made way for her to pass. She went through them without a glance. She scarcely even saw them.

She went to her cabin and lay down, but she knew at once that sleep would not come to her. Her eyes burned as though weighted with many scalding tears, but she could not weep. She could only lie staring vaguely before her, and dumbly endure that suffering which she had vainly fancied could never again be her portion. She could only strive—and strive in vain—to shut out the vision of the man she loved standing alone at the altar waiting for the woman who had played him false.

The dinner hour approached. Mechanically she rose and dressed. She did not shrink from meeting the eyes of strangers. They simply did not exist for her. She took her place in the great dining saloon, looking neither to right nor left. The buzz of conversation all around her passed her by. She might have been sitting in utter solitude. And all the while the misery gnawed ever deeper into her heart.

She rose at last, before the meal was ended, and went up to the great empty deck. She felt as if she would stifle below. But, up above, the wash of the sea and the immensity of the night soothed her somewhat. She found a secluded corner, and leaned upon the rail, gazing out over the black waste of water.

What was he doing, she wondered. How was he spending this second night of misery? Had he begun to console himself already? She tried to think so, but failed—failed utterly.

Irresistibly the memory of the man swept over her, his gentleness, his chivalry, his unfailing kindness. She was beginning to see the whole bitter tragedy by the light of her repentance. He had loved her, surely he had loved her in those old days when she had tricked him in sheer, childish gaiety of soul. And, for her sake, that her suffering might be the briefer, he had masked his love. She had never thought so before, but she saw it clearly now.

It had all been a miserable misunderstanding from beginning to end, but she was sure, now, that he had loved her faithfully for all those years. And if it were against all reason to think so, if all her experience told her that men were not moulded thus, had not his chosen friend declared him to be one in ten thousand, and did not her quivering woman's heart know him to be such? Ah, what had she done? What had she done?

"Oh, Pat!" she sobbed. "Pat! Pat! Pat!"

The great idol of her pride had fallen at last, and she wept her heart out up there in the darkness, till physical exhaustion finally overcame her, and she could weep no more.

XI

"Won't you sit down?" a quiet voice said.

She started out of what was almost a stupor of grief, to find a man's figure standing close to her. Her eyes were all blinded by weeping, and she could see him but vaguely in the dimness. She had not heard him approach. He seemed to appear from nowhere. Or had he, perchance, been near her all the time?

Instinctively she drew a little away from him, though in that moment of utter desolation even the sympathy of a stranger sent a faint warmth of comfort to her heart.

"There is a chair here," the quiet voice went on, and as she turned vaguely, almost as though feeling her way, a steady hand closed upon her elbow and guided her.

Perhaps it was the touch that, like the shock of an electric current, sent the blood suddenly tingling through her veins, or it may have been some influence more subtle. She was yielding half-mechanically when suddenly, piercing her through and through, there came to her such a flash of revelation as almost deprived her for the moment of her senses.

She stood stock still and faced him.

"Oh, who is it?" she cried piteously. "Who is it?"

The hand that held her tightened ever so slightly. He did not instantly reply, but when he did, it was on a note of grimness that she had never heard from him before.

"It is I—Pat," he told her. "Have you any objection?"

She gazed at him speechlessly as one in a dream. He had followed her, then; he had followed her! But wherefore?

She began to tremble in the grip of sudden, overmastering fear. This was the last thing she had anticipated. What could it mean? Had she driven him demented? Had he pursued her to wreak his vengeance upon her, perhaps to kill her?

Compelled by the pressure of his hand, she moved to the dark seat he had indicated, and sank down.

He stood beside her, looming large in the gloom. A terrible silence fell between them. Worn out by sleeplessness and bitter weeping, she cowered before him dumbly. She had no pride left, no weapon of any sort wherewith to resist him. She longed, yet dreaded unspeakably, to hear his voice. He was watching her, she knew, though she did not dare to raise her head.

He spoke at last, quietly, without emotion, yet with that in his deliberate utterance that made her shrink and quiver in every nerve.

"Faith," he said, "it's been an amusing game entirely, but you haven't beaten me yet. I must trouble you to take up your cards again and play to a finish before we decide who scoops the pool."

"What do you mean?" she whispered.

He did not answer her, and she thought there was something contemptuous in his silence.

She waited a little, summoning her strength, then, rising, with a desperate courage she faced him.

"I don't understand you. Tell me what you mean!"

He made a curious gesture as if he would push her from him.

"I am not good at explaining myself," he said. "But you will understand me better presently."

And again inexplicably she shrank. There was that about him which terrified her more than any uttered menace.

"What are you going to do?" she said nervously. "Why—why have you followed me?"

He answered her in a tone which she deemed scoffing. It was too dark for her to see his face.

"You can hardly expect me to show my hand at this stage," he said. "You never showed me yours."

It was true, and she found no word to say against it. But none the less, she was horribly afraid. She felt herself to be utterly at his mercy, and was instinctively aware that he was in no mood to spare her.

"I can't go on playing, Pat," she said, after a moment, her voice very low. "I have no cards left to play."

"In that case you are beaten," he said, with that doggedness which she was beginning to know as a part of his fighting equipment. "Do you own it?"

She hesitated.

"Do you own it?" he insisted sternly.

And, yielding to a sudden impulse that overwhelmed all reason, she threw herself unreservedly upon his mercy.

"Yes, I own it."

He stood silent for several seconds after the admission, while she waited with a thumping heart. At last, half-grudgingly it seemed to her, he spoke.

"You are a wise woman," he said, "even wiser than I took you for, which is saying much. The game is ended, then. But you will pardon me if I refuse to surrender my winnings. Such as they are, I value them."

She bent her head. Her subjection was complete. She was too exhausted, physically and mentally, to attempt to withstand him, and undoubtedly the ultimate victory was his. Had he not witnessed those agonizing tears?

"You are welcome to anything you can find," she said, smiling wanly. "I suppose all experience is of value. At least, I used to think so."

Again for a moment he was silent. Then: "It is the most valuable thing in the world," he said, "if you know how to turn it to account. But, sure, that is a lesson that some of us are slow to learn."

The Tidal Wave and Other Stories | 201

He paused; then, as she remained silent, "You are going below to rest?" he said. "Don't let me keep you! You have travelled hard, and need it."

There was a hint of the old kindliness in his tone. She stood listening to it, longing, yet not daring to avail herself of it and make her peace with him.

But, whatever his intentions, it was apparently no part of Hone's plan to allow himself to be conciliated at that stage, for, after the briefest pause, he bowed abruptly and stepped aside.

And Nina Perceval went humbly away, as befitted one who had played a desperate game, and had been outwitted by the adversary she had dared to despise.

XII

During the whole three weeks of the voyage Hone took no further action.

Nina saw him every day of those interminable weeks, but he made no sign. He did not seek her out, neither did he avoid her, but continually he mystified her by the cheery indifference of his bearing.

He became — as was almost inevitable — an immense favourite on board. He was in the thick of every amusement, and no entertainment was complete without him. No rumour of the extraordinary circumstances that had led to his undertaking the voyage had reached their fellow passengers. No one suspected that anything unusual existed between the winning, frank-faced Irishman and the silent young widow who so seldom looked his way. No one had heard of the wedding party that had lacked a bride.

But everyone welcomed Hone, V.C., as a tremendous acquisition, and Hone, V.C., laughed his humorous, good-tempered laugh, and placed himself unreservedly and impartially at everyone's disposal.

Nina never saw him in private. In public he treated her with the kindly courtesy he extended to every woman on board. There was not in his manner the faintest hint of anything deeper. He would laugh into her eyes with absolute friendliness. And yet from the depths of her soul she feared him. She knew that he was continuing the game that she had wantonly begun. She knew that there was more to come, that he had not done with her, that he was merely waiting, as an experienced player knows how to wait, till the time arrived to play his final card.

What that final card could be she had not the remotest idea, but she awaited it with an almost morbid sense of dread. His very forbearance seemed ominous.

On the night before their arrival there was a dance on board. Nina, who had not joined in any of these gaieties for the simple reason that she had no heart for them, rose from dinner with the intention of going to her cabin. But as she passed out of the saloon, Hone stepped forward and intercepted her.

"Will you give me a dance, Mrs. Perceval?"

She looked up at him, meeting his eyes with an effort.

"I am not dancing," she said.

"Just one," he pleaded, with that air of gallantry that cloaked she knew not what.

She hesitated, and then, almost in spite of herself, with something of the old regal graciousness, she yielded.

"Just one, then, Major Hone, since to-morrow it will be good-bye."

He thanked her with a deep bow, and promptly led her away.

They danced the first waltz together in unbroken silence. Nina kept her face studiously turned over her shoulder. Not once did she glance at her partner, whose quiet dancing and steady arm told her nothing.

When it was over, he led her to a seat in full view of the other dancers, and sat down beside her. For a few seconds he maintained his silence, then quietly he turned and spoke.

"Are you going to stay in London?"

The direct question surprised her. Somehow, though he had given her small reason to do so, she had come to expect naught but subtle strategy from him.

"I shall spend one night there," she said, after a moment's thought.

"No longer?"

She faced him calmly, though her heart had begun to leap and race within her.

"Why do you ask?"

"Why don't you answer?" said Hone.

He was smiling faintly, but there was determination in the set of his jaw.

"Because," she said slowly, "I am not sure that I want you to know."

"Why not?" said Hone. She shook her head in silence. "It's sorry I am to hear it," he said, after a brief pause. "For if it's to be a game of hide-and-seek I shall soon run you to earth."

She raised her eyebrows. Had they been alone together she knew that she could not have disguised her fear. It had grown upon her marvellously of late. But the publicity of their intercourse endued her with a certain courage.

"What is it that you want of me?" she said.

He met her eyes with absolute steadiness.

"I will tell you," he said, "the next time we meet."

She tried to laugh to hide the wild tumult his words stirred up.

"Is that a promise?"

"My solemn bond," said Hone.

She rose.

"I shall stay at the Seton Ward Hotel for a week," she said. "Good-night!"

He rose also; they stood for a moment face to face.

"Alone?" he asked.

And again, with a reckless sense of throwing herself upon his mercy, she made brief reply.

"I haven't a friend in the world."

He gave her his arm.

"Any enemies?" he asked.

They were at the door before she answered.

"Yes—one."

For an instant his arm grew tense, detaining her.

"And that?" he questioned.

She withdrew her hand sharply.

"Myself," she said, and swiftly, without another glance, she left him.

XIII

The roar of the London traffic rose muffled through the London fog. It was a winter afternoon of great murkiness.

In the private sitting-room of a private hotel Nina Perceval sat alone, as she had sat for two dragging, intolerable days, and waited. She had begun to ask herself—she had asked herself many times that day—if she waited in vain. She would remain for the week, whatever happened, but the torture of suspense had become such as she scarcely knew how to endure. Something of the fever of restlessness that had tormented her at Bombay was upon her now, but with it, subtly mingled, was a misery of uncertainty that had not gripped her then. She was unspeakably lonely, and at certain panic-stricken times unspeakably afraid; but whether it was the possibility of his presence or the certainty of his continued absence that appalled her, she could not have said.

A fire burned with a cheery crackling in the room, throwing weird shadows through the dimness. Yet she shivered from time to time as though the chill of the London fog penetrated to her bones. Ah! what was that? She startled violently at the sound of a low knock at the door, then hastily commanded herself. It was only a waiter with the tea she had ordered, of course. With her back to the door she bade him enter.

But, though the door opened and someone entered, there came no jingle of tea things. She did not turn her head. It was as though she could not. She was as one turned to stone. She thought that the wild throbbing of her heart would choke her.

He came straight to her and stood beside her, not offering to touch so much as her hand. The red firelight beat upwards on his face. She ventured a single glance at him, and was oddly shocked by the look he wore. Something of the red glow on the hearth shone back at her from his eyes. She did not dare to look again. Yet when he spoke, though he uttered no greeting, his voice was quite normal, wholly free from agitation.

"I should have been here sooner, but I was scouring London for an old friend. I have found him at last, but, faith, I've had a chase. Do you remember Jasper Caldicott, the parson who went out with us on the *Scindia* eight years ago?"

"Yes, I remember him." She spoke with a strong effort. Her lips felt stiff and cold.

"He has a parish Whitechapel way," said Hone. "I only found him out this morning. I wanted to bring him to see you."

"Yes?" At his abrupt pause she moved slightly. "But he wouldn't come?"

"He will come some day," said Hone. "But he had some scruple about accompanying me there and then, as I wished. In fact, he wants you to visit him instead."

"Yes?" She almost whispered the word. She was holding the mantelpiece with both hands to steady her trembling limbs.

"Sure, there's nothing to alarm you at all," Hone said. "It'll soon be over. He wants you to do him the honour of being married in his church and there's a taxi below waiting to take you."

"Now?" She turned and faced him, white to the lips.

"Yes, now! By special licence." Sternly he made reply, and again she felt as though the fire in his eyes scorched her.

"And if I—refuse?" She stood up to her full height, flinging her fear from her with a royal gesture that was almost a challenge.

But Hone was ready for her. Hone, the gentle, the kind, the chivalrous, stepped suddenly forth from his garden of virtues with level lance to meet her.

"By the powers," he said, and the words came from between his teeth, "I wonder you dare to ask me that!"

She laughed, but her laughter was slightly hysterical, and in an instant he seized and pressed his advantage.

"It is the end of the game," he grimly told her. "And you are beaten. You told me once that you didn't always pay your debts. But, by Heaven, you shall pay this one!"

By sheer weight he beat down her resistance. Against her will, in spite of her utmost effort, she gave way before him.

A moment she stood in silence. Then, "So be it!" she said, and, turning, left him.

When she joined him again she was so thickly veiled that he could not see her face. She preceded him without a word into the lift, and they went down in utter silence to the waiting taxi. Then side by side through the gloom as though they travelled through space, a myriad lights twinkling all about them, the rush and roar of a universe in their ears, but they two alone in an atmosphere that none other breathed.

It was a journey that neither ever afterwards calculated by time. It was incalculable as the flight of a meteor. And when at last it came to an end, for an instant neither moved.

Then, as though emerging from a dream, Hone rose and alighted, and turned to give his hand to his companion. A little group of ragged urchins stood to view upon the muddy pavement. There was no other pomp to attend the coming of a bride.

Silently they entered a church that was lighted from end to end for evening service. They passed up the aisle through a haze of fog. They halted at the chancel steps....

The knot of urchins had grown to a considerable crowd when they emerged. Women and half-grown girls jostled each other for a glimpse of the bride. But the utmost that any saw was a slender figure wearing a thick veil that walked a little apart from the bridegroom, and entered the waiting motor unassisted.

XIV

Back once more in the room where the fire crackled, newly replenished, and electric light revealed a shining tea-table, Hone turned to the silent woman beside him.

"Can I write a message? I promised to send one to Teddy as soon as we were married."

She pointed to the writing-table; and moved herself to the fire. There she stood for a few seconds quite motionless, seeming to listen to the scratching of his pen.

He ceased to write, and turned in his chair. For a moment his eyes rested upon her.

"Take off your hat!" he said.

She obeyed him in utter silence. Her hands were stiff and numb with cold. She stooped, the firelight shining on her hair, and held them to the blaze.

Hone rose quietly, and came to her side. He held his message for her to read, and she did so silently.

"Just married. All well. Love.—PAT."

"Will it do?" he said.

She glanced up at him and shivered.

"Is all well?" she asked, in a tone that demanded no answer.

He made none, merely rang the bell and gave orders for the despatch of the message.

Then he came quietly back to her. They stood face to face. She was quite erect, but pale to the lips. She stood before him as a prisoner awaiting sentence, too proud to ask for mercy.

Hone paused a few moments, as if to give her time to speak, to challenge him, to make her defence, or to plead her weakness. Then, as she did none of these things, he suddenly laid steady hands upon her, drew her to him, and, bending, looked closely into her eyes.

"And is there any reason at all why I should not take what is my own?" he said.

She did not resist him, but a long shiver went through her.

"Are you sure it is worth the taking?" she said.

"Quite sure," he answered quietly. "Shall I tell you how I know?"

Her eyes sank before his.

"You will do exactly as you choose."

He was silent for an instant, still intently searching her white face. Then:

"Do you remember that night that you fainted in my arms?" he said. "Do you remember opening your eyes in the boat? Do you know—can you guess—what your eyes told me?"

She was silent; only again from head to foot she shivered.

He went on very quietly, as one absolutely sure of himself:

"I looked into your soul that night, and I saw your secret hidden away in its darkest corner. And I knew it had been there for a long, long time. I knew from that moment that, hate me as you might, you were mine, as I have been yours for so long as I have known you."

She raised her eyes suddenly, stiffening in his grasp.

"And you expect me to believe that of you?" she said, a tremor that was not of fear, in her voice.

"You do believe it," he answered with conviction.

She raised her hands with something of her old imperious grace, and laid them on his arms, freeing herself with a single gesture.

"And all those years ago," she said, "when you made me believe you had been trifling with me—"

"I lied!" said Hone. "It was the hardest thing I ever did. But something had to be done. I did it to save you suffering."

She turned abruptly from him, moving blindly, till groping, she found the mantelpiece, and leaned upon it. Then, her back to him, she spoke:

"And you succeeded in breaking my heart."

A sudden silence fell. Hone stood motionless, his hands fallen to his sides. The dull roar of the streets beat up through the stillness like the roar of a distant sea, bringing to mind a night long, long ago when first he had met his little princess, when first the gay charm of her personality had been cast upon him.

With a resolute effort he spoke.

"But you were scarcely more than a child," he said. "It—sure, it couldn't have been as bad as that?"

At the sound of the pain in his voice she slowly turned.

"It was much worse than that," she said. "While it lasted, it was intolerable. There were times when I thought it would drive me crazy. But you—you were always there, and I think the sight of you kept me sane. I hated you so. I had to show you that I didn't care."

Again he heard in her voice that tremor that was not of fear.

"As long as my husband lived," she went on, "I kept up the miserable farce. As you know, we never loved each other. Then he died, and I found I couldn't bear it any longer. There was no reason why I should. I went away. I should never have seen you again, only Mrs. Chester would take no refusal. And I had put it all away from me by that time. I felt it did not greatly matter if we did meet. Nothing seemed of much importance till that day I saw you on the polo ground, carrying all before you—Achilles triumphant! That day I began to hate you again." A faint smile drew the corners of her mouth. "I think you suspected it," she said, "but your suspicions were soon lulled to rest. Did it never cross your mind to wonder how we came to pair on that night of the river picnic? I accused you of cheating, do you remember? And you were quite indignant." A glimmer of the old gay mischief shone for a fleeting second through her tragedy. "That was the first move in the game," she said. "At least you never suspected me of that."

"No; you had me there." There was a ring of sternness in Hone's voice. "So that was the beginning?" he said.

She nodded.

"And it would have been the end also, if you would have suffered it. For that very night I ceased to hate you." A faint flush tinged her pale face. "I would have let you off," she said. "I didn't want to go on. But you would not have it so. You came after me. You wouldn't leave me alone, even though I warned you—I warned you that I wasn't worth your devotion. And so"— again her voice trembled—"you had to have your lesson after all."

"And do you know what it has taught me?"

Again there sounded in his voice that new mastery that had so strangely overwhelmed her.

She shrank a little as it reached her, and turned her face aside. "I can guess," she said.

"And is it good at guessing that you are?"

He drew nearer to her with the words, but he did not offer to touch her.

She stood motionless, her head bent lest he should see, and understand, the piteous quivering of her lips. With immense effort she made reply:

"It has taught you to hate and despise me, as—as I deserve."

"Faith!" he said. "You think that—honestly now?"

The mastery had all gone out of his voice. It was soft with that caressing quality she knew of old—that tenderness, half-humorous, half-persuasive, that had won her heart so long, so long ago. She did not answer him—for she could not.

He waited for the space of a score of seconds, standing close to her, yet still not touching her, looking down in silence at the proud dark head abased before him.

At last: "It's myself that'll have to tell you, after all," he said gently, "for sure it's the only way to make you understand. It's taught me that we can both be winners, dear, if we play the game squarely, just as we have both been losers all these weary years. But we will have to be partners from this day forward. So just put your little hand in mine, and it'll be all right, mavourneen! Pat'll understand!"

She moved at that—moved sharply, convulsively, passionately. For a moment her eyes met his; for a moment she seemed on the verge of amazed questioning, even of vehement protest.

But—perhaps the grey eyes that looked straight and steadfast into her own made speech seem unnecessary—for she only whispered, "St. Patrick!" in a voice that trembled and broke.

And "Princess! My Princess!" was all he answered as he took her into his arms.